LANCASHIRE COUNTY LIBRARY

This book must be returned on or before the date marked below

THE BRIAR PATCH

The world of the Young Ladies of Miss Pelham's finishing school at Portelet-sur-Seine was a world of decorum, a neat, beautifully-mannered, well-ordered world in which "coming out" bulked large. The world of the Jewish orphan boys at the Hostel on the other side of the Place du Triangle was a world of war, violence, sadism, the deprivations and degradations of the concentration camp. In the wild, wary dark eyes of these youths were reflected all the things Miss Pelham's charges should never see. Between the two establishments there was a tacit arrangement that the inmates should not meet.

But Deirdre, a seventeen-year-old Irish beauty with the most sheltered of backgrounds, met Max, and of all M. Wolff's boys Max, with his memories of Auschwitz, striking looks and lively brain, was the one on whom Inspector Granier kept closest watch, even before the murdered corpse of a certain unhonoured citizen of Portelet was fished from the Seine.

By *the author of*

THE
BRIAR PATCH

CHARITY BLACKSTOCK

Bred and born in a briar patch, Bre'er
Fox, bred and born in a briar patch!
From UNCLE REMUS by Joel Chandler Harris

LONDON
HODDER AND STOUGHTON

FOR

la bande

WITH LOVE AND THANKS

1104

Chapter One

THE Place du Triangle lay in the centre of Portelet-sur-Seine. Portelet-sur-Seine was forty-five minutes from St. Lazare. It was, as M. Quiqueran always told visitors, a town of historic importance. The Seine flowed thinly through it and on its far bank was a forest where the nightingales sang. There was a market-place that was three hundred years old; in its centre was a war memorial, of which one of the sides was dedicated to the Jews of Portelet-sur-Seine who had lost their lives in the war which had now been over for four years. There was a château where Henri IV had kept one of his mistresses. The mistress was long since dead, and so was the château, which had fallen into hopeless decay; it was now used as a Hostel for some of the few Jewish boys who had survived.

It was all very picturesque, but the long, thin houses were the colour of a sad, decayed lion, and the trees in the Place smelt of autumn, for all it was now mid-summer. The air was parched and dusty; even the bright shutters were faded. Visitors came and went; they seldom stayed. There was a Hôtel du Nord, a Café Niçoise, a variety of *tabacs*, and two vast blocks of flats where the outer door opened mysteriously as one pressed the bell.

"It is awfully dirty," Deirdre wrote to her mother, "and all the poor animals look half starved, it makes me wretched to see them."

She spelt it "retched". She could never spell.

The College—Rosedene College for Girls—was clean. Miss Pelham saw to that. Miss Pelham herself was as clean as she was English. The first thing she did when she reopened, after the war, her finishing school for young English girls, was to instal new bathrooms and lavatories, then, when the school began to flourish again, she painted the outer walls white. M. Wolff, who ran the Hostel opposite, and who was always entertained by the sight of the little English misses taking their supervised promenade, declared that this was symbolic of their virginal status.

"*En principe,*" said Max, repeating this remark to Inspector Granier. And he smiled his enchanting, ravaged smile as he spoke, while his vast, dark eyes roamed over the front of the College, as if he were seeing it as a fortress to be stormed. But then he saw M. Quiqueran making his jaunty way towards the Syndicat, and his smile changed in quality. Inspector Granier, noting this, seized his arm and said quite fiercely, "Ah, for God's sake, Max! Do you think I want to waste my handcuffs on you? Leave the poor devil alone. It's all been over, a long time ago. Anni's got supper waiting for you, and Patricia won't go to sleep till you kiss her good-night. Come on—" And he almost pulled him into the courtyard of the flats where he lived.

M. Quiqueran—*Bitteschön* Quiqueran they had once called him—saw Max, and his jaunty step flagged. His sunburnt face tightened, and one hand went instinctively to the hair sleeked across the bald patch on his crown. Sometimes the wind caught that swathe of hair and it stood up straight like a feather. He had been gazing at the College with a kind of wistful lechery, but now he almost ran through the doorway of his office, which he kept open late on summer evenings to deal with English and American visitors.

The Syndicat d'Initiative was at the apex of the Place du Triangle, and Inspector Granier lived on the hypotenuse. Rosedene College was on one side, and the château where the Jewish boys lived was—from Miss Pelham's point of view, most unhappily—on the other. She considered the matter now, as she waited for Deirdre's knock. Her twenty-five girls, all aged between sixteen and eighteen, were strictly forbidden to speak to the boys, and in this matter she and M. Wolff were entirely at one. Indeed, they were so much in accord that they even had a kind of respect for each other. He had no wish for his Jewish boys to speak to the Christian girls and, from Miss Pelham's angle, the boys were entirely impossible. She was sorry for them, of course, for they were all without families, and they had all been in concentration camps; but when they first arrived, three years ago in 1946, a horde of young barbarians, it was to her as if the tribes of Gaul had besieged her, and she had nearly closed the College in sheer despair.

They were all so foreign, and their fierce, gaunt faces appalled her. They moved together like a pack of wolves, and their eyes were such as she had never seen in human beings—wild, wary eyes, the eyes of hunted beasts out for the kill. The thought of her young girls coming into contact with these savages choked her with terror. It was as if those eyes reflected everything her charges should not see. Her world was a world of decorum, a neat, patterned world with a white wedding at its end. Her girls all came from good families—with the possible exception of Nora, but then in these days one had to accept money as a substitute for good breeding. And Nora was a good girl. They were all good girls, and she did her best to train them in such things as were essential for their futures. They all learnt to speak French with a pretty accent, they could, when she had finished with them, cook and dance, bath a baby and make polite conversation. The weekly lecture on current affairs, the artistic appreciation and diction classes, alone, were worth the enormous fees that the parents paid. Miss Pelham had a sincere belief in what she was doing, and her girls, when they left her, could hold their own in any society.

This outer world that had edged in on hers was no world for her girls. Miss Pelham, when she first saw them, felt as if the ordered, sweet-smelling beauty of her College were blasted from her, as if she were slipping into a darkness of obscenity and horror, a nightmare of despair and death.

But now, three years later, the boys were very much like other boys. On the whole, they behaved themselves very well. They sometimes whistled when she took the girls out, and there were constant murmurs of, *"Pas mal, celle-là,"* and so on, but that was to be expected of all boys, and in any case they were out at work all day, so trouble could easily be avoided.

Miss Pelham, still waiting for Deirdre—the child was dreadfully unpunctual—stepped over to the window and, blinking in the bright sunlight, watched with some amusement as the Hostel's youngest boy stepped out into the Place, scuffing up the sandy soil as he did so.

His name was Jean-Louis. He was the cosseted baby and he was ten years old. He was one of the few French boys in the Hostel; most of them came from Eastern Europe. How pretty these young Jews could be. He was as charming as a Greuze, with tight curls, enormous eyes and a delicately tinted complexion. She was on the point of calling out to him to offer him a chocolate, when she saw him stand at the kerb, unbutton himself and, without the least self-consciousness, relieve himself in the gutter.

Miss Pelham, rather to her own surprise, flushed and stepped back into the room. She stood there for a moment, a slim, elegant woman of forty-seven, then sat down at her desk. She was aware of a quite disproportionate anger and revulsion. It made her take a cigarette out of her handbag and light it. She did not permit her girls to smoke (though Nora, as she knew perfectly well, did so whenever she could), and usually she only smoked herself in her private room, but really, she must do something to calm herself.

She knew it was absurd. All French children behaved like that. And he was only ten. Yet she could not rid herself of the idea that it was a deliberate affront, and what was even worse, it reminded her that outside the cool, white walls of the College was another world, a world of danger, to threaten the pure, enclosed garden she so preciously protected. At that moment she almost hated Jean-Louis. She thought he might at least have gone indoors; she felt that if that pretty little face had been within striking distance, she would have boxed his ears.

Then she was ashamed of herself, and grew the angrier for her shame. When Deirdre, moving in her usual, vague, indolent fashion, at last made her appearance, she spoke to her sharply.

She said, "You are extremely late. I don't like being kept waiting. Why didn't you come at once? What have you been doing?" Then she exclaimed in irritation, "My dear child, your hair—" She broke off, shocked by her own nagging voice. She said more calmly, "Sit down, please. Well? What have you been doing?"

"Nothing, Miss Pelham," said Deirdre, as might have been expected. The soft voice, with its faint Irish accent, invested the words with a kind of beauty, as if doing nothing were well worth while. She sat down obediently, moving with the sweetly flowing grace that Herrick loved in his Julia; there was no class that could add to Deirdre's elegance, and the disordered hair fell about as lovely a face as any poet could desire. But Miss Pelham, surveying the thick, fair hair, and lowered, long-lashed, grey eyes, was stirred to exasperation again; she found herself thinking it was a pity that the landed gentry produced offspring so singularly dumb and so singularly unsophisticated. This was heresy, for without such products her College would not have existed, but nonetheless her temper still flickered; she put out her cigarette and began to speak in a voice that stabbed sufficiently to make Deirdre raise her dreaming eyes.

"You say you have been doing nothing. That I can well believe. Deirdre, I want to have a little talk with you."

"Yes, Miss Pelham," said Deirdre. Her eyes strayed to the window, where the June sun struck back from the tawny street.

"Will you please pay attention to me?" And she thought, if that child says "Yes, Miss Pelham," again, I shall really lose my temper.

"Yes, Miss Pelham," said Deirdre.

Then Miss Pelham laughed. "I don't know what to do with you," she said almost cheerfully, "but of course you've only been here a couple of weeks. Are you happy with us?"

"Oh yes."

"There's nothing troubling you?"

"No."

"A tiny bit homesick, perhaps?"

Deirdre said suddenly, "I wish I could have Rusty here."

"Rusty? Is that—is that your brother?"

"Oh no. Rusty's my dog. He's an Irish terrier. He's terribly intelligent. He's mad on fighing, of course, but all Irish terriers are like that. I miss him very much."

Miss Pelham fell silent, mentally reviewing Deirdre's family history. Of course, there was no brother. She remembered that now. Irish father, a Brigadier, English county mother, both elderly. There was a sister, but she was ten years older than Deirdre, and married. The girl was virtually an only child and had obviously been left far too much to herself; she seemed to have fallen into a gentle wildness where she roamed the hills with Rusty at her side.

She said, "What interests you, my dear?" She added, with a faint irony, "Apart from Rusty. My colleagues say you make no effort at all to join in anything. I know your French is exceptionally good, but apart from that—Where did you learn to speak so well, by the way?"

"I had a French governess."

"Ah, I see. But you need more than French. We pride ourselves on being a happy little family here, you know. We all have to pull our weight. After all, next year you'll be coming out. You have to learn how to mix with people. You don't want to be a wallflower, do you?"

She glanced at the bowed head as she spoke, and found her own words a little ridiculous. If Deirdre were a wallflower, it could only be from her personal choice. That strange, dreaming face, with its beautifully pencilled brows, would compel many a young man to open his poetry books again. But beauty was not enough. The girl must be made to see that. And the reports on her were really shocking—

"I'm sorry, but she cannot stay in my choir." This was the singing mistress, after a disastrous episode when Deirdre's voice, raised obediently in song, soared so startlingly off the note that everyone else was reduced to giggles. Miss Pelham had been tempted to retort that she did not care much for Deirdre in her play-reading class, either. She had been lured by that lovely face into casting her as Cleopatra in the Shakespearian session. It had been an unforgettable experience to hear her say:

"O! withered is the garland of the war,
The soldier's pole is fall'n; young boys and girls
Are level now with men."

It was as if Kensington, with a shopping basket on her arm, had stepped by mistake on to Egypt's sands. Miss Pelham had learnt, in the course of her profession, to take a great deal, but these words, soft-spoken without the faintest understanding or expression, had nearly broken her. And the child was almost illiterate, into the bargain; her spelling was unbelievable, and her schoolgirl writing sprawled across the page.

She said briskly, "Well? What does interest you? Something must. Do you like reading?"

Deirdre shook her head. She raised her eyes to meet Miss Pelham's half-despairing gaze. One could almost believe the girl to be a moron, yet the eyes were not a moron's eyes; it was more as if she were away in some dream-world of her own.

"I'm going to speak quite frankly," said Miss Pelham. She rose to her feet. The impulse to seize Deirdre by her shoulders and shake her into some display of animation was alarmingly strong within her. There had always been difficult girls. Some, like Nora, were precocious, and many were wilful, childish and spoilt, but until now she had never met anything like this sleeping beauty. She said, "You are a very pretty girl, Deirdre, as I have no doubt you know. I expect you think that is sufficient. But, believe me, my dear, it is not. Young women, these days, are expected to know what is happening around them, to be able to hold their own in conversation. You are not, after all, a Victorian miss with a vinaigrette. You will soon find that young men become bored with you if you have nothing to talk about. You are not, I hope, waiting for a fairy prince. I assume you do want to get married?"

"Oh yes." This, unbelievably, was almost animation. "And I want at least six children."

"Are you so fond of children, then?"

"Oh, I adore them. Babies are so sweet. I have a little nephew, you know. He's five. He's a sweety. My sister lets me look after him, sometimes."

Miss Pelham would never have voiced this, even to herself, but, like another and more famous lady, she thought privately that breeding and good-breeding did not go together. She was a little startled by this outburst. She said dryly, "Well, you'll have to find yourself a husband first."

"I suppose so," said Deirdre in her former apathetic way.

"What do you mean, you suppose so! Of course you will. My dear child, you really must pull yourself together. I understand that you moon about the place from morning to night, half the time you don't even listen to what is said to you, and you don't even make much effort to get on with the other girls. Don't you like them?"

"They're all right," said Deirdre.

"You don't sound very enthusiastic—Tell me. Do you by any chance keep a diary?"

"Oh no."

"I think it might be a good idea if you did so. I'd like you to try. Just write down what happens during the day, and what you think about it. You needn't show it to me, if you don't want to, though of course I should be delighted if you did. I think it will help you to express yourself. And I want you to make a special effort to be more sociable. Shyness isn't really very attractive, you know, except when one's very young."

"I'm not shy," said Deirdre.

"Oh, I think you are. A little bit. But you'll soon overcome it. You do like people, don't you?"

"I don't know," said Deirdre. Then, as if aware of the growing exasperation in Miss Pelham's face, she said with some difficulty, "I don't think I like girls very much. I've never really met them *en masse* before. Our house stands on its own. I have lessons with my friend, of course. But then I've always known her. The chauffeur takes me over and brings me back. But we never see people. We don't entertain much. Daddy's writing his book on the war, and Mummy's not very strong, she doesn't care for going out. I listen to the radio in the evenings, but I don't like it very much."

"Well, now," said Miss Pelham, encouraged by this comparatively lengthy speech, "you're meeting lots of girls and you will be able to make plenty of nice friends of your own class. We have several outings to concerts and theatres during the term, and you will have a chance to see a great

13

many Paris churches and museums. And of course the Louvre. You'll have no chance to be bored—"

"I'm never bored," said Deirdre.

"Of course you are. You must be. No one can sit around and do nothing without being bored."

"I think sometimes people are more boring than doing nothing."

Miss Pelham gave her a sharp glance, but there was no insolence in the grave, young face looking into hers. Deirdre, it seemed, was simply making a plain statement of fact. She felt she could take no more. She said, "I am sure you will settle down very nicely." She added with a smile, "At least I'm certain you will cause us no trouble. Don't forget about the diary, will you? Here's a nice, new notebook for you."

Deirdre, back in her room, looked out of her window, across the Place du Triangle. She saw Max and the Inspector walking into the block of flats. She watched them for a moment, then sat down at her desk, opening the notebook and caressing the white pages with loving fingers.

Each girl had her own room. The rooms were little more than cubicles, but Miss Pelham was a great believer in privacy. "They all have their little sanctum," she wrote to the parents. The rooms were all white, with chintz curtains, and bedspread and chair-covers to match. On the wall, above each bed, was a small, framed notice, informing the occupant, "If you want a mistress in the night, please ring." This had greatly edified the American army who stayed in the school after the liberation. The lamp-shade was pink, and so was the rug beside the bed. Everything was pretty and dainty and girlish, and Deirdre surveyed it, her full mouth going down at the corners. Her eyes turned briefly towards the photo on her dressing-table, of herself in jumper and skirt, with Rusty at her side. Then she looked again at the notebook and picked up a pencil.

She wrote in her atrocious handwriting, "June 2nd, 1949," underlined it twice. Then she wrote, "I think Miss Pelham is an awfully silly old woman." And suddenly she began to draw, and beneath her pencil emerged a long, thin face, a little like that of an aristocratic sheep; every feature was cruelly caricatured, from the over-large teeth to the wrinkled throat. The nose jutted out, making a vast shadow; the pencilled brows revealed the natural outlines underneath. And then she drew groups of little faces like bunches of flowers gathered together—prim, surprised, silly, gaping little faces—all of which would have surprised Miss Pelham very much, for she would never have understood, any more than Deirdre did herself, how a drawing eye could perceive what the normal eye would not so much as notice.

*　　*　　*

Max was bathing Patricia; he did this most professionally. Anni complained that he made more mess than the baby, but her eyes were gentler than her words, for she loved Max and thought he was a charming boy. There were not after all so many young men of nineteen who would trouble themselves with a baby, and Patricia adored him, shrieking with delight whenever he came near her.

"A very dangerous young man, you know," said her husband as they paused at the end of the corridor, listening to the noise of riot from the bathroom.

"I can never understand why you say such things," said Anni, a little crossly. "I suppose it's your tummy again." For Inspector Granier was a worrying man, and suffered badly with his digestion; it attacked him whenever he was overworked, and he was overworked most of the time. She went on, "He's so sweet with Patricia. Don't you remember when she was ill at Christmas? He came every evening, and made those delightful wooden toys for her.

How many boys of his age would take so much trouble? I think that people who are nice to children must be nice people. It's no good your looking at me like that, Jean. Max is a darling. And when you think of all he's been through—" She put a hand on Granier's arm. "Does he ever talk about it?"

"No." He said suddenly, "He worries me. Oh, it's no good your making faces. There's something wrong with him. There's something that's just not here, any more. Yes, yes, I know. He can be kind—When he chooses to be. Ever spoken to Quiqueran on that subject?"

"That pig!"

"Well, that's as may be. All right. He's good with Patricia. He's a charming and handsome young man. But— How shall I put it? There's a kind of veto that operates with most of us some of the time, and with some of us most of the time. It tells us we mustn't do things. Like stealing and making love to other people's wives—"

"Huh!" said Anni.

He smiled at her. "Since when have I made love to anyone but you? Or wanted to? It tells us not to murder, too. We all feel like murder sometimes. But we don't. We say, *Je m'en fous*, like that little pest, Jean-Louis, and do a bit of gardening instead. But with our friend there, the veto no longer operates. The world has taught him to kill or be killed. I wouldn't care to be the person standing in his way if he really wanted something."

"Yet you're always playing chess with him!"

"Yes. He usually beats me, too. But one day I'll be putting the handcuffs on him. If he doesn't kill me first—Well, Max? Have you drowned my daughter? You look rather as if she's drowned you."

The young man came out of the bathroom. He had slung the nine-months-old baby across his shoulder. The water was dripping from his black hair, his shirt was drenched, and his face, which was a remarkable one, was twisted into mock ferocity. "You have the devil of a daughter," he said. "I'm exhausted." He swung up his free fist so that it brushed gently against Patricia's chin. "Wait—I'll just dump her before she maims me for life."

He stooped to pick up the discarded clothes hanging on the bath-rail, and stepped swiftly into the room across the landing. They could hear his voice raised in song:

B'Telaviv haiti,
B'ir yafah haiti,
Im lo achshav e matai,
E matai!

Anni looked sideways at her husband. "Sure," she said. "Sure, sure, sure. A desperate young man. I wonder you dare to have him in the house—You haven't shaved. I think you look much more dangerous than he does. Supper will be ready in a quarter of an hour."

Granier said to Max, in his heavy, abrupt fashion, "I want you to lay off Quiqueran."

The dark eyes, mourning, derisive, were instantly veiled. The smile remained. Max said, "Haven't I been a good boy? Has he been reporting me?"

The Inspector listened for a moment to the sound of his wife in the kitchen. Then he stretched out a hand and gripped Max's forearm. It felt young and frail beneath the cheap, cotton shirt. He said, "You're going to listen to me, boy, whether you like it or not. Of course he's been reporting you. He's always reporting you. You scare the poor devil out of his wits."

"Poor M. Quiqueran," said Max. He suddenly jerked his arm away.

"Max," said Granier, "you're not going to like this, but be damned to you. After all, you can always walk out. But I'd like you to remember that the time may come when you won't be able to walk out, and I'd prefer to say what I have to say while you have the choice."

"That's very gentlemanly of you," said Max. He pulled out a packet of Gaulloises. "Cigarette, sir?"

"They kill my throat—Listen now. And take me seriously, will you? I'm saying this for your own good. You've had a hell of a time—" He saw the dangerous change in Max's face, and added quickly, "Oh, listen, damn you. You can knock me down afterwards, but listen to me first. Of course you've had a hell of a time. It's not a thing we've ever discussed, and I don't propose to discuss it now, but let's face it, it's a bloody miracle that you survived at all. But it's over and done with, Max. It's been over and done with for four years. And you've survived. A great many didn't, but that's by the way. You've survived, and so has all the hatred stewing inside you. Which you are now turning on to old Quiqueran. I think you could find someone more worthy of your steel."

"He collaborated with the Bosches," said Max calmly. He moved over to the window, the cigarette hanging from the corner of his mouth. He looked at the white walls of the College, then down to meet the eyes of a plump, dark young woman who was opening the gate. He grinned at her, and winked.

Granier, coming up behind him, caught at his shoulder and pulled him round, saying roughly, "Will you listen!"

Max snapped in a thin, harsh voice, "There's no need to manhandle me. Let go. I don't like being touched. You're not arresting me yet."

"It's what I'm hoping to avoid," said Granier, moving away from him. "Will you let me finish now? All right. Quiqueran collaborated with the Germans. So did a great many others. I'm surprised you find it so astonishing. I wonder if any of us, in certain circumstances, would dare to swear we'd never collaborate."

"Did you?"

"I was in the army. And you'd no choice, had you? You're a Jew. I don't think you can take much credit to yourself for non-collaboration. But suppose you weren't a Jew. Suppose you were an ordinary French citizen, with a wife and kids. You might want to make the heroic gesture, but suppose the price were their life. I wonder if you'd care to pay that price. I wonder if your patriotism would stand up to seeing the Bosches rape your wife and beat your kid's brains out. Do you think your heroism would support you then? I didn't marry till the end of the war. I was only responsible for myself. That way it's easy—Max. Will you be so good as to honour me with your attention? I should have thought your religion would deter you from making eyes at the young ladies from the College."

"I have no religion," said Max. His face was the face of a fallen angel, ruined, beautiful and, just then, as hard as a diamond. "And I am not interested in the young *anglaises*. That particular little piece is called Nora. I heard the dragon calling her. But she doesn't interest me, either. Go on, sir. You have my full attention."

"Oh, what's the use?" said Granier wearily. "I only want to explain that you can't altogether blame that poor old bastard. I don't like him. He's a fraud and a most shocking coward. One day I'll probably run him in for pinching little girls in cinemas, or something. It's about all he's capable of. He never had any guts. Of course he collaborated. What do you expect? You've only got to say boo, and he backs away, howling. He didn't do any real harm. He said, Yes, sir, and, Thank you, sir, and smiled when they kicked him. He didn't inform on anyone. He's not responsible for what happened to you." He added deliberately, "Or to your parents."

Max glanced at him, then lowered his lashes. His face was impassive, and the hand that selected a fresh cigarette as steady as a rock. He said in a quiet, pleasant voice, "I'm surprised that you, as a policeman, do not believe in collective responsibility. Aren't we all responsible for each other? That's what you're always preaching at me. Quiqueran may be a harmless little man. But it's Quiqueran and the millions like him who are responsible for—as you are kind enough to remind me—the deportation of my parents and my sister. Don't forget my sister. Do you really imagine I have any pity for him? If I could kill him and get away with it, I'd kill him, this instant. You're a slobbering old sentimentalist. Sentimentality may be a civic virtue, but to me it's quite obscene. What use is Quiqueran to the world? He's a coward and a lecher and a hypocrite and a fool. He poses as a Don Juan, but all the whoring he does is to drool over underclothes in lingerie shops. No one believes in him, not even himself. He's a phoney through and through. Even down to his precious visiting card."

Granier listened to this in silence. He was growing more and more aware of the nagging pain inside him; it was always worse when he was disturbed.

Max went on, "Didn't you know about that? It bears the inscription: '*René Quiqueran, Chargé des Cours de la Sorbonne. Conferencier de l'Office du Tourisme (Syndicat d'Initiative de Portelet-sur-Seine)*'. It sounds grand. It's a pity he was never near the Sorbonne."

"Very amusing," said Granier sourly. Then it seemed as if Max's derisive smile jerked the words out of him. He went a brick-red. "I'm going to ask you a question. You say, 'What use is Quiqueran to the world.' Well, my friend, what use are you?"

In the ensuing silence, Anni's voice was raised: "Supper's ready."

Max said not a word. His face was dark with the blood that had rushed into it. He stared at Granier. His breath was coming quickly.

It was the Inspector who turned away. He ran an embarrassed hand through his hair, mumbling, "Oh, never mind. I'm sorry, Max. I shouldn't have said that. Only we—we like you, my wife and I, and to Patricia you seem to be the sun and the moon. It hurts to see you setting out so blindly for damnation—Where are you going? Aren't you staying for supper?"

"No. I am not staying." Max's colour had faded. His voice was as sharp as a lash. "I prefer to set out for damnation. If it was anyone but you who said that, I'd kill him."

"Anni will be very disappointed."

"That's too bad." The hysteria shrilled in his voice. "That's too bloody bad. Anni will be disappointed and Patricia will need her nappies changing. Find yourself another nursemaid!"

Granier raised his hands in a despairing gesture. He was wondering what Anni would say to him, and cursing his appalling lack of tact.

"And if I meet Quiqueran, I'll break every bone in his blasted body. And cut his throat—I'll damn well cut yours in a moment—"

Granier, despite his distress, grinned at this, and Max met that smile with a white rage which immediately began to dissolve and change. Then he gasped out, "You can't leave well alone, can you? You're a policeman, aren't you, not a bloody preacher." With a strange, melodramatic gesture, he put a hand to his heart, spreading out long, slender fingers against the check pattern of his shirt. He turned his head sideways to peer up at Granier who was four inches taller than he was. His mouth twisted in a bitter smile. "Ah," he said, "why the hell must you make me lose my temper? It hurts. I shan't be able to to eat for days."

Granier said eagerly, "Have a drink. That'll settle you. It always helps me."

"No. I'm going."

"You won't do anything silly, will you?"

"If I do," said Max, "you'll feel a hell of a responsibility for it, won't you?"

And with this he swung on his heel and was out of the door.

*   *   *

He came into the Café Niçoise, and said good-evening to Madame Dupont. He shook his head when she offered him dinner.

"If you're *fauché*, you can have it on the house," she said. She had a weakness for this wild, handsome boy. He had once come to her help when she had a couple of tough and drunken lorry-drivers who refused either to pay or to leave. He could not be more than five foot seven, and he was slight of build, but the lorry-drivers had quickly slunk out; there had been no scene, no brawl. She looked now at his haggard, exhausted face, with the enormous eyes, and thought it was a shame that he had no mother, nor even a nice, comfortable girl-friend to look after him. She said coaxingly, "A nice plate of soup, now. It's good. I made it myself."

He shook his head. "Thank you, auntie, but it'd be wasted on me. I couldn't keep it down."

"What's the matter with you? Is it your stomach? I've got something the doctor gave me—"

"No, my love," he said. "It's not my belly, it's my temper. It's the kind of thing one's smacked for when young. Don't be sorry for me. It's my own fault." He slid his arm round her thirty-six inch waist. "Give me some wine. It's all right. I've got the money. I was paid this morning." And he fell on to the nearest chair as if he were done for, giving her a wide, desperate smile that made her want to cry, for he was too young to look like that; at his age he should not have a care in the world.

22

"Have a drink with me," he said. "Come on, auntie. Sit down and give me the local gossip."

He stretched out his hand for the bottle of wine. Her eyes fell to his wrist, where the number 8935 was branded. He saw the direction of her gaze and moved swiftly so that the cuff of his jacket shot down and covered it.

She said, "And how are all the pretty English misses opposite?"

He gave her a half-smile. The wine had restored him a little. "Oh, I don't know. They don't interest me." He checked himself. "I'm a liar. That's not true. They interest me very much. But not as girls, if you know what I mean. Imagine, auntie—they come from an era that's dead and done. They are all *jeunes filles, bien elevées*. They have a lot of money, and their papas all drive in a Mercédès-Benz or Cadillac, and here they are to learn how to curtsey and how to hook a husband. But I think they're like lost children, wandering in a world that was smashed to pieces, four years ago. What future is there for them? And what will happen when they meet reality?"

"They aren't all lost," she said. Her shrewd blue eyes glinted wickedly. Thirty years ago she had been a very pretty woman. "There's one little girl who isn't all that *bien elevée*, either. She once came in here for some cigarettes. She speaks like a French girl, and her French doesn't come out of the drawing-room. I've seen her looking at the boys. Old Quiqueran has an eye to her, but she snubbed him good and proper."

"I know the one you mean," said Max indifferently. "Her name's Nora. Has old Quiqueran been bothering you again?"

"Oh," said Madame Dupont, "he comes in here for a free meal, from time to time. If I don't give it him, he sends me no more clients. He's full of his conquests. He says there's an American lady who's madly in love with him, and wants to have a child by him. I must say, I find that very hard to believe. I sometimes wonder how his wife puts up with him."

"His wife? I didn't know he was married."

"He hardly knows it, himself. He leaves her in Paris with the children. Why don't you get married, M. Max?"

"Me? Good God!"

"Why not? There'd be someone to look after you and prevent your losing your temper. You'd better give me that jacket. There's a button coming off. If you had a wife, your buttons would be looked after."

He said, with a twisted smile, "I'm not sure if that's the main reason for marriage, darling. I'll never get married. First, there's no decent woman will put up with me, and secondly, I couldn't put up with a decent woman for more than a week at a time."

"That's young man's talk," said Madame Dupont placidly. She adjusted her spectacles to examine the dangling button, then threaded a needle. "There's plenty of girls would be glad for you to smile at them."

"I'll smile at them, then. No one can call me disobliging," said Max, watching her dexterous fingers. "But marry—no. What's the use? You marry. You bring children into the world. And then, bang, bang, bang—no children, no wife, no world. Do you remember the last war but one, auntie?"

"Perfectly well," said Madame Dupont. She sighed. "One invasion is very like another. One Bosche is very like another, too. They are a strange people. They lack, I think, imagination."

"There was a cartoon," said Max, taking the mended jacket from her and slinging it about his shoulders, "Thank you. You're a dear. It was about the Treaty of Versailles. There's Clemenceau and Wilson walking down the steps, and one of them says, 'Strange, I thought I heard a child

24

weeping.' And there's a naked baby behind the pillar, with a little halo round its head that says, '1940 Class'." He rose to his feet, smiling down at her. "It might have been me, auntie. There must be plenty of babies weeping now for the next war. I'm going to bed. I'm dead-beat." He added, half-angrily, "And I'm so damned fed-up. I hate the whole bloody world. The old so-and-so's right. I'm no use. Good-night, old dear. Don't pay any attention to me. I've got the *cafard*."

"You'd feel better if you had something to eat."

"I tell you, I couldn't keep it down. My guts are not what they used to be. Granier and I are a pair. Good-night." He bent his head to kiss her cheek. "Thank you for mothering me. If I ever do get married, you shall do my wedding breakfast for me."

*   *   *

M. Quiqueran came out for a breath of air and a possible glass of wine. The evening was stiflingly hot. When the slender shadow brushed against him, he jumped. Then he saw who it was, and turned white, casting frenzied glances around him.

Those frightened eyes blew Max's temper to white heat. His head was aching badly, as it always did after an emotional outburst, and there were shooting pains in his belly, a memory of the time when he had starved and caught typhus on top of it. He said between his teeth, his voice tight with rage and hate and self-disgust, "I hoped I'd meet you. I wanted to tell you again what a swine you are. One day I'll kill you. I carry a knife, you know. Shall I show it you?" And suddenly he flicked out the blade so that it almost touched M. Quiqueran's chest.

The unhappy man leapt back, still looking frantically for help. There was no one in sight. Only on the top floor of Rosedene College a light still burned. He turned his eyes towards it, half opening his mouth to cry out, then, as the young man burst out laughing, began to tremble.

"The Bosches must have had fun with you," said Max. "Did you fall on your knees to them, and crawl and weep? This knife accounted for a couple of them, if it interests you." He snapped the blade back. He said scornfully, "O.K. I'm not going to kill you now. It'll come one day, when you least expect it. Were you going to ask the English girls to protect you? I'll call them for you. I speak English, you know. I was in England for two months." Then he swung round, cupped his hands to his mouth, and roared out "Mees! Mees! English Mees! Help! Fire! God-damn!"

"For pity's sake," began M. Quiqueran, then watched in fascinated horror as the lights came on, like a procession of glow-worms. He heard the sound of windows shooting up. In a moment Miss Pelham would appear. M. Quiqueran detested Miss Pelham, and was scared to death of her. She had once spoken her mind to him; she told him if he ever said one more word to her girls, she would instantly inform the police. He longed to run away, but curiosity held him there; he waited for the vision of this English old maid who would undoubtedly appear with a nightcap on her head and a candle in her hand.

Max, silent now, stepped back. He stared up at the windows, his eyes glimmering, his black hair wild about him. The lights were going out again, one by one. Miss Pelham did not appear. Only the top window remained open, as Deirdre leant across the sill to stare down at this extraordinary young man who had so atrociously serenaded her.

Max did not see her, for her light was now out. He was shaking with anger and hysteria; his eyes were dilated. But Deirdre saw him clearly enough, and continued to stare, for he was like nothing she had ever seen. He was plainly mad, but he was also very beautiful; he stood with his head flung back, his hands a little raised as if he were inviting her to come down. The she saw that M. Quiqueran had noticed her, and she slipped back into the room, sitting down rather breathlessly on the chintz-covered bed.

M. Quiqueran said in a weak, scared rage, "This is a fine thing, waking everyone up at this hour of night. It's disgraceful. I shall report it first thing tomorrow morning."

"Oh, go to hell," said Max in a snarl, and he gave M. Quiqueran a shove that all but sent him on to his face. He said savagely, "I meant what I said. I'll kill you yet. You damned fascist!"

Then, exhausted, his mind whirling with confused and bestial images, he screwed up his eyes, turned his back on M. Quiqueran, and walked into the Hostel.

The lights were out there, too. It was after eleven. The older boys left early for their work in Paris and the younger ones, who were still at school, were supposed to be in bed by nine. Max did not switch the lights on. He walked down the hallway that even on this hot evening smelt chill and stale. He came into the big ground-floor room that served as a dining-room, and stood there for a while, leaning against the table, cigarette dangling from his lips.

The château had stood there for over three hundred years. Once it had gleamed and glittered; here a gay, light lady had welcomed her royal lover. Once marquise and duchesse in powdered wigs and hooped skirts had danced the minuet, danced away the country's wealth, until the dancing changed its tune, with tumbril and descending knife to make its beat. The minuet became the carmagnole, and now the carmagnole had turned into the *horah*. The elegant slippers had mouldered into dust, and rebellious Jewish feet from Eastern Europe tramped the boards in their stead. Corydon and Phyllis had fled to the woods they had sworn never to re-enter, while the children of David followed their yellow star, battering down shepherd and shepherdess in alien song.

This charming, useless, hopelessly uncomfortable mansion had been allowed to sink into ruin, until M. Wolff took it over. The boys lived in a kind of aristocratic squalor, with taps that barely trickled into ornate basins, elementary sanitation, scarcely any heating, and elegant, high-ceilinged, panelled rooms where the draughts whistled down.

Max had no mind to the ghosts that stirred about him, rustling their silken skirts, flashing their swords before his exhausted eyes. It was his own ghosts that surrounded him, and now, sick and exhausted, he had no power against them. Their skeleton fingers closed clammily over his, drawing him back remorselessly down that long, bleak corridor of the mind, to the final memory, with the smoking chimneys at the end, back to sights and sounds of a world where hope was gone.

He stood there, pressing his fingers against his eyes. His head was swimming. The desolation that consumed him was so strong that he groaned at the agony of its impact. *There* it had been different. *There* there had been the urge to fight. *There* all one's energies were assembled for survival. But now the struggle was done. One was left in a world that trundled along as if nothing had happened. *What use are you?* The lighted cigarette end began to quiver and tremble, and at that moment there was a movement against his leg; he recovered himself and grabbed at something that squealed and swore in protest.

He recognised both the squealing and the swearing. He caught at the curly head that butted against him, and shifted his grip to a pyjama collar. He said in a fierce whisper, "What the hell are you doing here at this hour of night? Why aren't you in bed? What devilment are you up to now?"

Jean-Louis whined, "Oh, Maxy, don't, don't—" The

whining was purely hypocritical and assumed. He was well
aware that Max would not hurt him. He was the privileged
darling of the Hostel, being six years younger than any of
them; everybody spoilt him. But he continued to wail, and
the wailing beat on Max's nerves so that in his exasperation
he cuffed him hard. The wailing changed to swearing of
such gutter indecency that Max fell into an ominous silence,
and Jean-Louis at last grew silent, too.

Max said grimly, "Have you finished?"

"Yes, Maxy," said the little boy in an angelic voice.

"You're sure?"

"Oh yes, Max."

Max could see the whites of the enormous eyes that
peered up at him. Suddenly he laughed, swung out his
clenched fist as if to strike, and shoved the little boy away
from him. "Get up to bed," he said. "Get up to bed at once
before I skin you. You disgraceful little *chaser*. Who taught
you such language? I've never heard anything like it."

"We had a visit today," said Jean-Louis, ignoring this.

"What? Oh God, not another of them." Max for the
moment forgot the need for discipline. He lit another
cigarette and stared down at the child in half-amused
exasperation. He said, "Who was it this time?"

"A lady from Paris. And there are two American ladies
coming tomorrow. They are doing a survey on the effects
of the camps. M. Wolff wants you to be the interpreter."

"Well, he can want," snapped Max.

These erratic visits were the bane of M. Wolff's life.
The Hostel was run on a most precarious financial basis, so
he dared not discourage visitors who might be persuaded
to make a little gift, but these visitations upset both the
routine and the boys, besides causing a great deal of unnecessary work.

"She was ever such a grand lady," said Jean-Louis.
"She kissed me. They always kiss me."

"God knows why."

"They like kissing me." His voice piped up. *"Quel âge as-tu, mon petit?"* He imitated the fluting Parisian voice with some skill, and Max choked, then cleared his throat to say in stifled tones, "Shut up. How long did she stay?"

"She stayed to supper. Where've you been, Maxy? Old Wolff was asking about you."

"It's nothing to do with you where I've been. Did she give any money?"

"Ten thousand francs." Jean-Louis burst out laughing. "Oh, old Wolff was just furious—"

"Ssh! You'll wake the whole house."

"And she was stinking with money. She was stinking with scent, too. We had to sing for her. She went into the synagogue. I don't think she'd ever been in a synagogue before. We sang *Ba Menuchah*. She said it was a pretty little song. She said I was a pretty little boy, too." And once again he began to chant, *"Quel âge as-tu, mon petit?"* interspersing the mimicry with succulent sounds of kissing.

"I'll give you a good hiding in a moment," threatened Max, then he began to laugh again, for he, too, in his time had suffered from these fine ladies; they had not offered to kiss him, but their patronage had been hard to endure, and he would never forget the bright, shining eyes that dwelt so greedily on suffering.

Jean-Louis giggled, then said again, "There'll be the two American ladies. They've got funny names. I don't remember them. They are from New York. Perhaps they'll take me back with them. Why aren't you going to be here, Maxy? It's Sunday. You're not working."

"I've told you I'll not be here. And now you're going back to bed."

"Oh, Max—"

"Did you hear what I said?"

30

Jean-Louis recognised the note of finality. He scuttled across the hallway, and Max walked slowly behind him.

He could see the candles burning in the room that served as synagogue. The great embroidered Star of David gleamed in their light. It meant nothing to him, except that it signified the only home he knew. It brought no comfort to him, and he came silently into the small cell that served as his room; the four eldest boys in the Hostel had rooms of their own, and he was one of them.

He lay on his bed, and the ghosts crawled like maggots in his brain. It seemed to him that his loneliness was more than he could endure; it was all the more terrible because human companionship could not touch it.

He recognised, quite impersonally, that the black mood was coming upon him. It was like insanity. It shut him off from the world. The fits had grown less and less frequent, but even now a chance word could spark them off, and the word had been spoken, and the devil again possessed him. Soon he would have to get up, for he would not be able to sleep; at the moment the nightmare so weighed upon him that he could not even bring himself to stir.

And as he lay there, sweating, moaning a little, his face white, crucified, Deirdre, also unable to sleep, was writing painstakingly in her diary, "Their was a most peculiar thing tonight. A young man came and shouted up all sorts of quear things at us, I suppose he was drunk." She added, after some reflection, "He was awfully good-looking."

But the words meant nothing to her, and suddenly she stopped writing and started drawing, instead; out of her pencil grew a sad, fallen-angel face, tormented and beautiful, so beautiful that her own pencil faltered at what it produced.

And presently Max, dragging himself in silence and pain, crossed the Place du Triangle.

Chapter Two

On Sunday, in the Place du Triangle, everybody stayed in bed until ten or eleven o'clock. Granier lay there, and Patricia sat on top of him, rolling about on the eiderdown while Anni made coffee. M. Quiqueran did not get up until midday. Sleep was his escape; in its comforting warmth he could slip into a world where neither Germans nor Jews frightened him, and where women were soft and amenable. He lay there with the bedclothes over his head, thinking vaguely that he should go to Paris to see Marie and the children; presently the delicious languor stole upon him again and he fell asleep.

Only in the Hostel and the College was there activity. Miss Pelham always conducted her girls to the English church at the far end of Portelet-sur-Seine; now, at a quarter past ten, they walked out of the main gate, hatted, gloved, prayer-books under their arms. Miss Pelham stood on the path like a general and inspected them. Nora's skirt was too short and much too tight. It was really quite indecent. It was a miracle that the child could sit down in it. She must be spoken to after the service. Miss Pelham kept her fancy as much under control as she did her bosom, but she could not help thinking that Nora in this skin-tight skirt, with her plump figure and black fringe, resembled the product of an older finishing school than Rosedene College.

Then a natural exasperation drove all thoughts of Nora from her mind.

"Where," she demanded, "is Deirdre?"

"Deirdre?" they all repeated, one after another, like well-bred parrots, "Deirdre, Deirdre, Deirdre?" And their charmingly groomed heads all turned, as if they expected Deirdre to materialise at their shoulders. Their clear voices all pealed out the same note; to Miss Pelham's irritated eye they seemed like chorus girls, so perfectly timed were their gestures and voices.

She said in annoyance, "Yes. Deirdre. Where is she?"

"I expect she's still in her room, Miss Pelham." This was Nora. There was nothing in the remark that could possibly be suspect, yet Miss Pelham glanced at her sharply. However, she only said, "Well, please go upstairs and tell her she's keeping us all waiting."

Deirdre came down a minute later. She made no attempt to apologise. She looked untidy, and Miss Pelham, too genuinely angry to scold—"Never lose your temper with the girls"—tweaked her beret (so unsuitable) into place and, in a grim silence, buttoned up the rather shabby light coat. It was, she could not help noticing, a model coat; it had probably been worn by her sister, ten years ago.

Deirdre slipped into her place. She said nothing, only pushed back the heavy fair hair with a black-gloved hand. The glove had a hole between thumb and first finger; it left a dusty mark on the white forehead. Her grey eyes stared ahead. What a waste of a lovely day—At home she would be walking the hills with Rusty at her side. The wind would be blowing through her uncovered hair, stinging the colour to her cheeks. The ghosts of the Irish past would keep her company; warring O'Byrnes and O'Tooles would be bloodily trampling the grass, giants in their clanking armoury of gold, thrusting their skeens into each other, and cursing the name of Lord Deputy Strafford with every whisky-laden breath. And then she would go home, and there would be hot scones for tea, and she could sprawl in the armchair and dream and draw and dream again.

And here were tawny, dusty houses, with shutters still drawn. The harsh sunlight beat upon her eyes, and the air smelt of drains and petrol and garlic and cheap tobacco; even the dogs and cats that lay sunning themselves on the pavement were shabby, mangy things, with suspicion in their eyes.

She turned her gaze upon her companions' faces. Her fingers moved a little as if she were holding a pencil. If only something would happen. If only she could get away for a little while—

Miss Pelham spoke. "We are very late," she said. "Please walk as quickly as you can."

And so they set forth, twenty-five pretty little girls, a decorous ballet of brides-to-be, material for the *Sketch* and the *Tatler*, next year's debs, descended from a handful of lords, a scattering of knights, a brush of generals—little flowers of the wordly world, with a thousand thoughts milling in their heads, and a well-bred indifference sculptured on their delightful faces.

*   *   *

M. Wolff was preparing for the American visitation. He was doing this, as always, by sweeping out of sight everything that should not be seen. As the crocodile passed, he clicked his fingers to the boys who were helping him, and beckoned them to the window to watch the show. They stood there in a lounging silence, their eyes on the prim procession. There was Chaim from Poland, and Baruch. There was Nathan from Czechoslovakia, and Moishe from Germany. There was Jacob and Saul and Binem. Their hair was black, red, blond. They came from all over Europe, and the brand of their race was on their wrists and on their memories. They looked at the sugar-candy English misses, and whistled softly beneath their breath, while M. Wolff said, sighing, "And all for sale," then quoted:

"Filles, veuillez vous entremettre
D'escouter pourquoy pleure et crie;
C'est pour ce que ne me puys mettre,
Ne que monnoye qu'on descrie.

The girls swept by. It is possible that they were aware of the inspection, but no observer could have guessed it; not one uplifted chin faltered. Only Nora's black eyes shifted sideways in a glance as swift as the flicker of a snake's tongue. Then the crocodile vanished round the corner of the Place du Triangle, and a slow grin spread from face to face, ending in a concerted splutter of laughter that grew in volume as M. Wolff's face lengthened in sardonic disapproval.

"Come," he said at last, "there's work to be done."

"I like the little blonde," said Nathan, who was ginger and resembled Harpo Marx, but Jacob shook his head, saying, "No, she's only a baby. I'll take the little black-haired *poule* for choice——"

"That will do," said M. Wolff. Then he said suddenly and sharply, unaware that a similar remark had just been made by his colleague across the way, "Where is Max?"

There was a pause. He witnessed again that strange drawing together; it was a thing of the spirit, for their bodies scarcely moved. He glared at them, his heavy-jowled face settling into lines of resignation and disgust. They had little bond, these boys of his, but there was the odd, unbreakable freemasonry of a common suffering, as could be seen in the waiting-room of a hospital, where the sick were compelled towards each other, with nothing more than a pain, a limp, a disfigurement to bind them. Between these young men was something infinitely remote from friendship, love or common interest. For the most part they endured each other very well, though Baruch the Pole disliked Moishe the *yekke*; French mistrusted German, and German mis-

35

trusted French. But in any crisis they swung together like parts of the same machine; they would lie themselves to death for one another, defy authority to the last drop of blood. When M. Wolff first met them, they had been a gang of savages, standing back to back, knives drawn. And now, for all they might detest each other, they would be together in a flash if one of them were threatened.

He saw their wooden looks, their eyes grown expressionless. He wondered with a sudden stab of apprehension if Max were in trouble again. He was for nine-tenths of the time a dependable boy; he was doing excellently in his work. Yet there had always been bad moments with him, and once or twice the moments had been very bad indeed, especially when he was off on one of his fugues. There was M. Quiqueran, for instance. M. Wolff liked Quiqueran no better than anyone else, but he would have preferred his executioner to be someone else than one of his own boys. Max in one of his black moods could be violent, ruthless, unscrupulous and unpredictable. God knows what he was up to now.

He repeated angrily, "Well, where is he? Doesn't he know these two American ladies are coming today? I'll admit his English isn't up to much, but he does at least speak a little, and I don't suppose these fine ladies from New York speak a word of anything else."

He broke off, looking so disturbed and furious that the boys moved a little away from him. American financial help was so essential, and these two ladies with their damned survey—did the Americans never do anything else but make surveys?—might just possibly bring a few so indispensable dollars into the Hostel account. He glared around him at the damp patches on the walls, the flaking ceilings, the uneven floor. He saw the inadequate furniture, the poor lighting, remembered how in the depths of winter the central heating was never reliable, even when there was sufficient fuel. The small private dream he had once cradled now seemed something in another world. A comfortable sitting-room with armchairs. A decent record-player for boys whose greatest bond was music, perhaps even the television. It was surely not so much to ask. And now these two women were coming, full, perhaps, of the best intentions (preferably green-backed) and he would scarcely be able to exchange a word with them.

He roared, "Damn the blasted lot of you! Where is Max?"

He saw them shrug. The old man's off again, silly old b—. Eyelids drooped. Lower lips protruded. "*Je ne sais pas.*" They had been saying, "*Je ne sais pas,*" almost since they were weaned. They had said it to the police, Nazis, camp-guards, interrogators. That it should now be turned on him was an irony he did not appreciate. He was preparing to flay them, when Jean-Louis piped up:

"He's gone out, M. Wolff. He went out at two o'clock this morning."

"Two o'clock!"

"Yes, M. Wolff. I heard him. I looked out to see who it was. I said hallo, but he didn't answer." Then he fell silent, his eyes wide, for he remembered Max's face as he walked blindly down the stairs; his look had been such that the greeting had only been a whisper and he had not dared repeat it. The ruined, handsome face turned briefly to his was that of the damned. Jean-Louis, who loved him, had shrunk back into his dormitory with beating heart, as if the damnation might be turned on him.

M. Wolff, who had been stacking up old newspapers, stood for a moment with his back to the room. His face was working; he chewed his lower lip. His thoughts eddied and swirled. What the hell do you expect? What the bloody hell do you expect? You take 'em as kids, you beat the daylights out of them, you destroy everything they could hold on to, you show 'em conclusively that men are brutes and fiends. You throw them into the sewer, sink or swim, and you wait on the bank to knock them on the head if they emerge for breath. Oh God, he thought, then shut his eyes, looking then an embittered, disillusioned old man.

He supposed he should have foreseen this. It had happened before. He wondered what had caused it. Perhaps it was himself. It needed so little. Of course it might be nothing. Max was a boy; perhaps he felt like walking, perhaps he wanted a girl, perhaps, perhaps, oh, perhaps anything. But then with him one never knew. A handsome face, a lithe body, a swift mind, a bright imagination. He had all these. What more could one want? One could say he had everything. Except the one thing, just the one small thing—.

There had been that black market business. And that fight in the bar. Once something even uglier. Next time it would be the police.

He swung round on the boys. They were pretending to work, but he knew that Max was with them as much as if he had been in the room. He spoke harshly, wishing he did not always feel so tired, wondering if the job were growing too much for him, "I'm going out. If Max comes in while I'm gone, tell him I'll wring his neck for him. And get this place tidy. It looks like a pigsty. If the ladies arrive before I get back, show them into my office and get cook to make them coffee."

It was a pity that pity could not last. Once compassion turned to charity, pride became a luxury one could not afford. M. Wolff was an arrogant man, but he would have crawled down the garden path for a few hundred dollars; he knew it and hated himself for it. He stepped into the blazing sunlight, and met Granier wheeling Patricia in her pram.

"Is Max with you?" he asked, without preamble.

Granier went red. He was a big man, and this habit of blushing had always caused him embarrassment. He cleared his throat. He said, "No. Why?"

"He's walked out," said M. Wolff.

Granier knew what this meant well enough. He did not know as much of Max's private life as M. Wolff, but this was largely deliberate; no one was more aware than he of the potential danger that lay in the boy. He said, answering an unspoken question, "I met Quiqueran, a few minutes ago." Then he cried out furiously, for he had already quarrelled with Anni about this, "I suppose it's my fault. But he shouldn't be so easily upset at his age. He's neurotic."

"And what do you mean by that?" said M. Wolff. He was blowing himself up with rage. He looked like a truculent frog.

Granier told him. "I only asked him what use he thought he was. I was perfectly justified. He goes on like a young gangster, and I know he carries a knife. What does he expect? He talks of murder as the English talk of the weather. Why can't he pull himself together and make the best of things? Other people do. Other people have suffered just as much, only they don't bellyache about it all the time——"

M. Wolff interrupted him in a whisper. "You said *that* to him?"

"I did. And I'd say it again."

"You damned fool," said M. Wolff; then savagely, "Of course your trouble is you're anti-semitic. You're down on Max because he's a Jew."

Granier refused to answer this, and they stood facing each other in the middle of the Place du Triangle, two middle-aged men, both unhappy and angry. Granier was very tall, and M. Wolff very short. They looked a little absurd, and M. Wolff had stalked out in such a hurry that he had forgotten to remove his kappel. But their indignation and shared apprehension blazed about them; they could only stare at each other in a kind of horrified rage.

Then M. Wolff sighed. "All right," he said. "I suppose he asked for it. I suppose I might have said the same. I don't blame you for being anti-semitic."

"I am nothing of—"

"I am myself at times. All Jews are. Let me tell you a story, sir. It will help to blow away the fumes."

Granier gave him a resigned look. M. Wolff was addicted to stories, and they often went on for a very long time.

"It's about the Englishman, the German, the Frenchman and the Jew. They all set out to write a book about elephants. The Englishman produced a fat volume called 'Elephant Shoot'. The German wrote six volumes on: '*Die Analyse von Freud und die Mythologie vom Elefant*'. The Frenchman had an elegant tome privately printed: '*L'Elephant et l'Amour*'. And the Jew? He gave it up. He said that elephants were too anti-semitic."

Granier merely looked at him. Patricia, who was growing bored, gave a sudden shout and threw her toys out of her pram. Her father and M. Wolff both stooped to pick them up and banged into each other. They raised flushed faces, and M. Wolff began to laugh.

"Ah," he said, "I'm going to change my job."

"Try mine," said Granier bitterly.

"After all," said M. Wolff, "what are we expected to do? If people want to go to the devil, they'll go to the devil, and neither you nor I can prevent them. You put them into prison. I put a fireguard round them. It doesn't make a tinker's damn of difference. As fast as you put things back in the pram, baby throws them out again, and you're back where you started."

And indeed, Patricia, delighted to be the centre of

attention, had hurled her teddy-bear back on to the pavement.

The crocodile was returning from church. M. Wolff watched them, remarking, "Well, for all I know, Max may have thrown himself into the Seine, but the American Joint is visiting us, this afternoon, and come death or damnation, I must have an interpreter. I am not losing dollars for Max or anyone else. We are, after all, poor, bloody Jewish refugees, and we need dollars more than anything else in the world. I am going to secede from the religion of my fathers. I am going to ask the help of a Christian and a virgin. This is a major crisis, and no scruples, Inspector, racial, religious or any other, are going to stand in my way."

He prepared to cross the road towards Rosedene College, only he half-turned to snap over his shoulder, "Another time, Granier, you might curb your moralising tongue. It surely required only a grain of common sense to realise that when dealing with a desperate young man, one doesn't ask him what use he thinks he is." He saw that the Inspector was discomfited, and this pleased him. He shouted out, as *coup de grâce*, "Why don't you ask yourself what use you are? The answer might astonish you."

Granier did not reply to this. Patricia threw her teddy-bear out once again, and he meekly bent to retrieve it. And, as he did so, M. Wolff boldly rang the bell at Rosedene College front door.

*   *   *

M. Wolff and Miss Pelham had known each other for a long time and had—though neither would have admitted it—a kind of acidulated affection for each other.

They sat now in Miss Pelham's study. The room was fresh and white. A bowl of roses stood on the desk. At its side was a framed photograph of two children. They were the children of Miss Pelham's niece. She was a most devoted aunt. She looked at M. Wolff. She was as always immaculately tidy and clean. Her waved, lacquered hair was brushed glossily back. He noted this, and glanced down with a rueful self-mockery at his badly pressed trousers, and jacket fraying at the wrist. He gave a push to his kappel, sending it over one eye. He said, "And how are all your little virgins today?"

Miss Pelham wished he would not speak like this. Foreigners were so outspoken, and Jews tended to be worse than any of them. She was too sophisticated to be shocked, but M. Wolff seemed to her a gross and common little man and, as she thought this, she had a violent desire to brush the ash off his suit and put needle and thread to the button hanging from his open-necked shirt. She could see the hair on his chest glistening with sweat. She averted her eyes. She said, "They are all very well, thank you. How are your boys?"

"Oh, fine, fine," said M. Wolff. He thought, as he had thought before, how strange it was that here on the left were two dozen young girls, and there on the right, almost the equivalent number of boys, yet the Atlantic might flow between them for all they had in common. He said, knowing this would exasperate, yet speaking in bitter earnestness, "Do you know, madame, I sometimes wonder which are the more lost, yours or mine."

"I really don't know what you mean," said Miss Pelham coolly. She bent her head to smell one of the roses. "Would you like a cup of coffee, M. Wolff? A glass of sherry, perhaps?"

"No! It would send me to sleep. Madame, do you know what my idea of heaven is? You can keep your stars and angels and Abraham's bosom, too. I don't want them. All I want is bed. Ah God, to lie in bed and sleep and sleep and sleep. I believe I could do it for the rest of my life. A boyless world and a soft mattress."

"I seldom get tired," said Miss Pelham. This was by no means true, but somehow she had to sound entirely efficient before this sad, fat old man who sprawled in her chair, his stomach bulging over his trouser belt, his sorrowful, cynical eyes surveying her, taking her to pieces and putting her together again.

He said again, "After all, they belong to the past, your little girls and my boys. My young men come from a world no one will ever see again—Did you travel a lot when you were young, madame?"

"I have been over most of Europe."

"Did you dance in Vienna, madame? Did you drink apricot brandy by the banks of the Danube, with the gypsies playing? I come from Vienna. In my day they said, *'Gruss Gott'*. When I left, they were saying, *'Heil Hitler'*. I don't know what they say now. It doesn't matter. It's all gone. Maybe it was bad and feudal and unfair. But it had something. The young will never know what we have known."

Miss Pelham found herself resenting this enforced partnership of her carefully preserved self and this old man gone to seed. But sentimentality stirred within her, and suddenly, to her astonishment, the tears pricked her eyes. She said sharply, "I don't know why you think my girls belong to the past. I assure you they are entirely modern."

"Ah," he said, "their world is done, too. They're anachronisms. They're a hundred years out of date. The money trickles through their pretty fingers, and they've nothing to do but curtsey and use the right knife and fork, until some noble English lord marries them to breed more pupils for you. It's not a finishing school you run, madame. It's finished. What equipment have they for this modern, tough, armour-plated world?"

"Really, M. Wolff," said Miss Pelham. She gave a little high-pitched laugh.

He said reflectively, "The thing that has always amazed me is that none of my boys has ever made love to one of your girls." He saw her expression, and grinned. "It's all right, my dear. I'm not changing profession in mid-stream. Such a situation would not please me at all. But the young don't always see the barriers as plainly as we do, and they're not so bad-looking, our children, when you come to think of it—not so bad-looking at all."

He broke off. He remembered the good-looking boy who was the cause of this whole conversation. His smile vanished. He said rather grimly, "However, to business. I'll put it briefly. I've got a couple of American ladies on my hands. I want you to lend me one of your girls for a couple of hours. To act as interpreter." His eyes swivelled up. "I promise her diplomatic immunity. I guarantee that my boys will treat her like a princess."

He had never in all their acquaintance made such a request. Miss Pelham could not decently say it was unreasonable. She was, however, startled and disturbed. It was breaking the unwritten law that had always existed between the Hostel and the College. She suspected that M. Wolff thought this, too, for he added in a grumbling voice, "Well, we shan't eat her. If you can suggest someone else.... Perhaps you'd care to come, yourself."

"I'm far too busy!"

"All right. All right. I tell you we shan't eat her. Surely," said M. Wolff, in a rough voice, "you know that Jews only eat Christians at Pesach. At the moment we are glutted and safe. Pesach has been over for two months. And it's only for a couple of hours. All the child will have to do is to translate a handful of damn silly questions and interpret the answers back. She'll be returned to you intacta."

Miss Pelham wanted most passionately to refuse. Instead she found herself saying calmly, "Very well. I'll see what I can do."

44

"All your girls speak French, don't they?"

Miss Pelham did not answer this for a moment. She was considering the matter. All her girls spoke a reasonable French when they left, but there were only two who already spoke it fluently. One was Nora—and she was not sending Nora into the Hostel—and the other was Deirdre.

Deirdre.

The child lived in such a dream that probably she would not realise what was happening. But it might be good for her. It might wake her up.

She said, "Yes. I think I know who I'll send. She's a nice child and she speaks very good French. She had a French governess when she was little. Her name is Deirdre O'Brien. When do you want her to come over?"

"Oh, in an hour's time, perhaps. She can have dinner with us, then there'll be the interrogation." He rose heavily to his feet. He cocked an eye at her. "Any time you feel that a boy would be of—be of service to you—"

"Thank you, M. Wolff," said Miss Pelham. "If such an unlikely contingency arises, I shall be sure to let you know."

And presently she sent a messenger up to Deirdre's room, asking her to come to the study.

*　　　*　　　*

Max sat in the café with his three acquaintances. He had been drinking and smoking a great deal. The ash-tray was piled high. Food he had not touched; it would not have stayed in his stomach for five minutes. He was not drunk, but he was violently excited, and the emotions, all of them disintegrating, flared across his gaunt, beautiful face. He could not stay still for a second. He was perpetually stubbing at a cigarette, gesturing with the slender hands, shifting in his chair, drawing nearer to the table, then jerking away. An occasional shudder ran through him, and the eyes which explored incessantly his companions' faces were enormous and bright with fever.

He looked at them, cigarette dangling from lower lip. "I don't know," he said, "I'll have to think about it."

He was not a fool. He had been a great many things in his brief life, and he had done things that not even M. Wolff knew about, but he was not a fool. He had learnt not to be a fool seven years ago. He had been a beautiful little boy. People had sometimes associated that beauty with silliness. In that they were, as they sometimes discovered, very much mistaken. This he knew was a turning point. He had slid his foot many times over the boundary, but this was a little more. It was as if Granier stood at his shoulder. His face set suddenly in ugly, menacing lines. He looked at that moment every inch the gangster he had been called. The damned old bastard—what bloody right had he to talk like that? He was just a *flic* like other *flics*; he'd shoot the handcuffs on as soon as look at you. But never mind Granier. Granier didn't matter. Max, blowing smoke-rings, pouring himself out another glass of wine, saw clear before him the black hinter-land of the hunted, where he had lived his days. At that dread vision his soul instinctively faltered. His right hand clutched greedily the sword of danger, yet his left flinched from its steel. In this second of decision the danger might be always with him; he would live beneath its shadow, knowing that this was for always, this time there could be no turning back, never, never again.

"Make up your mind," said the man on his right. He called himself Jacques. It was not his name. "It's nothing much, after all." His voice lowered. "And there's money in it. You've as much right to that money as anyone else."

Max's temper blew out in a streak of flame. "You leave me alone," he said between his teeth, "I'll make up my mind in my own good time. I don't need you to tell me what to do." And his hand shot out, as if on a catapult, knocking the half-filled glass on to the floor, spilling the wine so that it lay in a pool at his feet.

The proprietor took one look at his face, ghastly in the dim light, and rushed out from behind the counter. His great hand came down on Max's shoulder, only to be withdrawn as if stung when the thin knife-blade flicked out, scarcely an inch from his belly. His head jerked down to look at it, then up to meet the set, smiling face. He muttered in a hoarse, trembling voice, "Get out. Get out, the pack of you. I'm going to ring for the police. You won't show your faces here again, if you've any sense. Get out!"

His companions were already on their feet. Max sat there, thrusting his legs out, leaning back in his chair. The blade snapped back, but the knife still lay on his palm. He waited in silence, always smiling, and the proprietor, liking the look of him not at all, backed, while the other customers watched with the impassivity of those to whom such scenes were no novelty.

Then Max rose to his feet in a swift, feline movement, and with a nod and a grin walked out into the street. He said to his companions, who were staring at him resentfully, "I'll let you know, boys. I'll meet you here tonight, when I've had time to think about it."

Then, without waiting for a reply, he turned away.

He was shaking from head to foot. He grew aware that he felt most dreadfully ill. It was like the onset of death, for fear accompanied it. He put a hand to his forehead, rubbed it viciously as if the pain of this would keep him from falling. He threw away his cigarette. Another puff of it would make him vomit. It was three in the afternoon, and he had had nothing to eat since lunch-time the day before. The reaction was already setting in; he knew it for what it was and fought desperately against it, against the corroding weakness, the sickness, the wild, frantic temper that could tear at his very guts, and the final humiliation of tears that would not, could not be checked. The self-hate was already devouring him; his legs were trembling so that they would scarcely bear his weight. It was always the same. He had accepted stoically the beatings, the torture, the non-stop hail of questions, and then, when it was done, and his persecutors gone, he had collapsed. There should have been victory in him, but there was nothing but a hell of defeat and despair.

Already the world had lost reality. The faces of the passers-by were distorted in fever. They were no longer the faces of human beings. They were the faces of Bosche's demons, vile, depraved, bestial in stupidity. The houses threatened to topple on his head, the pavement was keeling beneath his feet like a ship on a stormy sea. Yet somehow he managed to keep upright. He made his way towards the Seine. He reeled as he walked, gasping, clinging on to the last thread of his sanity.

He reached the river at last. He could not have said why, but he had to reach the river. He collapsed on to one of the benches and buried his face in his hands. He sat there for a long time. And slowly, as the day went by, he came back to his senses. The sweat was pouring off him, his hands shook like leaves in the wind, but he was in the world again, alive and free. At last he raised his head. His face was stripped of colour. The aquiline features stood out starkly, as if on a death mask. There were deep, graven lines from nose to mouth, and the eyes sank back into troughs of shadow. He stared at the river, grey now in the late afternoon. It seemed to him, and he thought this without melodrama, that it would be peaceful to be dead, but he did not want to die, he was young and the vitality was surging up again.

Then he thought, To hell with them, I'll do it. Why not? It would be exciting, something to exercise his ingenuity; it would enable him to pit his wits against an authority that for him would to the end of his days wear a swastika on its arm.

He rose unsteadily to his feet, to meet the eyes of a girl who, as he suddenly realised, must have been watching him for some time.

This angered him. He could not endure that anyone should witness his weakness. He turned so wild and ugly a look on her that her smile faltered and she backed a little. She wore very high heels and an almost skin-tight skirt. Then he recognised her. This was one of the English young ladies, and she was called Nora. He had once winked at her. She did not seem to him much of a young lady, and she did not look English, either, with her black hair and slanting eyes that fluttered their lashes at him. He half turned away from her. He thought contemptuously that the dragon must have her work cut out with this one, who wobbled towards him on her stiletto heels, flaunting herself like any tart from the streets. She did not interest him. She even disgusted him a little, for he was more fastidious than he would ever have admitted. She reminded him of others he had met, who had sold themselves to the German officers, who had laughed and danced while their compatriots were being murdered. He would have passed her by in silence, but she planted herself in his path. She smiled at him. She said, "Hallo."

He looked at her bleakly, without a smile. He said nothing.

"Do you often come here?" she said. She spoke French without a trace of accent. Her smile widened, revealing very white teeth.

Then he detested her to the point of longing to hit her. She seemed to him to come straight from his fever world; he thought her vicious and ugly and depraved. He said, "No, I do not. Good-afternoon," and brushed past her, walking swiftly so that in a moment he was out of her sight.

Nora stood there and watched him go. There was disappointment, surprise and anger warring in her face. Her hands, little, plump hands with bitten nails, clenched. She began to chew her lower lip. She looked almost as if she were going to cry. Then she shrugged, and followed after him in the direction of the College, moving with little, high-kicking steps, owing to the extreme tightness of her skirt, and ignoring the occasional whistles and comments of the young mashers of Portelet-sur-Seine, who found her worthy of their attention.

Chapter Three

DEIRDRE accepted Miss Pelham's request without surprise, protest or enthusiasm. Indeed, she took it so calmly that Miss Pelham was more exasperated with her than ever. She began to wonder if the girl were mentally arrested. There was certainly something very odd about her. She had not expected giggling or coyness, but it was natural, after all, for a young girl to be pleased at the prospect of meeting a number of extremely personable young men. Most girls would be very excited. She said, "You do realise what you'll have to do, don't you?"

"Yes, Miss Pelham," said Deirdre.

It was as well for Miss Pelham's peace of mind that she had no idea whatsoever as to what was going on behind that calm, beautiful face. Deirdre, up in her room—"See your hair is tidy, my dear, and I think perhaps your best afternoon frock. After all, you are going as our representative. You must do us credit"—gave several little skips of pure pleasure. Her face, which irritated Miss Pelham so by its lack of expression, broke into a wide, delighted smile. Oh yes—she had an afternoon frock, and a very pretty one, too. Mummy had brought it back from London, and she had never yet worn it. It was very expensive and very lush; it still lay in its tissue paper. There was even a string of pearls to go with it. Oh, thought Deirdre, brushing away at her golden hair, how wonderful to get away from all these silly girls who talk of nothing but clothes and dances, and reading ghastly plays and doing boring dictations. And oh how gorgeous to meet lots of boys—

For Miss Pelham had grossly underestimated Deirdre's

awareness of her own attractions. There were not many young men in County Wicklow who were suitable for her, but Deirdre's limpid eyes had not failed to notice among those she had met a sudden change of expression as soon as their gaze lit upon her and, though she had never done more than receive bashful kisses and have her hand squeezed, she had enjoyed this very much, and was now looking forward with a dancing heart to the effect she could not fail to have on an all-male establishment.

It was even better for Miss Pelham that she was unaware not only of these disgraceful thoughts but also of the final betrayal simmering in Deirdre's mind, repeated with every stroke of the brush, every touch of the powder-puff, every line of the lipstick: I am going to see the young man who shouted up at us, he must be quite mad, but he's gloriously handsome—

But there was none of this in evidence as Deirdre came into the study before setting out. Only a faint misgiving, that was half pride, stirred in Miss Pelham's heart as she looked up at her. The child was really incredibly lovely, with the pearls gleaming against her throat, and the soft blue dress she was wearing might have been styled for her. She studied the face with a sudden suspicion. But there was nothing there, not even interest. She felt compelled to say, "You look very nice indeed. I do wish you'd always take so much trouble with your appearance."

"Yes, Miss Pelham," said Deirdre.

*   *   *

On the other side of the Place du Triangle, a state of siege had already been declared. M. Wolff was saying fiercely to his silent assembly of young men, "I hope you all realise that my reputation—the whole reputation of this Hostel—depends on your behaviour today." In this he was virtually repeating what Miss Pelham had said, but he was quite unaware of this, and continued, more fiercely than ever, "If one of you—if one of you so much as says one word out of place to this young lady, I'll break every bone in his body—"

The young, secretive faces confronting his, cracked slightly at these frightful words; elbows found their way into adjoining ribs; eyelids fluttered down. Then, as M. Wolff turned his scowl upon them, gravity instantly returned. He glared suspiciously at the wooden countenances, the young bodies standing stiffly at attention. He said, "This is after all a situation without precedence. I can only hope you all realise how vitally important it is for you to make this young lady welcome."

Nathan muttered out of the corner of his mouth to Baruch, "And all this for a *schicksah*."

"What did you say?" snapped M. Wolff, whirling round.

They all stared at him, in injured astonishment. Who had said what? Nobody had said a word. As if anyone would dare, when M. Wolff was speaking—

"Well," said M. Wolff, tightening his lips, "all I can say is that if anyone misbehaves himself in any way whatsoever, there's going to be a dead boy on the premises. And I mean that."

However, *schicksah* or no *schicksah*, there was a scramble for the douches, a vigorous amount of shaving and a startling display of clean shirts. The boys of the Hostel did not by any means lead the segregated life of the girls of the College, but it was not often that they entertained someone young and pretty and, though they would have died rather than admit this to M. Wolff, they knew as well as he that this really was something of an occasion.

The two American visitors, arriving just before Deirdre, were agreeably surprised at the well-groomed young men who came forward to greet them. They were extremely well-groomed, themselves. M. Wolff welcomed them in his fragmentary English; the ladies spoke an equally fragmentary French, and he was thankful that Miss Pelham's little miss would be there to help him.

The visitors, well-tailored and looking, to M. Wolff's disillusioned eyes, as alike as peas in a pod, managed to explain to the dead silent semicircle of young men that they were members of a committee set up to investigate the after-effects of the concentration camps.

"Buchenwald," said one of them, in her clear, high-pitched voice, "and Auschwitz, you know."

She turned her eyes on the boys as she spoke. She thought these names would help them to understand what she was talking about. She gave them a faintly self-conscious, compassionate smile. Their faces remained impassive. It was almost as if they did not hear. It was a little embarrassing, but then the other lady saw Jean-Louis, and exclaimed, "What a dear little boy. What is your name? *Qu'est-ce-que c'est votre nom?*"

M. Wolff directed a look of the most menacing kind at Jean-Louis, but the little boy merely raised an angelic face and answered in a shy whisper.

"Jean-Louis," repeated the lady, unaware of the sigh of relief breathed by everyone around her, "that's a nice name. You must be a little French boy. And what are the rest of you called?"

M. Wolff, who understood this, rapidly translated, and the young men stepped forward to answer, one after the other. And just as this ended, the bell sounded. There was a faint, indrawn breath as shoulders straightened, heads turned, hands moved furtively to already sleeked-down hair. M. Wolff, very stiff, very self-conscious, at once went to open the front door.

Never in her life had Deirdre made such an entrance. She stepped a little shyly into the room, to be greeted by some twenty perfect gentlemen who almost rushed to shake her by the hand. She stood and looked at them. Her blonde hair gleamed in the sunlight streaming through the window. She raised her long lashes to meet stares of the frankest, most undiluted admiration. A faint dimple fluttered in her cheek. She glanced surreptitiously from one to the other. She did not see the American ladies at all, for the boys encircled her, hiding them from her view. Her grey eyes roamed from Nathan's fiery head to little Polish Baruch, wizened and blackavised, from handsome Moishe to Jacob, whose hair was as blond as her own, lighted for a second on Jean-Louis, then lowered.

There was no sign of the handsome young man with the black hair.

She was conscious of the sharpest disappointment. But she had no time to dwell on this, for the next instant she was introduced to the visitors, who, delighted to be able to talk in their own tongue, at once burst into conversation.

At table she sat opposite M. Wolff, who beamed at her, enchanted by her beauty, beguiled by her air of youth and simplicity. There was a certain edging and shoving for the privilege of sitting beside her. She found herself sandwiched between Nathan and Moishe, who was six foot two, and as good-looking an escort as anyone could desire. They were most punctilious and tended to pass the same thing at an identical moment, and Deirdre's dimple, which Miss Pelham had never seen, was much in evidence, to the delight of M. Wolff, who was enjoying the play and thinking that after all his grumblings he had a remarkably nice lot of boys and that this kind of social occasion was very good for them.

But the particular young man whom Deirdre would have liked to be at her side still did not make his appearance, and presently, to submerge her disappointment, she concentrated on the novelty around her, all of which her pencil would soon set down. She noted the little black caps that the boys wore, and was fascinated by their faces, some of which were beautiful and all of which were strange. Her eyes wandered to the well made-up faces of the two visitors who sat on either side of M. Wolff; she found them a little brittle and unreal, with their quick nervous gestures, as if they were oppressed by the overwhelming vitality of the boys around them.

She bowed her head dutifully during the benediction, though it seemed to her of inordinate length, and listened to the singing that succeeded it; the harsh, young voices stirred her, and made her think again of her wild, dark young man; she longed to ask where he was and did not dare.

The interviewing started after lunch, and took place in M. Wolff's office. She sat down beside the two American ladies, and Jean-Louis tailed her as her shadow, looking at her with a kind of wistful adoration that touched her very much. She heard the murmurs as she left the dining-room. She heard Moishe say, "*Mais elle est ravissante,*" and her mouth curved faintly; she did not for one second believe he was talking of the two visitors.

There was nothing to prepare her for what was to come. She translated easily enough, and at first did so mechanically, for the incessant talk of concentration camps made no impact on her. Her parents had never talked of such things; the names were simply names, with no significance. It was only after a while that two things forced themselves upon her. She began to register at last the monstrosity of the questions that she was turning into French, and then that the answers were growing more and more unrepeatable.

She was not accustomed to deception. There had never been any need. She had been interpreting the replies and missing out words she did not understand, but when Moishe, who had been so gentle and courteous with her at lunch, said savagely, "*Oh, elle m'emmerde, cette vache,*" she stopped dead, flushing scarlet; she had little knowledge of the more colloquial French, but she knew well enough that this was something she must not repeat.

"What does he say, my dear?" persisted the American lady. "Didn't he understand? I want to know if any of his family have survived."

Deirdre, almost in tears, met Moishe's eyes. His expression changed. He gave her a wry, ironic smile. He said gently, in French, "It's not your fault, is it? All right. What does she want to know now?"

Deirdre faltered, "She—she asks if any of your family have survived."

"Tell her, No."

She stared at him. She could not believe him. He had no family, this handsome, heavily-built boy, with the honest eyes, with the look of one who had spent his life on a farm. None of them had any family, even little Jean-Louis. It was surely not possible, and the things that the ladies were so glibly putting into words were not possible, either—all about gas-chambers and tortures and beatings-up and death. She did not find it easy to assert herself, but at last, after half a dozen of these interviews, she turned a flushed, distressed face on the older of the two ladies, and stammered, "Do you really think we ought—I mean, it seems so awful to ask them such personal things. It must hurt so to have to remember."

"Oh no, my dear," said the lady kindly, "I'm sure they're pleased that people are interested. Besides, it's all for a good cause, isn't it? One has to have these surveys."

Deirdre did not answer this. But her face set in obstinate lines, and for the rest of the afternoon she behaved in a fashion that would have astonished Miss Pelham as much as it would have done M. Wolff. The organisers of the survey were never to know this, but not only did she not translate the questions correctly, she also made up the answers. She simply asked such things as, How long have you been living here? and reported the appropriate answer to the ladies who were charmed by her fluent French and surprised by the speed with which the interviews were conducted.

They thanked her very much. She received their thanks with a slightly withdrawn expression. And a few minutes later the boys escorted her back to the College, across the Place du Triangle. M. Wolff was not at all sure if Miss Pelham would welcome this, but the spectacle afforded him considerable sardonic amusement and, perhaps, a little regret. He had said a very tender good-bye to Deirdre. He took both her hands in his, saying, "You're a very nice girl, and I'm more grateful to you than I can say. I'm almost glad Max was away. You did it a great deal more prettily than he would have done."

Max. So his name was Max. Deirdre bestowed her most enchanting smile on M. Wolff, hugged Jean-Louis, who implored her to come back again, and arrived at the door of the College, a Christian general with an army of twenty young Jews following behind her.

M. Quiqueran watched this extraordinary sight with popping eyes. He could hardly believe it. He was bursting with curiosity. He had never witnessed such a thing in his life.

Inspector Granier, too, noticed the phenomenon. But he understood well enough what had happened, and it appeared that it was largely his doing. There was still no sign of Max. He had quarrelled with Anni throughout the day. "Why can't you control your tongue?" she cried out furiously to him. "I suppose that as a policeman you just don't consider that people have any feelings. When you think of all that poor boy's been through—To say such a thing to him! I believe I've married a monster. Why, he— he may have thrown himself into the river."

"I think that's most unlikely," said Granier very wearily.

If he were a monster, he was a sad and exhausted one. Then, as she burst into tears, he shouted at her, "Oh, for God's sake, Anni, do you want to drive me mad?"

And he strode out into the town, with a stomach-ache, and looked into all the cafés, starting with the Café Niçoise and ending with the most sordid little pull-ups in the town. But he did not find Max, who was at that moment almost fulfilling Anni's prediction, and still sitting on the banks of the Seine.

*   *   *

"Well, tell me all about it," said Miss Pelham to Deirdre. She had watched the processional return. It had jolted her a little, but, like M. Wolff, she recognised its inevitability. Only there was one brief, disturbing moment when it struck her as strange that there should be anything strange about it at all. Here were two dozen boys. There were two dozen girls. Looked at dispassionately, it was perhaps a little odd that the width of the Place du Triangle must always lie between them. But of course anything else would be quite impossible. Heaven knows what the parents would say if they learnt that their darling daughters were going out with penniless young Jews. She recognised the finality of those farewell handshakes. The boys would never speak to Deirdre again, except in purely formal greeting. They knew this as well as she did. They stood there in a line as Deirdre opened the door. They really were an exceptionally good-looking collection, and their white shirts gleamed in the sunshine. Then the ranks broke, and they dived back for the Hostel in their usual noisy, jostling fashion.

Deirdre was as uncommunicative as usual. Yes, she had enjoyed herself. Everyone had been very nice to her. She had managed the translating all right. The American ladies? Oh, they were quite pleasant. There had been a good lunch.

"So you think M. Wolff was pleased with you?"

"Yes, Miss Pelham," said Deirdre.

Miss Pelham gave it up and concentrated her attention on Nora, who had just come in; that tight skirt was really too dreadful, and coupled with the high heels gave a most unfortunate impression.

Deirdre sat in her room and filled her diary with pictures of the two Americans and the boys. Her pencil, so cruel in comparison with her gentle face, portrayed clearly the excellent permanent waves of the ladies, their bright smiles, their figures compressed and uplifted in all the right places. But when she came to the boys, she found that her mind was a strange confusion of pity and horror so that her pencil skidded over the paper, as if it were performing automatically. And from it grew a strange nightmare place with smoking chimneys and the criss-cross of barbed wire, with gaunt, skeleton faces peering hopelessly through. And the faces were the faces of the boys who had all been so kind to her, who had clasped her hand so warmly, whose eyes had glowed with admiration. She was appalled by her own work. She dropped the pencil, and put a hand to her throat.

It was only then that she discovered that her pearl necklace was missing.

*   *   *

Max turned up almost immediately after Deirdre had left. This was deliberate. He had no wish to meet her. He saw her vaguely through the window, and retreated into the château grounds, which had long since fallen into ruin. He was in no state to meet anyone. He huddled in the summer-house where a king had once embraced his mistress, and waited until he saw the crowd emerge from the Hostel and the car driving back to Paris, with the American visitors and their questionnaires inside. Then famished, exhausted and a little drunk, he came silently in.

M. Wolff was busy finding all the things he had hidden away. He had taken off his jacket and rolled up his sleeves. Humming a tuneless little song to himself, he was restoring disorder with such vigour that he did not even perceive Max was there until he grew suddenly aware of the silent figure standing a couple of yards away from him.

He dumped a pile of records down on the nearest chair, and straightened himself, wiping his dusty hands on his trousers. He looked as old and tired as he felt. He had always hated these visitations. He suspected that this present one would bring in no money at all. The ladies had been very agreeable. He had taken pains to point out to them that the boys had nowhere comfortable to sit in the evenings. He had emphasised the necessity for something better than an ancient gramophone and an even more ancient radio. A few armchairs, he suggested, would make the place look more like home and less like one with a capital H. Surely, he said, rolling his eyes quite shamelessly at the older and less attractive, there were some rich American Jews who, when Yom Kippur came nearer, might be willing to salvage their souls at the cost of a few dollars. The ladies were polite but non-committal. American Jewry had already been so generous, and there were still so many calls upon it. The committee were ardently Zionist, and their funds were destined to go to Israel.

"This is Zion, too," said M. Wolff, growing angry as he always did. He opened the door of the room that served as synagogue. He pointed his finger, almost menacingly, at the Star of David.

The ladies smiled and nodded. "Of course, of course." And, "So very good of you to co-operate with us, dear M. Wolff. It'll be a real pleasure to send you a copy of our survey."

"I nearly told them what they could do with their blasted survey," growled M. Wolff to Moishe afterwards. "Only they wouldn't have understood, and I could hardly expect that nice little girl to translate for me. Just a damned schnorrer, that's all I am. What else is there to be?"

He looked grimly now at Max. His eyes took in every detail of that haggard face, ghastly with exhaustion and every destructive emotion; his heart sank as his fury rose.

"And where," he began in an ominously hushed tone, "have you been?"

"Around," said Max. His hand came down to grip the table edge, as if without its support he could no longer stand upright.

"You forgot, I presume, that two ladies from the American Joint were coming today?"

"No."

"You knew they were coming?"

"Yes."

"And you still went out?"

"Yes."

"Realising that I should be left alone without an interpreter?"

Max shrugged.

"Fine, fine," said M. Wolff. Then his temper blew into flame, and the words spurted from him. "Where the hell have you been? You've been drinking. And by the disgraceful look of you, you've been doing worse. What is it this time? Murder, perhaps. Why not? It doesn't matter to you, naturally, that the police will close this Hostel down." Then he shouted, "Doesn't even that matter to you? You live here, don't you? This is supposed to be your home. But we could all drown, for all it would bother you. You fly into a paddy like a spoilt child and then you have to disappear, digging your nose into God knows what filth, giving us all a bad name, probably losing us the little grant we have. And you don't care. You just don't care. I'm beginning to think it would be a good thing if the police did get you and put you in prison where you belong. At least it would keep you out of harm's way. If you were younger, I believe I'd give you a thrashing."

"Would you?" said Max. His face was a mask of icy rage. Then he said in a soft snarl, "This is my home no longer. Not that it ever has been—I'm going. Tonight. You won't be troubled with me again. Do you imagine I'd stay here another minute after what you've just said to me?"

He broke off with a gasp that was nearly a sob, and M. Wolff, too, was silent. He was thinking with a cold dismay, Oh, it's time I went. I can't do my job properly any longer. He's right, after all. He's not a child. It's not my business to swear at him. And then he thought, If only I weren't so damned tired. When you're tired, you don't feel any longer, you do things because you have to, and you forget you're dealing with human beings who are as tired and fed-up as yourself.

He briefly closed his eyes. Then he lifted up the pile of records and held them out to Max. "Put these on top of the gramophone, will you?" he said.

There was a long pause. Then Max took the records and, without a word, did as he was told. He gave M. Wolff a look, and walked out of the room.

M. Wolff called after him, "Go and get yourself something to eat." Then he sat down heavily, his hands flat on his knees. He knew Max would not go. He might detest the Hostel, he probably did. But he would stay, because for him, as for the others, it represented the only place he could call his own, the only place that signified security. M. Wolff, disgusted at himself, let his head sink down on his chest, let his mind trundle back along a long-obliterated path, at the end of which had been a wife and family, and happiness and peace.

He sat there, rocking a little, permitting the slimy self-pity to creep over him. So tired, so tired—He was roused from this by a squealing and protesting, which came recognisably from the one member of the Hostel who might be permitted to indulge himself.

He rose, grumbling, to his feet, and came into the dining-room, where Jean-Louis, scarlet with temper, was dancing up and down, flailing with his fists at the older boys who surrounded him.

M. Wolff could not but notice the similarity in behaviour, and a faint, bitter smile came briefly to his lips. There had always been days like this, when it was as if a mistral blew through the Hostel. He said, "What's all this about?"

"He won't go to bed," said Moishe.

"He won't go to bed? Oh, he will, you know. Why do you imagine you won't go to bed?"

"I don't want to," shrieked Jean-Louis. "I want to go and see the English miss. I'm not a little boy, any longer. Why should I have to go to bed before everyone else?"

M. Wolff wasted no time in argument. He said calmly to Moishe, "Take him upstairs. If he won't undress himself, you'll have to do it for him. If he wants to behave like a baby, he shall be treated like one."

Moishe, with a half-grin—for they were all very good to Jean-Louis, even if sometimes they swore at him—seized the little boy under his powerful arm. But Jean-Louis continued to struggle and kick, and suddenly something slid snakewise out of his pocket and landed on the floor.

It was a string of pearls.

Moishe dropped Jean-Louis so violently that he landed with a thud. His howling stopped. There was an aghast silence. M. Wolff, staring at the necklace, thought, Oh, my God, then he said in a carefully composed voice, "And what is the meaning of this?"

He met Moishe's eyes as he spoke. He saw in them a full awareness of the disaster. They both knew that, come what may, this must somehow be hidden from Miss Pelham.

Jean-Louis began to whimper, then to sob.

"Get up," said M. Wolff, touching him with the toe of his shoe. "Did you take this?"

Jean-Louis wailed, "She gave it me—"

M. Wolff saw that Max, with a large hunk of bread and meat in his hand, had come in from the kitchen, and was surveying the scene. He ignored him. He said grimly, "That's a lie. You took it. This, I must say, just about puts the lid on everything. We invite one of the young English ladies over to help us, and we repay her kindness by stealing her jewellery." He let the string of pearls run through his fingers, remarking almost in surprise, "These are real— Why did you take them? I want to know the truth now."

It took several minutes to get the truth. Jean-Louis, seeing that this was serious, sobbed piteously. Then, as this was received in a stony silence, he at last burst out with the story. By now he was really frightened. His tear-blurred eyes turned to Max, then, finding no encouragement there, back to M. Wolff. The necklace had fallen off. He had not been able to resist it. It was so pretty, and he didn't think it was anything valuable, he would keep it to remind him of the beautiful *anglaise* who had been so kind to him.

M. Wolff walked away. He would not use violence on those who had already endured so much of it, but this was one of those times when he could not trust himself. His anger was such that he would not even permit himself to speak until the length of the room was between himself and the offender. The only consolation was that he had found out about this before Miss Pelham; she would surely have rung him immediately. The humiliation was more than he could bear. He ignored the howling culprit. He said very quietly, "I am going to ring up the College. We have just found the necklace. Under the desk in my office. One of you will have to take it round—" His eyes lit on Max. "You will take it round. After all, it's your fault that this ever happened. You will hand it to Mademoiselle Deirdre in person, and make her an apology for the trouble you have caused. And before you go, you will take this—this beastly little thief up to bed. See he's undressed and in it before you leave. Lock the door on him. He'll have no supper."

And he walked up to his office, refusing even to consider that his command might be disobeyed.

Max, his mouth twisted, watched him for a moment. Then, still holding the sandwich, he jerked his head silently at Jean-Louis, then, as the little boy hesitated, shoved him forward with his knee. Jean-Louis, still snivelling, trotted sulkily out before him.

In the dormitory, Max stood there in a forbidding silence as Jean-Louis undressed. His face was expressionless; once or twice he glanced at the pearls that M. Wolff had pushed into his hand.

Jean-Louis took off his clothes. He started with a deliberate and sullen slowness, then he met Max's eyes and his movements grew quicker and quicker. He put on his pyjamas with such speed that he tripped over the cord. He hurled himself into bed, and tugged at the blankets with a force that jerked them away from the mattress; his feet stuck out at the end. He said, "*Je m'en fous.*"

Max said, "Pick your clothes up."

"I won't," said Jean-Louis, rather doubtfully.

"Pick them up!"

Jean-Louis glared at him from under the silky lashes. Then, his lower lip jutting out, he leant over the bed, snatched up the garments and hurled them on to the chair at his side.

"Fold them up and put them over the back," said Max.

"*Je m'en fous,*" said Jean-Louis.

Max took a step towards him, and he grabbed at the clothes again and, with a perfunctory folding of them, did as he was told.

66

Max went towards the door. Jean-Louis lay there, glaring at him, saying again in a wretched, whining voice, "*Je m'en fous.*" Then, "Max!"

"Well?" said Max, not turning round, his hand on the light switch.

"You won't tell her I took them?"

Max swung round to look at him. He said, "I'll see."

The tears were crawling again down Jean-Louis's cheeks. He said piteously, "Oh, please, please don't. She's so pretty."

"I tell you, I'll see. Now shut up and go to sleep." He switched off the light and stood there for a second, hesitating. Then he stepped swiftly over to the bed, with one hand boxed the culprit's ears and with the other deposited the sandwich on to his pyjama'd chest.

He closed the door behind him, and locked it.

*　　*　　*

Miss Pelham was not at all pleased to hear that one of M. Wolff's boys was now actually stepping over Rosedene's threshold. She was beginning to regret that she had ever agreed to the first proposition. If this went on, there would soon be a series of most undesirable social calls. She hesitated, the receiver in her hand. M. Wolff heard the hesitation. He knew exactly what she was thinking. He had no intent of sparing her. He wondered what she would say if he told her that this particular boy was the most dangerous character in his Hostel. He heard her sourly agreeing. Silly old woman, he thought, and then, She's not half as silly as I am.

And he pulled open the top drawer of his desk and began to work on the interminable weekly accounts.

*　　*　　*

It was Nora who told Deirdre that one of the boys from the Hostel was waiting in the lounge to see her. "He looks a fine young tough, too," she said shrewishly, for she had caught a glimpse of Max as he paced up and down the soft, beige carpet, and was very taken aback to see who it was. She had neither forgotten nor forgiven his rebuff, and she glared at him resentfully. She was also very angry because Miss Pelham had gently teased her about her skirt. She said to Deirdre, "It's the one I saw, this afternoon. He was roaring drunk. You'd think they'd find someone more presentable to send over. What on earth can he want, anyway?"

"I've no idea," said Deirdre vaguely. She saw Nora's eyes light on the notebook in front of her. As she was not entirely lacking in shrewdness she suspected that Nora would take a look at it the moment she was out of the room. She picked it up and put it under her arm; she walked slowly down the stairs.

Max's eyes roamed over the lounge. It was next to Miss Pelham's study and faced the back of the house, overlooking a beautifully kept garden. It was as much to his taste as a hospital. He looked at the comfortable armchairs which, like the bedroom furniture, were covered in a floral chintz. He stepped across to examine the pictures on the white walls. They were excellent reproductions of French paintings. By the far window was a cabinet with some good china behind the glass-fronted doors. It was all entirely charming and feminine, from the pink-shaded standard lamp to the small rosewood piano, with a volume of Chopin nocturnes laid upon it. The taste was impeccable; it was gracious living epitomised. It aroused within him a crude, vicious anger; he wanted to shout out, like Jean-Louis, "*Je m'en fous.*" Yet, in spite of this, he grew painfully aware of the fact that he had not changed, that his shirt was sweaty and his chin unshaven. This made him angrier than ever, and when Miss Pelham, who had been listening for Deirdre's footsteps, hastened to precede her by opening the door and remarked, "How very kind of you to come— I'm sending some tea in for you," he turned a face of such

68

startled resentment upon her that her polite smile faltered.

He heard her say to someone outside, "Here's the young man with your necklace, Deirdre. I was just telling him how much we appreciate his taking the trouble to bring it over." But he could not, fortunately, read her thoughts which were, Good heavens, what a terrible looking young gangster! We must get him off the premises as soon as possible.

Deirdre came in, her notebook under her arm.

Max swung round to meet her. He began to speak, to say, "Here are your pearls—" then he saw her clearly for the first time. He fell into a complete silence, and she, too, did not say a word, her eyes fixed on his face. They stood motionless, with the width of the carpet between them. His fierce expression was slowly changing into one of incredulity and delight. He had never seen anything so lovely in his life. He supposed he had seen her before, setting out in the crocodile, but then she had been one among many; he had not even noticed her, he had not been interested. Interested—He was interested now. His breath began to come a little quickly. His lips curved faintly into the smile which was so enchanting in the fallen-angel face. His eyes took every liberty with her; his imagination began at once to weave such fantasies as would have made Miss Pelham telephone the police. He could not stop looking at her. She was gorgeous, she was unimaginably gorgeous, and she wasn't finding him repulsive, either, not if he could go by her startled, rapt face. He thought, I must have her. I will have her. And then, with the familiar excitement gripping him, upheaving his belly, And I will, too, in spite of them. She's a young lady. She's English. She's a goy. To hell with it all, I'll have her yet, she shall lie in my arms, she shall let me kiss her, and she'll kiss me back, *and* she'll kiss me back and like it, too—

He made her a little inclination, smiled and held out his hand. "*Bonjour, mademoiselle,*" he said.

Deirdre put her hand in his. Her thoughts ran along a more naïve, less defined path, for all she knew was that here was the dark young man who had shouted up at her, and he was obviously liking her very much; it was fate, it was destined, it was terribly exciting, and really, she was quite resigned now to staying in Portelet-sur-Seine for the rest of her life. She returned his smile with a look that was at the same time innocent yet inviting; it disconcerted him a little so that his brows met, and the hand still holding hers, tightened. This in turn startled Deirdre; the notebook fell from her grasp, opening as it touched the floor.

Max at once stooped to pick it up, then, crouching there, exclaimed, "But this is magnificent." He looked down at the strange, tortured drawing of the barbed-wire enclosure, with the young, crucified faces staring out of it. His heavy brows began to meet again. He stared up at her, almost in awe. His shoulder brushed against her skirt. He whispered, "But how can you possibly know?"

They heard the sound of the tea-trolley outside. Miss Pelham's clear voice said, "Open the door, my dear, will you? I thought we'd all have a nice cup of tea together."

Deirdre's anguished gaze fell to the notebook, and Max, in one swift, economical gesture, snatched it up and slipped it inside his jacket, just as Miss Pelham and the trolley made their appearance.

Miss Pelham had not at first meant to have tea with them, but that one glance at Max had decided her that on no account could she leave one of her girls alone with such a desperate looking character. She glanced again now at that dark, ravaged face. She did not see the brief, conspiratorial look that passed between them; she did not notice that Deirdre's cheeks burned with heightened colour. She only looked at Max's deep-set, shadowed eyes, the fierce, proud curve of his mouth, the indented nostrils, the finely modelled bone contour and winged brows. To her it was an arrogant face, and a dangerous one; she recognised its beauty, for indeed she could scarcely do otherwise, but this was not the kind of beauty she wished her girls to meet; it was too violent, too strong, too evocative of all the many things the polite world preferred to ignore.

She said pleasantly, "Do you take milk and sugar in your tea, or do you prefer lemon?"

It did strike her at that moment that possibly these words were a little out of place. It was rather like asking Lucifer to drink a nice orange squash. The thing that disconcerted her was that the young man, who now raised his eyes to hers, seemed to be struck by the same idea. She was sure there was a flash of mockery in his gaze, but then he said with perfect civility, "I should prefer lemon, madame."

"Of course," she said. She gave a little laugh. "It's only the English who have the bad taste to prefer milk. I hope you've thanked this young man, Deirdre, for bringing back your necklace. We're very grateful to you, M.— M.—"

"Max." His eyes moved momentarily to Deirdre's again, but Miss Pelham was pouring out and did not notice. Only she grew aware of Deirdre's continued silence, and this annoyed her. She said sharply, "I suppose the catch is loose."

It was Max who answered. "It is a little," he said. He pulled the string of pearls out of his pocket, and laid it over his knee. He bent his head to examine it. Both Miss Pelham and Deirdre were impelled to watch him. They both saw how the strong, black hair fell across his forehead. They both remarked the broad shoulders, and the elegance of the hands that so delicately touched the mechanism. They were both entirely aware of the disturbing quality of his masculinity. But there their thoughts diverged, for Miss Pelham was thinking quite passionately, The sooner I get him out of here, the better, and Deirdre was thinking with equal passion, How am I going to see him again, I must see him, oh I must.

Max said gravely, "You'll find that it's quite safe now." He laid the necklace in Deirdre's hand. His fingers brushed almost imperceptibly across her palm. He shot her one swift glance, then his lashes drooped down.

"Is that part of your job?" inquired Miss Pelham offering him a plateful of small, home-made cakes, baked by the girls in their cookery class. "I mean, do you do this kind of work in a shop?"

"No, madame. I am an electrical engineer."

"Oh, that must be very interesting. Have you been doing it long?"

"Three years. I am still studying for my certificate."

"Well, we'll know where to go when our lights fuse, won't we, Deirdre?"

"Yes, Miss Pelham," said Deirdre.

Miss Pelham shot her a glance of pure exasperation. She wanted to shake her. She looked back at the young man, and a quite startling anger stabbed through her. He should be shy, embarrassed, awed by the cool beauty of his surroundings. And there he sat, with all the calm in the world, as if every day of his life he ate little cakes and drank tea out of Minton cups. She had of course noticed immediately that his shirt was dirty and he smelt of sweat, but not even this, not even the black stubble on his jaw, could conceal the fact that he was infinitely more at ease than she was. She saw that he was regarding her, and something indefinable in his expression put her instantly on the defensive. She was resolved not to leave him alone with Deirdre for one second. The child was in many ways as simple as a baby, and heaven knows what this young ruffian might choose to say to her.

She continued to talk for a while, and grew more and more disturbed as she did so, as if, half-consciously, she were aware of the emotional atmosphere between them.

She talked easily of a film the girls had seen, a book everyone was reading; she passed lightly over such subjects as the world situation and a recent strike in the Metro. It was part of her job to make easy conversation, and her clear voice, speaking French with the slightest of English accents, went on with scarcely a pause. Both Max and Deirdre listened to her, she with a half-sulky impatience, he with lowered eyes and an impassive face.

Miss Pelham began to think it was high time that Max left. She began to stack the tea-things, after saying, "You're sure you won't have just one more cake before you go?" But he would not take the hint, so she rose to her feet, saying, "I'm afraid we must say good-bye to you. We believe in early hours. We are all in bed by nine-thirty, you know. And Deirdre has a little homework to do for to-morrow, haven't you, my dear? So nice of you to have come round. And don't be surprised if we suddenly ring you one day and tell you that all our fuses have blown. It will be very useful to have a tame electrician so near to us, won't it, Deirdre?"

He, too, rose to his feet. His eyes measured hers, like a duellist's. He was scarcely taller than she was, and she saw now that, despite the broad shoulders, he was slightly built, but anything less tame could hardly be imagined. Miss Pelham had a sudden and horrid conviction that her deliberate patronage had by no means escaped his attention. But he only said with a smooth and irreproachable civility, "I am afraid that's not my job, madame, though of course, I should be delighted to help if I could. However, if you do need an electrician in a hurry, I can give you the address of someone who might be useful. I'll just scribble it down for you."

Miss Pelham opened her mouth to say that there was already an electrician attached to the College, but remembered her preceding remarks and fell angrily silent.

73

He pulled a little notebook out of his breast pocket, and wrote down a couple of lines. He held this out to Miss Pelham. "Mention my name, will you?" he said. "He'll be glad to oblige you, if you're a friend of mine. He's good at all kinds of other jobs, too. I expect you're often in need of a handyman. Housekeeping must be hard work. He's not expensive, and he's entirely trustworthy."

She stared at him, the colour rising in her cheeks. This, she was sure, was deliberate insolence, yet his face was perfectly grave. She said coldly, "I am not the housekeeper, young man. I happen to be the Principal of this College."

"Oh, I beg your pardon," said Max.

There was no mistaking it this time, any more than there was any mistaking the faint smile that accompanied the apologetic words. Miss Pelham was an intelligent woman, but she was not to know she was being subjected to a small experiment in applied psychology. She reacted as she was expected to react. She took the piece of paper, looked at it disdainfully, then handed it to Deirdre. "You'd better give this to the housekeeper," she said.

"May I just add the telephone number?" asked Max. He looked a little confused. He obviously realised that he had made a mistake in speaking to her in such a fashion. This appeased her a little, and she watched with a more kindly smile as he scrawled down the number, then put the paper in Deirdre's hand. She said, "Thank you for all the trouble you've taken." She opened her handbag and took out a five-hundred-franc note. "Buy yourself a little something," she said.

"Thank you, madame," said Max, and he slipped the money into his pocket. He did not look again at Deirdre. He seemed to feel no embarrassment in taking the money.

Miss Pelham saw him to the door. She watched him cross the Place du Triangle. Deirdre, choked with mortification and very red in the face, could scarcely mutter good-bye to him. Not a vindictive girl, she wished at that moment that Miss Pelham were dead. It was all over. He would never speak to her again. That last insult would make him so angry that he would probably avoid her if they even met in the street. It was dreadful, unspeakable, and what a fool he must think her, that she should sit there, a witness of his humiliation, and not be able to say a word. The tears were rising in her throat. She looked down wretchedly at the piece of paper in her hand, and opened it to see what kind of handwriting he had. She would keep it. It was a poor kind of lover's token, but it was all she was ever likely to have.

Then she gave a little gasp, and shot one frantic look at Miss Pelham, who was still watching Max's progress as if she were determined to see him safely away. She was indeed so busy watching that she did not see her pupil's mouth open, her eyes dilate.

Deirdre was realising that Max as a lover was not so easily daunted. There was nothing poor about this token, at all. The address was written down clearly enough, and under it the words: "Meet me at ten, outside."

Meet me at ten—The cheek of it! Under Miss Pelham's very nose—Deirdre's teeth sank into her lower lip, the laughter was swelling in her throat.

"Poor lad," said Miss Pelham, closing the door. "You know, really those boys have survived their experiences remarkably well. They're uncouth, of course. But what else could one expect? He's really quite a decent boy, and would look almost presentable if he shaved and took more pains with his appearance. Don't you think so?"

"Yes, Miss Pelham," said Deirdre with positive enthusiasm, and the smile she bestowed on her Principal was so captivating that Miss Pelham's reproaches remained unspoken; she said pleasantly, " Good-night, Deirdre. Sleep well."

"Good-night, Miss Pelham."

Miss Pelham watched her run up the stairs. It was quite obvious that the boy had made no particular impression on her. And of course nothing like this would ever occur again. It was just after nine o'clock.

Chapter Four

MAX swung out of the College into the Place du Triangle. The savage young man who had stalked so grimly into the pretty chintz lounge was gone. His face was triumphant, his eyes aglow. He looked up at the clock. It was just on nine. In an hour's time he would be seeing her again. He never doubted for a second that she would come. He saw her again as he had first seen her—with her pale gold hair, the big grey eyes, the mouth that had twitched into an involuntary smile. He was about to go into the Hostel, but now he stopped and stood there, very still. He swallowed so that his throat muscles rippled up and down. Then he bounded forward, bursting into song as he did so, and it was thus that Granier, coming drearily home to a nagging wife, and his own by no means appeased conscience, set eyes on him.

Max swung off the Hostel steps, and walked impudently up to him, swaying and swaggering like a stage gangster. He was grinning from ear to ear. He clenched his fist, and brought it down with a resounding thwack against Granier's shoulder. Then he struck an attitude, arms folded across his chest, eyes moving insolently up and down. "Well, *M. le flic?*" he said. "Have you been laying assassins by the heels all day? Shut up any desperate criminals? Tell me. Do they pay you a commission to lay off them? I always understood that was how policemen made their living—so much per cent for whores, so much for thieves, so much for dirty Jews—"

"When you've finished," said Granier stonily.

"Old boy," said Max, "the real trouble with you is that you haven't any sense of humour."

"Where have you been?"

"You see what I mean!"

"I asked you where you've been."

"Anything to do with you, old boy?"

"That's what I'd like to know."

"Well," said Max reflectively, digging out a crushed packet of cigarettes, "where have I been now?" His eyes flickered to the clock. It was two minutes past nine. He gave a sudden crow of laughter, and peered over the match-flame at Granier's perplexed and exasperated face. He held out the match. "Blow!" he said.

Granier slapped the hand away; he growled, "Stop playing the fool."

"But I'm trying to remember where I've been, old boy—"

"And stop calling me old boy."

"Sorry, old boy. Well now—I can tell you what I've been doing. After all, you're an old friend of mine, and there should be no secrets between old friends. At eight o'clock this morning—no, at three and a half minutes past eight—I cut an old woman's throat. Krrr! Like that. Poor old girl. She was left weltering in her gore. Very sad. However, there it is. One mouth less to feed, and all that. Then by nine I was drinking an aperitif. It's exhausting, cutting throats, you know, though I expect it comes easier after the first half-dozen. But by half past, I was quite recovered, so I broke into a bank. I had to bump off the manager and a couple of clerks, which was a pity, but then they would interfere, and I don't like interference. Anyway, that's not my concern, it's theirs. And think of all the *grisbi*—ah, Inspector Granier, *le grisbi*—"

Granier suddenly seized his arm, so suddenly that Max, a great deal lighter in build, was almost thrown off his balance. The grin vanished. His face contorted. He smacked the arm away from him, saying between his teeth, "You're too free with your hands, M. Bloody Inspector. I told you not to manhandle me. I won't have it. The next time you lay hands on me, I'll knock your teeth down your throat." Then he stopped, drew in a gasping breath. He sprang aside and burst out laughing. "Ah, *merde alors*—You thought I meant that, didn't you? You thought I was going to kill you. But I wouldn't do a thing like that. You're not a bad old sort. A bit of a bore, perhaps, but then you're growing old, that's your trouble. Poor old man, weighed down by your belly and family cares. You'll never be young again. What a shame it is—I'm sorry for you. You see, I'm still young. And it's ten past nine. Ten past nine!"

"I don't know," said Granier, staring at him. "What is all this?"

"That's your trouble, friend. You just don't know."

"You seem very full of yourself, tonight."

"Why shouldn't I be?"

"You realise that we've all been very worried about you?"

"*Tiens, tiens,*" said Max, and he clicked his tongue sorrowfully, while his mocking eyes shone with suppressed laughter.

"Well, you've been known to do extremely silly things when you go off like this," said Granier heavily. "I wish you'd grow up, Max. It's time you buried the past. All these fugues of yours—If I upset you, I'm sorry, I didn't mean to, but I still can't see that there's any reason for you to fly off the handle like that. If you're going to rush to the devil every time something annoys you, you'll end in jail before another year is out. You ought to settle down. Do you want a game of chess tonight?"

"Tonight? Let me see," said Max, his mouth tilting up. "No, old boy, I don't somehow think—"

"I told you not to call me that. What's the matter with you? Have you been drinking?"

"It's a fine thing," said Max, "that if one laughs too loudly, sings in public or merely looks happy, one is considered mad or drunk. I am neither, my dear M. Granier. And I'll give you a game of chess, some other time. And beat you hollow—You know, your trouble is that you don't see a sufficient number of moves ahead. You can only see the pieces as they are on the board before you. If you are really going to play chess properly, you have to see the board as it will look some twenty moves ahead. That is why I so often beat you."

"I might remind you that I taught you the game."

"Have you never heard of a pupil being better than his teacher?"

"Have you never heard of the sorcerer's apprentice?"

The look Max shot at him was for that second wary and dangerous. He did not reply.

"One day," said Granier, "you'll plan out all your moves, and then you'll look at the board and find a piece there that you've forgotten all about. It might upset your calculations."

M. Quiqueran had slipped out of the Bureau for a breath of fresh air. Max and Granier were talking in the shadows, and he did not see them until it was too late. He wanted to back, nearly did so, then decided to step forward boldly, thus performing a strange kind of *pas seul*, as if he were dancing with himself.

Granier did not see him, and for a moment M. Quiqueran believed that Max had not seen him either. Only he could not stop himself from turning his head, and he found that the great dark eyes, hard now as stones, were fixed upon him in a cold, appraising stare that sent a shiver through him.

Max did not speak to him. Instead, he said fiercely to Granier, "I'll tell you what you're like. You're like some blasted mediaeval conception of Death, and I'm the miser-

able knight you follow around. You're a permanent bogey-
man there to haunt me, and you clutch your great, black
hood over your disgusting, skeleton face, then, whenever
I do something you don't approve of or don't understand,
you pull the hood back and roar at me, I am Death. Can you
blame me for going to the devil? He at least is amusing."

"Death played chess with the knight," said Granier.

"And lost. And lost, Inspector."

"Oh, I give you up," said Granier. "Anni and Patricia
seem to like you, but sometimes I really wonder why."

"I expect in their innocence they see my innate goodness."

"Then God forgive us all," said Granier. He moved on,
with a farewell gesture of his hand.

It was a quarter past nine. Max ran into the Hostel and up
the stairs to the top floor where the douches were. The
water was seldom hot, and the gutters were always being
choked up so that regularly, half a dozen times a year, there
was an overflow and part of the ceiling came down. But it
was one of the few modern installations, and Max, grateful
for it, stripped and stepped under the shower. It was cold,
and he scrubbed himself vigorously, talking between
splutters and gasps to Moishe, who was in the next
cubicle.

Moishe said, "You should have been here. She was
ravishing—But ravishing. It's a shame we can't see her
again. And sweet, too—She didn't like those two women."

"What were they like?" Max had turned off the shower
and was towelling himself down. He passed a tentative hand
over his roughened chin and grimaced.

"Oh, the usual silly bitches." He drew down the corners
of his mouth. His soft country voice grew rough with
contempt. "What does it feel like to be gassed? Do you still
hate the Germans? Ach! Why do you ask? You've heard it
all before. What good do they think they're doing?"

"Oh, I don't know. Perhaps it's something. Perhaps one

person will read their report, and remember. If even that matters—So you liked the little goy, did you?"

"She was enchanting. She speaks marvellous French. I wonder the dragon ever let her come. Talk of turning a little lamb loose in a pack of wolves—I wish I could see her again. Old Wolff would go mad if he heard me. Going out?"

"Uhuh."

"Anyone I know?"

"No. I only met her today."

"Nice?"

"Not bad," said Max casually. Then he grinned. "Not bad at all, at all! See you later. *Shalom*."

He stepped naked into the corridor. He stood for a moment by the window, his slender body pressed against the sill. He could see the College opposite. The lights were still on. She would be there, behind one of the windows. He wished he knew which was her room. What would she be doing? He had the idea that she would be doing nothing, sitting at a table, her chin propped on her hands, dreaming, thinking of him. Perhaps she like him was watching the hands of the clock, wondering if she could creep out, un-observed, wondering what would happen if Miss Pelham caught her.

The shivers of excitement were running through him again. This was adventure. This was life. The fact that it was so entirely forbidden raised the excitement to fever pitch. There had been plenty of girls. There had always been plenty of girls. He was not so ingenuous as Deirdre, and a great deal more experienced. He knew that girls liked him very much. Why not? He liked them. He had the looks and the wit and the impudence; he knew how to say things that pleased them, and he knew how to get rid of them when they no longer pleased him. He never pretended to disguise his ruthlessness. He believed that the sentimentality had long been knocked out of him.

He rummaged in the cupboard for a clean shirt. The first one had a button off, the second was frayed at the cuffs. The third seemed to be all right. He examined it minutely. He could find nothing wrong with it. He put it on the back of the chair, and shaved. Then he wriggled his arms into the shirt and began to dream again, not even bothering to tuck the tails into his trouser belt.

That first charming sight of her came to him again. He could smell the shampoo smell of her hair, hear the rustle of her dress. He stretched out a hand as if he could touch the pale, yellow hair, encircle the softness of her cheek in his palm. She was so clean and cool, she was like no one he had ever met. His desire to possess her was so strong that it made him feel a little dizzy. He combed his hair, polished his shoes, made sure his nails were clean; when the clock struck the half hour, he jumped and swore, and gathered up his jacket to brush it meticulously.

It was a quarter to ten when he came downstairs again. The evening air was heavy with heat. He slung his jacket over his shoulders. The moonlight caught the whiteness of his shirt. On the first landing he paused, hesitated.

Then he opened the dormitory door, very softly. Jean-Louis lay there alone, for his six companions did not come up until later. He was awake. Max could see the whites of the eyes turned towards him. He could see, too, the dampness glistening on the cheeks.

He stepped over to the bed. He put his hands on his hips, so that the sleeves of the jacket dangled down like a cloak.

"Why aren't you asleep, little *salaud*?" he said.

"I'm hungry," said Jean-Louis sullenly.

"You had a sandwich. It's more than you deserve. M. Wolff said you weren't to have any supper at all."

"I'm so hungry," whimpered Jean-Louis, sensing quickly enough his weakening.

"Well, here's a piece of chocolate for you. It's all you're

83

getting. You deserve a good spanking. You're a dirty little thief."

Jean-Louis ignored the threat. He said, "There was a phone call for you, Max."

"For me?" Max took a step backwards. "Who was it? What was it about? Look, my boy, you play the fool with me and—"

"I'm not playing the fool. Keep your hair on, Maxy. It's someone who rang at lunch-time."

"Oh." Max relaxed again. "What did he want? Didn't he leave a name?"

"He said his name was Jacques. He wanted to know if he'd see you, tomorrow."

Max was silent for so long that Jean-Louis stirred uneasily. He said in a small voice, "Are you angry?"

"What? No, I'm not angry. Why should I be? I was just thinking. I must go. Good-night, pest. Try to behave yourself, another time."

He was out of the door at five to ten. The address he had given Deirdre was in a side-turning off the Place, one minute's walk away, yet concealed from inquisitive eyes. He stood back in the shadows. From where he stood, he could see that the lights of the College were now out, except on the ground floor. He frowned a little. Miss Pelham was probably there, working in her study. She would be thinking that all her little chickens were safely in for the night. He prayed she would not hear stealthy footsteps, that she would not glance out of the window.

Then a sudden foreboding cramped his stomach. Suppose she did not come. Suppose—suppose she did not want to come. What a fool he was not to have thought of this before. He had taken it all for granted, and now he saw what an imbecile he had been. Why should she come? She didn't know him. She was a well brought-up little girl. What right had he to expect that for the sake of a Jewish boy she had never seen before she would brave convention, creep out to keep an assignation—

The clock struck ten. There was no sign of her. Max was beginning to shiver and shake. Oh, of course she wouldn't come. He was a bloody fool ever to have imagined it. He began to swear viciously to himself. Damn her for the stuck-up little bitch she undoubtedly was. She'd think herself too good for the likes of him. She was probably discussing it with her girl friends; they would be giggling together about it. But he'd show her—No girl was going to make a fool of him and get away with it. She'd be sorry, all right. Just let her wait—

It was ten past ten. He knew he might as well go back. Yet he stayed there, cursing her and cursing himself, unable to move away, with the cold apprehension so strong inside him that he was on the verge of tears.

He did not see her until she was almost on him. She moved very softly, a little shadow slipping down the narrow road. He drew in his breath, then the next instant he was at her side, had with a bold, possessive gesture, swept her arm into his, and was leading her along the road that led to the river.

They did not at first say a word. But she moved closer against him, and he stared down at the head almost resting against his shoulder, smiling at her from time to time, walking on without looking where he was going.

He said at last, very softly, his voice flattering and caressing her, "I thought you were never coming."

"It's that Nora," said Deirdre. "She's so nosy. I'm sure she suspected something. Every time I came out of the room, she opened her door. In the end I put on my dressing-gown and left it in the downstairs lavatory. I can put it on again when I come back, you see."

Max turned on her a look of delighted astonishment. He began to laugh. Miss Pelham would have been equally astonished, but it is doubtful if she would have laughed.

"She's not a very nice girl," said Deirdre.

"I'll beat her for you," said Max, showing the whiteness of his teeth.

"Where are we going?"

"According to our respective and respected Principals, to the devil."

"Oh, I see," said Deirdre peacefully, as if this solved all her troubles, and they moved on again. Then she said hopefully, "Do you think I could have an ice?"

He laughed again. "You shall have all the ices you can cram down." He looked at her sideways. "Your dear dragon shall stand you one."

"What do you mean?"

"You can have five hundred francs worth of ice. She gave me the money, didn't she? It was very kind of her to tip the poor Jewish boy. There's nothing I should love to spend it on more."

"She won't let us buy ices in the town," sighed Deirdre, her seraphic face wistful with greed. "She says they are bad for the teeth. Such nonsense. Foreign ices, she says, are impure."

"She'd probably say the same of me. After all, I'm foreign."

"Well, it's a shame because I love them so much."

He opened his mouth, then changed his mind. He said, a little dryly, "And what is the kind you love most of all?"

"Oh, the green kind. With a nutty flavour. You don't get anything like that at home. It's gorgeous. Oh, I am enjoying myself—But I was so angry when she gave you that money. Of course, the trouble with Miss Pelham is that she's not really very well-bred. She's silly, too, and so boring, you just can't believe. Do you know, we have to learn how to sit down. I ask you! And get up again. And how to cross a room. And we're simply not allowed to look at boys. I think I'm really doing something rather awful."

"It is just possible that you are," said Max.

"Do tell me—why did you shout up at us yesterday? You speak very funny English." She began to mimic him. "Help! Fire! God-damn! You sounded like our chauffeur when he gets drunk. Were you drunk?"

He was surveying her. He was a little bewildered. He began to feel rather as if he were taking out a school treat. He had no idea, of course, that Deirdre, according to Miss Pelham, was almost mute, but this flow of chatter surprised him. Yet he could not help enjoying the soft little voice, and he said, "For an English girl you speak French quite well."

She replied with spirit, "What do you mean, for an English girl? First of all, I'm Irish, and secondly, I speak French very well indeed."

"Oh là là!"

"Well, I do. I had a French governess. She wouldn't let me speak English at all. She was rather nasty, really. She smelt. She didn't wash very much. She looked a bit like a tortoise. But she said I had no accent at all. Anyway, I speak better French than you do English."

He imitated her: *"Je n'ai pas d'accong!"*

"Oh, I don't speak like that."

He spluttered at her, and they looked at each other, extremely pleased with what they saw—Deirdre enchanted to have so handsome and exciting a young man to tease her and buy her ices, and Max, glowing with a cold triumph in having stolen this strange little beauty from under the dragon's very nose, and already considering how and when he could make love to her.

He kept on stealing covert glances at her from under his thick, dark lashes. He could not keep his eyes off her. She really was quite lovely with the delicate colour of her cheeks, that soft corn hair that his hands ached to touch, and the wide, innocent, grey eyes. His gaze slid down a little then up again to her frank and charming face. He simply could not make her out. She had come out to meet him, in defiance of all convention, and from what she herself had said, had contrived this in a most practised manner. She could not be so inexperienced. She must surely know that if a girl planned to meet a boy late at night, it was not solely for the purpose of eating ices. Yet here she was, prattling like a little girl, talking to him as if he were her brother, moving against him, sometimes clutching on to his arm. With any other girl he would have known exactly where he was; now he felt lost, as if he had stolen a fledgling from the nest. This both disturbed and angered him, yet filled him with a half-resentful protectiveness; he still had this feeling for the very young, but it was preposterous to experience it for a young and pretty girl.

He said abruptly, and without smiling, "Your Miss Pelham will be furious with you."

"Oh," said Deirdre, her voice tilting up, "she'd never forgive me. I think she'd expel me. She'd think this was awfully wrong."

"And she'd be quite right," said Max. "You're a very naughty girl, if I may say so. And I'm not sure if you're not a very silly one, too."

His tone disconcerted her, for he sounded as if he meant it. She flushed up. She said in an offended voice, "Oh, if you don't want me to come with you, I'll go home. I'll go home this very instant."

"Will you?" he said. They were just outside the Café Niçoise. He made no attempt to touch her, and his face was unsmiling, a little grim. He had stopped dead; he was standing almost against her. His eyes stared into hers. He said again, "Will you?"

The atmosphere between them flickered and snapped.

Deirdre's breath caught in a gasp. Her eyes moved over the handsome face so near to hers. But she did not stir, and she said nothing; it seemed briefly to her that his body was taut as if he were some animal of prey about to leap upon her.

Then he stepped back violently. He gripped her wrist with such force that his fingers hurt her. He said in a rough voice, "Oh come on. You're not going home now. It's too late. You're going to sit down at this table, and I shall buy you an ice."

She sat opposite him. Her eyes were wide, like those of a child that knows he has done wrong. There was apprehension in every line of her body, in the way she sat upright, clasped her hands, primmed her lips. She kept on looking at him from under her lashes. She reminded him of Jean-Louis asking for the supper he knew he did not deserve. Then he began to laugh, and he went on laughing while Deirdre and Madame Dupont surveyed him, the one in bewilderment, the other in faintly ironic disapproval.

"If I told you what you deserved," said Max, "you'd never speak to me again." Then he added, bestowing on her his most wicked and enchanting smile, "But I'm going to give you what you don't deserve. Madame! This young lady would like a large pistachio ice. And for me, you can bring a *rouge*. I don't like sweet things. Not to eat." And he turned his smile on Madame Dupont, who, standing behind Deirdre, was shaking her head at him; at this smile she shrugged resignedly and went into the café.

Deirdre was unaware of all this pantomime. She sat there in silence, gesturing away the cigarette that Max offered her. Then she said a little timidly, "You're a funny boy."

He nodded at her, sucking in the corners of his mouth.

"And—and I don't even know your name. You're Max what?"

"Wrzonski, mademoiselle. Max Wrzonski. At your

service." He rose to his feet, clicked his heels like a German officer, then sat down again.

"What—what did you say?"

"Wrzonski. W-r-z-o-n-s-k-i. Pronounced 'Wejonski'. It's Polish. *Je suis polonais, moi.* I was born in Lodz. We came to France in 1939."

"Oh, I see." But she did not see at all, and she attacked her ice with the utmost vigour as if this were the one thing that really lay within her comprehension. She raised her eyes over a spoonful of the mixture, and said suddenly, "Your hair's all wet."

"I've just taken a shower. In your honour, mademoiselle."

She said angrily, for she could not miss the mockery in his tone, "Why are you calling me mademoiselle now? My name is Deirdre. Deirdre O'Brien."

"Oh," he said, sipping his wine, "I'm just a common Polish boy from the Hostel, and you are a young lady. I don't know how to sit down. I don't know how to cross a room. I'm quite uneducated. It's obvious that I mustn't become familiar."

She gave him a look. She might be childish, but he saw that she did not lack a temper. He knew perfectly well that she was longing to throw something at him, but did not dare. He smiled at her grimly, defying her, daring her. The hand that held the ice-cream spoon was beginning to tremble. She did not answer him, but dug her spoon in with a sudden vicious jab; the lump of ice flew off the plate and landed in her lap.

She gave a wail of distress and fury, and sprang to her feet. She shook the remnants of her ice out on the pavement, and stared helplessly down at her dress. She cried out, "It's all your fault! Oh, what am I to do? Why don't you do something to help me instead of standing there, grinning like—like a jackass!"

He came over to her and took her handkerchief out of

her hand. He crouched down in front of her and began to
rub at her skirt. Then he paused, staring up at her. With a
violent movement he was on his feet again, and had shoved
the handkerchief back at her. He said harshly, turning his
back on her, "Do it, yourself. I'm not a nursemaid."

She cried out, "Oh, I'm going home."

"Do," he said, without turning.

She was still rubbing ineffectually at the dress. He remained standing there. He was staring out at the street. On
the face she could see was an expression of the utmost
resentment, fury and astonishment. He would not turn his
head. Only when Madame Dupont came out and touched
him on the arm, did he swing round; what he saw made
him ask warily, "What is it, auntie? Is there something
wrong?"

"There's a young lady coming along the street," said
Madame Dupont. "I saw her through the window. I
thought you would like to know, M. Max. I think there are a
very strange lot of girls in the English school. This one is
dark and she walks—so. She has been here before. I thought
you'd rather she didn't see you. You can come through the
café. There's a back entrance."

Max pulled out Miss Pelham's five-hundred-franc note
and put it under the glass. He said abruptly to Madame
Dupont, "You can keep that as a little present," then seized
Deirdre by the arm and ran her into the café precisely two
minutes before Nora made her appearance. He said nothing,
only jerked her after him with neither gentleness nor
civility; he did not pause until they were out in Madame
Dupont's back yard.

She did not know what to make of this. She did not
realise what had nearly happened. She glared at him with
wretchedness and fury, her head a little bent, one hand
pleating her skirt. And he simply dug his hands in his
pockets, half turned his back on her and began to whistle.

Then suddenly he turned his head. Their eyes met. He came up to her at once. He took her hand, then very gently stooped his head and kissed her cheek. She tried to look angry, but she found his gentleness charming; the dimple flickered, despite herself, and the smile caught at her lips, the small, secret, proud smile of someone who knows she is loved and admired. The sight of that smile brought a lump into his throat. He said in a voice that had grown husky, "I'm sorry. I'm very sorry. I'm behaving like an absolute swine. Do you really want to go home? I was thinking that we might go for a walk by the river." He hesitated, then his voice came out rather more loudly than usual, so that to Deirdre it seemed as if he were shouting at her, and she stared at him. He said, "I won't hurt you." His voice sank again. "I won't hurt you at all. You'll be all right. You needn't be afraid."

"Why should I be afraid?" said Deirdre. "I never thought you'd hurt me."

He said, "Oh, my God!" He stared at her fiercely, as if he believed she was making fun of him. She met the intent gaze, the dark eyes fixed on hers, with a mild astonishment. Then he sighed. He put out his hand and touched her cheek, the cheek he had kissed. He saw the quick colour fly to his finger-tips. He said, almost bitterly, "Oh, you should still be in your pram. You shouldn't be allowed out."

"I am not allowed out," said Deirdre, with a quiver of her lips.

"I'm beginning to understand why." Then he took her hand in his, entwining his fingers. "Come," he said, "it's infernally hot here, and there might be a little breeze by the river. You've got to tell me all about yourself. I want to know everything, down to the smallest detail. I've never met anyone like you in my life." A sudden thought struck him, and he paused. "Do they lock the front door at night?"

92

"Oh yes," said Deirdre, "but there's a garden entrance."

"You seem to have it all remarkably well planned!"

"Well, I don't want to be found out."

"You defeat me—All right. Shall we go?"

"Yes. Yes, Max, of course."

"And you do trust me?"

"Yes." There was amusement in her voice.

He said with sudden savagery, "Why?"

"Because I—I think you're very nice."

He said, "I don't know how you've survived so long. Come then—"

Hand in hand they strolled down the path that led to the river. And as they walked, the freshness blew away the sultry heat of the little town, and then it was as if a change came upon them, as if for the moment their characters were reversed. It was Deirdre who walked swiftly on, in an easy stride, her face glowing and eager, and it was Max who hung back a little, no longer smiling, his eyes always on her, as if he would probe her secrets, the half-bewildered resentment smouldering behind his look.

He was utterly intent upon her, and so it was that he, by nature suspicious, always on the look out for the prowler with the knife, did not even dream that there was a watcher on the other bank, a startled, uncharitable watcher, eager to draw the worst conclusions from anything to hand.

M. Quiqueran was taking an evening walk by the Seine, a dreary, unaccompanied walk, for there was no one who wished to walk beside him. Portelet-sur-Seine did not bear him the bitter grudge that its Jewish immigrants did, but it had not entirely forgotten. There were ugly things to remember. Perhaps he had not done much active harm, but he had acquiesced, he had accepted. When the last of the German conquerors were gone, there were one or two incidents that were not easy to forgive, and people had not forgiven; they still looked askance at M. Quiqueran and did not return his over-willing smile. The deserted building at the side of the Mairie still stood; nobody ever went inside, but it was in the main street and people who passed it remembered, and M. Quiqueran was not a pleasant part of that memory. It had been the Nazi headquarters. The Germans had done their interrogations there. M. Quiqueran might insist with perfect truth that there was nothing that he could have done about it, but the screams that came from there had made the night hideous; it was a little difficult to remember those screams and then look kindly at someone who had been so very polite to the torturers and who, as a result, had had more bread to eat, more liberty to do as he pleased. After the liberation feelings had run high; M. Quiqueran had fled to the woods and stayed there for three shivering days. After that, he had returned for a while to his wife in Paris, and lived there in a quiet, unobtrusive manner, tending to slink into the shadows whenever anyone came near him. But now he was back again, had been back for three years. And he lived an ordinary life, and nobody threatened him any more, except the boys from the Hostel, and they were good-for-nothing ruffians from the most primitive parts of Eastern Europe. "Poor lads," said M. Quiqueran to people who knew nothing about him. "It's not their fault, really. What can one expect with such a background?"

But alone in his room he thought quite differently, especially of Max, who terrified him more than the whole German army put together.

It was strange to be so afraid of a boy, barely nineteen. But M. Quiqueran could not even see Max without his stomach turning over; that wild, dark face with its savage, taunting smile haunted his dreams at night.

"I'll get you yet," Max would say. "You just wait, M. *Bitteschön* Quiqueran. Maybe you'll not have to wait very long. What did they pay you to get us deported? I suppose you sneaked in at night with the information. How many people did you betray? Or isn't that worth remembering?"

It was no use for M. Quiqueran to protest that he had not betrayed anyone. He had acquiesced in the betrayal, and that was sufficient. Sometimes he had watched the deportation trains setting out on their trundling journey eastward to unknown destinations. The people herded into them like cattle had not been put there on his information, but he had expressed no horror, he had turned away without comment. And afterwards he had picked up his extra rations, and smiled and bowed to the German officers. He did not like Jews, but he had not, until he met Max, had violent feelings against them.

What amazed him was that nobody seemed to take Max's threats seriously, for all this was supposed to be a civilised world. Threats and violence were surely police matters. But no one cared. Granier, whose business it plainly was to protect innocent citizens, listened to him with a marked lack of sympathy. "What else can you expect?" he said.

"But he's threatened to kill me," cried M. Quiqueran.

"Oh, that's just talk."

"It isn't. It's sheer persecution. He actually waits for me—" Then he saw the look on the Inspector's face, the involuntary, if instantly repressed, contempt, and he knew he was making a ludicrous spectacle of himself and nearly made it worse by bursting into tears. "It's not fair," he wailed. "It's simply not fair."

"No sensible person expects life to be fair," said Granier. He was thinking that life had not been exactly fair to Max, either. For a boy of twelve to have to see his parents deported, and his sister, two years older than himself, raped and carried off, the word "fairness" must seem nothing but an obscenity. But he did not mention this, for officially he did not know. It was not Max who had told him, but M.

95

Wolff. However, it was admittedly his business to see that the laws of the land were upheld, so he tried, unsuccessfully, not to find M. Quiqueran revolting, and tried, too, not to visualise a gaunt and desperate twelve-year-old who had had in the space of a few moments his whole life broken about his head, who had been forced then to realise that he was alone against a bitterly hostile world. He said, "Has the boy ever actually struck you?"

"He has threatened—"

"Yes, yes. So you keep on telling me. I am asking you, M. Quiqueran, if he has actually hit you. With his fist or open hand—"

"I suppose I have to be murdered before you'll do anything about it."

"If you would kindly answer my question, it would make things easier for both of us. Has he hit you?" And he was thinking, somewhat unprofessionally, If this goes on much longer, I will.

M. Quiqueran said reluctantly, "Well no, not exactly—"

"What do you mean, not exactly? Either he's hit you or he hasn't."

"He's shown me his knife."

"All boys carry a knife."

"Not like this one, they don't," cried M. Quiqueran, then, hysterically, "But you don't care. You just damned well don't care. He could cut my throat before you'd lift a finger to do anything about it."

"There's really no need to exaggerate," said Granier wearily, knowing in his heart that this was true. He did not care. And he knew, too, that Max's knife—though he had never actually seen it—was not just a boy's knife; it was a knife to kill, it had already killed, it might well kill again.

But he spoke to Max. And Max listened with downbent eyes and grave face; in a few days' time M. Quiqueran was back again with more frantic, hysterical complaints.

Granier said at last in the heavy tones that so provoked Max, "M. Quiqueran, I want to put a point to you. Mind, I'm not preaching a sermon." (*"Tiens, tiens,"* Max would have said, but M. Quiqueran said nothing, only scowled.) Granier went on, "It might clarify the situation. I came back here, after the war, when I was demobbed. I came to see Anni. We were courting. I found her very pale and thin, as people are when they've not had enough to eat over a certain period of time. Her mother was dead. She needed medicines and treatment, and she couldn't get them, so she died. In normal circumstances she might still be alive. Well, she isn't. And Anni—Anni had had a pretty bad time, too. You can imagine I felt a bit sick, especially when I heard some of the things she had to tell me. And then I looked around, and there were other people, all fat and prosperous, just because they'd kowtowed to the Bosches. I am not blaming you," cried Granier in a roar, "I tell you, I'm not. Who am I to blame anyone? I'm only telling you what I felt. And if I felt like that, what do you imagine Max feels? He was in Auschwitz, you know. He's no family left. There's not a soul in the world who belongs to him."

"That's nothing to do with me," said M. Quiqueran, and at that Granier fell silent, for there seemed to be nothing more to say. And M. Quiqueran, who did quite honestly believe that it was nothing to do with him, went sullenly away, thinking, He'll kill me one day, and nobody will care, nobody.

And Granier was thinking, He'll kill him, one day. And what the hell shall I do then?

M. Quiqueran now surveyed his enemy. He could not see his face, but that gaunt, supple body had long entwined itself with his blackest dreams; he knew every line of it, and even now, with the width of the Seine between them, he quailed, as if the voice were whispering in his ear, *Ah, c'est mon cher M. Quiqueran—Comment ça va, cher mec?*

But Max was now otherwise concerned, and M. Quiqueran, peering from behind a convenient tree, turned his avid gaze on the young man's companion. Then his mouth fell open. He knew all the girls from the College. He could have described each one minutely. Miss Pelham would not have appreciated his descriptions for, with his usual flair for such things, he had reduced them all to the level of dirty postcards, tabulated their more striking physical characteristics and stripped them of their clothes while doing so. Deirdre, up till now, he had scarcely considered, even in his fantasies. Innocence was not a word in his vocabulary, but he knew there was nothing here for him; he had registered her beauty, dismissed her as cold and immature, turned his hopes on others more forthcoming.

She was holding Max's hand. They were staring at each other. If Max had had any idea how he was betraying himself and to whom, he would have instantly slit M. Quiqueran's throat. M. Quiqueran knew that, and shuddered. But he continued to gaze. He recognised desire easily enough; this was not just boy and girl out for a friendly walk together. He turned his hungry eyes on Deirdre again. How beautiful she was, but how beautiful— And not, it seemed, so cold.

He slid further behind the tree. His eyes veiled. This was a fine scandal. One of the Jews out with one of Miss Pelham's precious little girls. A faint giggle rose in his throat. The joke was almost beyond endurance. He wanted to go at once to the College. "Mademoiselle Pel-ham, have you not counted your girls? But you should. And perhaps *ce cher* M. Wolff would also care to count his boys—"

Then another idea came to him. He looked again. He looked for a long time. In that look innocence withered, as it had withered when the deportation trains thundered east. Only this time he did not say, It has nothing to do with me. This time he said, What is there here for me?

And very carefully—for God help him if Max saw him—
he retreated into the shadows, and presently he made his
meditative way homewards, with vengeance and lechery
cuddled small and cold in his smutty shell of a heart.

*   *   *

They stopped at last by the river. This was not the fine,
broad Seine of Paris, with its magnificent bridges and misty
quais. There it flowed grandly with history its pilot. Here
it was a provincial river; to its left the tawny houses were
dark against the sky, and to its right were the woods where
a king and his mistress had once hunted and killed. The
nightingales still sang in those woods; the blackbird could
out-sing them any day, but the poets had glorified them, so
they continued arrogantly in their three-part motif, ending
always on the same monotonous note.

Max listened, then whistled an imitation. And the Paris
train on the other side took up his whistle in a kind of
impudence; they could hear its puffing, hooting progress
towards the city.

"You'll be going home on that, one day," he said, "back
to England." As he spoke, he unfastened the top buttons of
his shirt, for it was still very hot and he was sweating.

"To Ireland," she corrected him with a little sigh, and her
eyes grew briefly vague and opaque as if they were seeing
again the green slopes of the Wicklow mountains.

"It's a long journey," said Max, his eyes upon her.

"Oh, it doesn't take so long by plane."

"Do you like flying?"

"I hate it when you go up and somehow your inside is
left behind. But otherwise, yes. Don't you?"

"I don't know," he said. "I've never flown. When I went
to England, I went by train and boat."

"Did you stay in England long?"

"Not very. I speak English. A little." He smiled. "A

nice cup of tea. Excuse, please. That's what the English say when you bang into them. Excuse, please. How do you do? Very well, thank you. God-damn."

She made a derisive noise, then flung herself down on the grassy bank. He, after a moment's hesitation, followed suit; he laid himself at her side then moved so that his head lay upon her breast.

She did not, as he had half expected, move away. Instead she touched his hair, and presently her fingers entwined themselves in its thick, black tangle, pulling and tugging a little, while his head lay heavy upon her, his eyes half-closed.

She remarked, "Your hair's dry now—How thick it is. When were you in England? Did you go to school there?"

"No, of course not. I went over with a party. We stayed with English families for a month."

"To learn the language?"

"If you like." Then he exclaimed, "Hey!" as she jerked at the rough, wiry hair; his hands shot up to seize her wrists.

"Well, it's so silly—Don't, you're hurting me—'If you like'! What does that mean? If you didn't go to learn the language, what did you go for?"

He did not answer this directly. His hands still clasped her wrists. He flung his head back so that he could stare into her face, bent over his. He said lazily, "I stayed with a very rich lady—You look so funny, upside down— We didn't speak the same language, but she did her best. She was very serious. She gave me some clothes that belonged to her son. She tried to turn me into a nice, respectable English boy. I think she was kind and meant well. We wrote to each other for a time, when I came back. But we had nothing to say, really. We were like two people in different elements. She was on the land, and I was fathoms under the sea. We could make gestures at each other. There was no contact. It was not her fault."

Deirdre did not answer this. He knew she did not understand what he was saying, any more than the rich Englishwoman had understood. But this was different, for here was something that they both understood very well, something that existed on land and sea. He moved his head again, deliberately snuggling into her, making himself comfortable, and still she did not protest, though he sensed a faint unease in her. He was holding her hands now, bringing them down so that they encircled him, entwined with his own on his naked chest. The thoughts were scudding through his mind; his good resolutions fast vanishing. There was a vast excitement stirring within him, and still they lay in silence, with the nightingales singing their repetitive hearts out, and the river sounds and the distant town sounds, and their own deep, quiet breathing.

She said suddenly, "What's that on your wrist?" And before he could stop her, she had turned his hand over. He turned it sharply back again; he did not answer.

"It's a number," she said. "Have you been tattooing yourself? Why do you want a number on your wrist?"

"It's my distinguishing mark," he said.

"It seems awfully silly to me."

Then he began to laugh, very softly, but she felt the laughter beating against her breast, and she said crossly, "I don't know why you always find things so funny. If you must laugh, please don't laugh on me. You don't know how peculiar it feels—Max!"

But he continued with this subterranean amusement, and he held her hands firmly, smoothing them with his thumbs; his head and shoulders lay heavy upon her, so that, despite her wriggling, she could not shift him. She fell back again on the grass.

He said, "Shall I tell you why I was laughing?"

"If you want to."

"I was thinking of your Miss Pelham, and what she would say if she saw us now."

"I can't imagine what she'd say," said Deirdre with some asperity, "and I can't imagine, either, why you always talk about Miss Pelham."

Max said suddenly, "I don't understand you. Tell me something about yourself. Where do you come from? What do you do? Did you live in Ireland during the war?"

"Yes."

"Were you bombed?"

"Oh no. I didn't really know much about the war. I was very young, you see. You must have been pretty young, yourself."

"I suppose I was."

"Daddy was in London. In the War Office. Mummy and I stayed on in County Wicklow. It's a place called Glendalough. It's very, very pretty. There are seven old churches there. It's where St. Kevin lived, you know."

Max did not know. He had never heard of St. Kevin. But he said nothing, only lay motionless, his face so remote and still that it was as if he were sleeping. His hands still held hers; her fingers were white against his sunburnt skin. He heaved a great sigh, then turned his head sideways against her.

She was staring across the river. She went on, in her soft, sweet voice, "The war really made no difference to me at all. When you're little, you don't bother about things. I used to go for long walks with Rusty. That's my dog, you know. He's an Irish terrier. He's a darling. I miss him very much. Oh, and we had lessons, of course. Celia and I had lessons together. Celia's my great friend. The chauffeur took me over every day. That was quite fun. We didn't work very hard, I'm afraid. The car would call for me again in the afternoon. Daddy would ring up sometimes at night.

But he didn't talk about the war. I suppose he wasn't allowed to. I—I think the only time when I realised how dreadful it all was, was when Peter didn't come home. He was Celia's brother. He was killed. He was shot down over Germany. He was in the R.A.F. It was dreadful when I heard. I remember it even now. I didn't go over for lessons, for a whole week. I cried a lot. But even then—You see, I was only twelve. It was in 1944. And twelve's so very young. I mean, you just don't take things in. There's always your mother to comfort you, and a sort of family routine. You know it's frightfully tragic, but you're still safe and—I suppose this is very selfish—there are still scones for tea and that sort of thing, and you forget, and everything goes on as it always did. But it was very dreadful. Peter was always so nice to me. He was only nineteen, poor boy."

"That's my age," said Max.

"Ah, but Peter's dead, and you're alive."

"I suppose I am." Max raised himself up, and leaning on one elbow stared down at her. He touched her gently on the cheek, then gave the soft flesh a little pinch. He said, "I am beginning to think that you don't know very much about anything, Miss Deirdre."

"That's what Miss Pelham says."

"Does she now—Were you in love with this Peter?"

"In love? Oh, don't be silly. How could I be? I told you, I was only twelve."

"But you've been in love many times?"

The dimple showed for a second. She would not answer, and he persisted, "Well, have you?"

"Why should I be in love?" said Deirdre.

"Why shouldn't you? You're not bad-looking, for an English girl."

"Oh!"

"Don't you like boys?"

"Oh, they're all right," she said, adding with an air of

great importance, her eyes defying him. "Next year I shall meet lots and lots of young men. I shall—I don't know how you say it in French—I shall be coming out." She spoke the last words in English.

" 'Coming out'? *Je ne comprends pas.* What is it, this 'coming out'?"

"Oh—" Her lashes drooped down. "I don't think you'd understand. It doesn't matter. After all, I'm not the interpreter now, as I was with those silly American ladies." Suddenly her eyes opened very wide. She jerked her hands away from him with such force that he was taken by surprise and lost his grip on her. "My book—My notebook! You still have it. With all my drawings in."

He made great, solemn eyes at her. "What book?"

"Oh, honestly—You know perfectly well what I'm talking about. The notebook you picked up and hid from Miss Pelham."

"Oh, that."

"Yes. That!"

"Ah."

"Max!" In her exasperation, she thumped him with her fist. "You're being impossible. Where is it? You've got it on you."

"Have I? *Tiens, tiens,*" said Max.

"It's in your pocket."

"Is it? Are you sure?"

"Well, I'm going to be," said Deirdre fiercely. She had flushed up. She leant towards the jacket which Max had flung down on the grass beside him. But before she could reach it, his hands came down on her forearms and, despite her struggles, she could not release herself. She began to fight him; in a second the quiet between them was broken as they fell into battle, the oldest kind in the world. He was much stronger than she was. He held her away easily, and when she struck at him and called him names, he only laughed in her face, saying again mockingly, *"Tiens, tiens!"* and kicking the jacket away so that it was beyond her reach.

Suddenly she fell still, and in that instant his arms came round her, pushing her back on the grass. She did not struggle any more; her face, pale in the evening light, raised itself to his. When his lips touched hers, she closed her eyes then, to his astonishment, brought up her hands to link them round his shoulders.

He brushed her lips with his twice, then kissed her on cheeks, nose and forehead. He raised himself a little so that he could look down at her. His face was convulsed with the violence of his emotions. Then, to her stupefaction, he said in a grim, menacing voice such as she had never heard from him, "You silly little idiot. I'm going to give you a good telling-off. It's time someone did."

Deirdre's mouth opened in furious, startled protest. She wanted to be kissed, not scolded. She could not understand what was happening at all. But before she could utter a word, he had clapped his hand over her mouth. "Shut up!" he said, using a crude colloquialism he might have employed on Jean-Louis, "You're going to listen to me, whether you like it or not. I've never met anyone so utterly stupid."

She was still struggling to speak, but his hand lay stiflingly on her lips. Her eyes blazed at him. She writhed beneath him in impotent fury.

"I am surprised," said Max grimly, "that your chauffeur didn't instruct you better." He added, interpreting correctly the convulsive movement beneath his palm, "Don't you dare! You bite me and see what you'll get—Now you'll just listen. Don't you know, you little fool, that you should never lie on the grass with young men you don't know? What do you know about me? I might be a frightful character. I might be a maniac. I might have been strangling girls for years. And here you are, behaving like any—any slut from the streets. You ought to be ashamed of yourself. Why, only the other day there was an account in the paper about a girl who got herself murdered just because she hadn't the sense she was born with. He strangled her with a stocking. And there was another case—There are always cases. And even if you weren't murdered, you might be landed with a baby. I don't think they teach you anything in that preposterous school of yours. As it happens—and it's your good luck, not your good sense—you're all right with me, because I know what a nitwit you really are, but next time you mayn't be so lucky. Lying there and putting your arms round my neck—It's a good thing for you I've got some self-control, and it's more than you deserve." The righteousness was blazing in his voice; by this time he really believed he meant it. "It's time you grew up," he said. "It's time you opened your eyes. You can't drink milk for ever. After all—"

He broke off with a gasp. Deirdre might be ignorant of the ways of young men on grassy river banks, but she possessed a primitive instinct for self-defence, and Max had been unwise enough to relax his grip in order to shake her. Her strong white teeth bit fiercely on his thumb.

He jerked his hand back. He swore at her. He swung out his hand to smack her across the face. But before he could do so she burst into tears, and at this his expression changed. He caught her to him as if she were a small child, soothing her, rocking her to and fro, saying in a voice of the utmost tenderness, "There, there—It doesn't matter. It's my fault. It's all my fault. Look, here's your notebook. I didn't mean to tease you. I was going to give it back in a moment. Don't cry. Sweetheart, don't cry."

But she only wept against his shoulder; the weeping and the convulsive movements of her body against his were almost unendurable to him so that he went quite white and shut his eyes, muttering to himself, while his hands continued to gentle her. He exclaimed at last in a voice of pure desperation, "For God's sake, stop it. I can't take any more. Deirdre. You must stop—"

She raised a tear-soaked face. She took the bitten hand in hers, gingerly touching the thumb. She exclaimed in heartbroken horror, "Oh, it's bleeding. What shall I do? It's bleeding quite badly."

He said in a more normal voice, "What the hell do you expect? You've got teeth like a horse." Then he grinned at her. "Oh, kiss it better. Go on." His arm round her shoulder gave her a shake.

"That won't stop the bleeding," said Deirdre. She pulled out her handkerchief. She said in a doubtful voice, "It's not very clean. It's got ice-cream on it."

"An infallible remedy for a bitten thumb," said Max gravely. "It prevents lockjaw."

She stared at him; the green-stained handkerchief dangling from her hand. She began to smile a watery smile. "Oh, Max," she said.

He gave a great sigh. Then he moved a little away, reaching out for his jacket. "Oh, never mind my bloody thumb," he said, "I've had worse. I shan't die of it." Then, "You draw so very, very well. It's strange that you should know so little and see so much."

"I shall draw your face," said Deirdre, studying him. "It has great lines and hollows. Like a mournful mountain range. It's a sad face. You mustn't be sad, Max. Why do you look so sad?"

He shrugged and threw his jacket on to her lap. "There are cigarettes there," he said. "Light one for me. Put it in your mouth and light it, then I'll smoke it."

"Why must I do that?"

"Why shouldn't you? You owe me something. You bit me, didn't you? I let you off. I wouldn't do that for most people. I don't know why you call me sad. I'm not, particularly. Not that there's much to grin at in this world. Sometimes I'd give everything I had to get away from it. I'd like to find myself an island, and lie there in the sun. Where's my cigarette?"

She gave a sudden exclamation. She had put her hand into his pocket and pulled out, not the packet of Gaulloises, but a knife which she now held in her palm. She stared at it, then at him. "What a dreadful looking thing. It looks like a real weapon." A faint curiosity crept into her voice. "How does it work? Do you press this knob thing?"

He snatched it from her, springing to his feet as he did so. He shouted, "For God's sake! Do you want to chop your fingers off? You really are the silliest girl—It works like this." He pointed it at the grass and pressed the spring. The blade leapt out, six inches of death, bright, slim, sharp.

She said, "Why do boys always carry knives? I think this looks very dangerous. You could almost kill someone with it."

"Do you think so?"

"Well, it could cause a nasty accident, anyway. I wish you wouldn't carry it around with you. You might fall and jerk the blade open. You could do yourself a really bad injury with it."

"Are you worried about my hurting myself, or about my killing someone?"

"Oh, honestly," said Deirdre. "You wouldn't kill anyone. I know that. But you really could hurt yourself with it. I tell you what, Max. When is your birthday?"

"I was born in February."

"I'll give you a proper pen-knife. Then you can throw this horrid thing away."

He was silent for a moment. He pulled out his packet of cigarettes and lit himself one. He had apparently forgotten his request. He stared down at the knife lying across his palm. His head was bowed so that she could not see his expression, but her drawing eye pencilled his every line. He stood there, legs apart, the jacket hanging from one shoulder. The cigarette drooped from his lower lip. The black hair, disordered in their struggle, fell across his forehead. He wore it longer than an English boy would have done. There was a strange intensity to him as if he were looking back into a darkness where her eyes might not reach. Then he raised his head. He shook back his hair, laughed and, closing the blade, threw the knife on to the grass by Deirdre's knee.

"A present for you," he said.

"But——"

"Keep it. Throw it away, if you like. I don't want it any more. It's yours."

She did not understand, but she was moved by him enough to sense that this was no ordinary gift. This was a gesture, this to him was something symbolic. She took the knife in her hand and put it into her handbag. She said in a little voice, "Thank you, Max." Then, "I'm sorry I bit you."

This made him grin. But he only said, "Give me something. You must, you know. Otherwise we'll quarrel."

"I—Yes, of course. But I haven't anything you'd want."

"I want that drawing. Of the camp."

"Of the *camp*?"

"Yes. Yes." His voice roughened.

"But I've never drawn——"

He took the notebook from her. He turned over the pages. He pointed at the picture of the young, haggard faces behind the barbed wire. "That—Will you give it me?"

"Yes. If you want it. Only it's just something I scribbled down. I don't quite know what I meant by it."

He did not answer this. He tore the page out, folded it

with great care and slipped it into his trousers pocket. Then he said, touching her arm, "We ought to be going. Do you know it's eleven o'clock?"

"Oh no!"

"In fact, it's nearly a quarter past. Don't worry. I'll see you home. You'll be all right. There are all sorts of ways of getting back into places you're not supposed to get out of."

They began to walk back through the side streets of Portelet-sur-Seine. They walked in silence, intensely aware of each other, yet not even brushing their arms against each other. Only once he caught hold of her arm when she stepped carelessly off the pavement; he rapped out at her, "Can't you remember that the traffic here goes on the right? For God's sake!" Then he released her at once, and they walked on again.

There were still a great many people abroad. On hot nights the town went to sleep later. The cafés were full. Nobody looked at them; they were just another boy and girl out for a stroll. From one of the cafés came the sound of an accordion. It sounded gay and Parisian; Deirdre paused to peer in longingly. But Max strode on with stony face, and she had to run to keep up with him. She said placatingly, "It sounded pretty. And I've been so dreadfully bored. The only music Miss Pelham likes is symphonies and things."

He glanced at her. She thought he looked as if he hated her. But he made no comment, only continued to walk on, rather as if he were a policeman, escorting her back to prison. And the thought of prison tangled with Rosedene College and then with sad faces from behind barbed wire; she lagged behind more and more until he seized her wrist, exclaiming, "Oh, do come on. What the hell's the matter with you? Do you want to be caught?"

She replied haughtily, snatching her wrist away and rubbing it as if he had hurt her, "It's none of your business if I am. If you're afraid, you can always leave me. I'm sure I don't want to get you into trouble."

Then they began to quarrel fiercely, as if they had both been waiting for this to spark it off. They quarrelled in whispers, still making for the Place du Triangle, and neither really understood what the quarrel was about. But the hot, bitter words spilled out of them and, as they spat and brawled, so they moved closer to each other, their shoulders touching, their breath upon each other's faces.

"You're a spoilt little baby," Max snarled at her, "you ought to be slapped." He began to jeer. "I wonder you didn't bring your chauffeur with you. I suppose at home you all eat off gold plate. Does Rusty have a gold plate, too? I expect he only eats chicken. He wouldn't eat bones like an ordinary, common dog. The bones would be kept for someone like me."

They were at the Place du Triangle now. They both moved instinctively to the shelter of the trees. Rosedene College was completely dark. In the Hostel the first-floor landing light had been left on. They stood under the branches, furious with each other, unable to part.

"I hate you," wept Deirdre. "I wish I'd never met you. I think you're absolutely horrible. I can't imagine why you ever bothered to speak to me. I suppose you enjoy making people cry. I suppose you despise me because I came out with you. I hope I never, never see you again."

He looked at her in such a way that she fell silent. He did not answer. Only his arms came round her, and at once they began to kiss, her lips salty against his, her tears wetting his cheek, her hands clutching on to his shoulders.

He said in a great sigh that lifted the hair falling about her face, "I suppose this is the end for us."

She burst out crying again. "The end," she sobbed, savouring this dreadful moment to the full, and the tragedy of it enveloped her like the still, dark night, so that her kisses grew more violent, and at last it was he who drew back, holding her at arm's length.

"I suppose," he said, "you couldn't meet me just once more?"

"Yes! Oh yes, yes, I could."

"Tomorrow night, the same time? By the river?"

"Yes. Oh Max—"

He glanced across his shoulder. There was nothing stirring in the Place, not even a stray cat. His breath caught in a sobbing sigh. He was ablaze with glory, with the danger and wonder of it. He said to her in a voice that did not seem to him to be his own, "I love you."

She half shook her head.

"I do. And I want to marry you."

"Do you really mean that?"

"Of course I mean it."

Their hands linked. They both turned instinctively to stare up at the two buildings from which they came. The candles still burned in the synagogue. Miss Pelham's roses still perfumed her room. The landing light was out now. The boys slept in their dormitories, the girls under their soft pink eiderdowns. Only at the far end of the Place du Triangle a small light shone: Granier was still up, writing his reports, a weary man longing passionately for his bed.

"We'd better not go together," Max whispered. "Will you wait for me by the river?"

"Of course."

"I'll get there earlier if I can."

"I'll be waiting for you."

"Will you be all right now?"

"Yes."

"Good-night, Deirdre."

"Good-night, Max."

They moved towards each other again, magnetised, and, as if this were a prearranged signal, Granier's light went

out and they were left in the darkness, staring at each other's
shadow, oblivious of the candles and the roses, lost briefly
in a no-man's world.

He gave her a little push forward. "You must go," he
said. He tried to make his voice firm, but it shook badly.
He stepped away from her, watching her stoop to take off
her sandals. Then she waved at him, and ran soundlessly
on her bare feet across the dusty road. He saw her disappear
through the garden. Suddenly taut, he stared up into the
College's eyeless windows, waited in a dreadful apprehension
for the angry blaze of light.

But the darkness stayed, and presently he walked back
into the Hostel.

Chapter Five

NORA was writing a letter to her dearest friend. She had draped a scarf over the lamp so that the light should not provoke Miss Pelham's interest. It was a red scarf, and it made a soft, pink glow. It was after midnight, and she had only been in for a few minutes, missing Deirdre by perhaps a quarter of an hour. Deirdre, in bed now and asleep, did not know how lucky she had been, for Nora's ears were as sharp as her curiosity, and her curiosity was as sharp as her pen.

"I'll never forgive Dad for landing me in this dump," wrote Nora. "You just can't believe what it's like. All these frightful girls, they'd make you quite sick. They look like little dolls and all their mas and pas are in the peerage or the army or both, and they've pints of money and no sense. They bore me to stitches . . . I feel as if I'm in a ruddy kindergarten. There's one who's very odd. A kid called Deirdre—what a name! I thought she was half-witted when I first saw her, but now I'm not so sure. Still waters and all that. She draws. I caught a glimpse of her notebook, it looked interesting. One day when she's out, I'll pinch it. I wish you could see Miss P. giving us lectures on culture and (hold everything!) deportment. She told me today my skirt was too tight!!! 'My dear,' she says, ever so genteel, 'you must not be offended if I say this, but it does look a little vulgar to wear something as tight as that.' And then she gives a laugh. 'I really don't know how you manage to sit down,' she says. Silly old bitch. I nearly took it off and asked her if she liked me better in my panties. Never mind, it won't last for ever, and oh how wonderful it will be when I get out. Sounds like prison, I know, but that's the way I feel . . . How's the gang? Is Nick still going round with Mary, and has Pat got over it yet? Oh, I must tell you something else. Hope in the wilderness! There are some dazzling boys in a Hostel opposite us. Of course we're strictly forbidden to speak to them. They're Jewish and, my dear, they are wildly good-looking. There's one of them I've got my predatory eye on. He's called Max and too wildly exciting for words—"

She broke off. She hunched up on the bed, her knees under her chin. She bit pensively at the nails of her left hand. The small, dark face grew hurt and angry as if the bright vulgarity of her letter had been smudged over. She raised her head. "Hell!" she said aloud, "Oh hell, hell, hell!" Then she went on writing, "When are you coming to Paris? I'll get leave to see you, if it kills me—"

*   *   *

Max was up at seven the next morning. He, like most of the others, had to catch the quarter to eight train to Paris. The housekeeper left a tray of coffee and bread in the dining-room; the boys gulped down a hasty breakfast, collected their sandwiches and ran to the station. The train reached St. Lazare at half past eight, so that they could dive into the Metro and arrive at work at nine.

Max stood by the table now, a mug of coffee in one hand and a hunk of bread in the other. It was the sour bread of post-war Paris, but he was used to it; he dunked it in his coffee and swallowed it down. He glanced at his companions without speaking. There was no time to talk, and they knew each other too well for trivial conversation. Only Moishe spoke to him, asking if he wanted to see a new American film at the *Montparnasse*. He and Moishe had been in Auschwitz together. Their friendship was far beyond friendliness. They knew each other with the strange, instinctive knowledge of people who had fought side by side for survival. It was not affection that lay between them, but something infinitely tougher and more enduring. It was as if their mutual knowledge was pared to the bone, as if by seeing each other's emaciated and maltreated body they had penetrated into the spirit so that their identities merged.

"No," said Max. "I've got a date."

Moishe nodded. He asked no questions. His eyes, mild, gentle eyes, looked briefly into Max's, then he picked up his sandwiches and moved off towards the station, a big, handsome boy more like a German than a Jew, who took life with an easy good-nature; he was one of the fortunate fifty out of two thousand who had survived two winters in Riga.

Max, despite the lateness, still stood there, and from time to time, over his coffee-cup, his eyes wandered from face to face. In one way they were still aliens to each other. They came from different countries. Their fathers had been cattle-drovers, tailors, doctors, shop-keepers, lawyers. Yet they were like beads on a string, threaded together by experiences they never mentioned, fused into a common background, isolated in their Jewishness which separated and bound.

A sudden sick revulsion came upon him. These faces had surrounded him for seven long years. If it were not Chaim from Poland, it was other Chaims. If it were not red-haired Czech Nathan, it was other Nathans, with red, black or blond hair. German Moishe had endured Auschwitz and the extermination camp in the bitter north, but there had been other Moishes and they had endured or not endured; if not, their bodies had joined the pile of their kinsmen's corpses, and others had stepped forward to take their place. There had been an endless trail of them; skeletons with vast, suffering eyes, sustained by hate or by God or by the simple will to survive, all encircled by the yellow star. So it had been and so, it seemed, it must always be. And the vileness of those unspoken memories beat upon him so that the coffee he had just swallowed surged up in his throat; he slammed the cup and saucer down. For behind those living faces, normal, healthy, youthful faces, crept the others, the myriad dead whom he had known, and the stench of the camp was about him like a fog, that dreadful stench of decay and death and despair; it seemed to him that they were none of them human any more, but things like lice left to crawl upon the barren earth.

He forgot his sandwiches. He picked up his brief-case, and ran out into the Place du Triangle, making his violent way towards the station. He passed by M. Quiqueran, who scowled apprehensively, but Max did not even see him; if he had done so, he would have said nothing, for his enemy was now supremely unimportant.

The thought was pounding with his footsteps: I must get away, I must get away. To be no longer bound—He had tried. They had all tried. M. Wolff could have told the American ladies that if they had been interested. There had come to all of them, M. Wolff included, a brief passion of revulsion when they had sickened at this enforced free-masonry, when they had cried out, Must deprived know only deprived, must the barbed wire always, always, always shut us out from the world where others, Jew, Gentile and Muslim, roam unfettered and free? And they had broken asunder the wire and stepped into that world, only to find themselves stateless, defenceless and alone. One by one, ashamed, shocked, they had crept back again to their little hole, forced into a communal life with little to bind them but a past that they only could understand.

"Max!" It was Jean-Louis going to school with satchel on his shoulder; the angelic face that was the bane of many a teacher's life turned sweetly upwards. "Max! Maxy!"

"What's the matter with you, *schlmiel*?" said Max, walking so fast that Jean-Louis had to run to keep up with him.

"Your—your telephone call—"

"Well, what about it?"

"Did you ring back?"

"What's that to do with you?" Max looked down at him. Even to him it was strange to know that Jean-Louis had been thrown on to the French countryside at the age of five, and had wandered for six months before a relief organisation had picked him up. He had been as savage as a cornered rat, a skinny starveling with every inch of him ripe for murder. Max had no illusions about him now. The cherubic face that visitors liked to fondle concealed as tough a gangster as ever roamed the city gutters; a knife was nothing alien to those small hands which still retained their baby softness.

"Oh, I don't know," said Jean-Louis, very innocent. He was, as Max knew perfectly well, devoured by curiosity. "If they ring again, do you want me to give them a message?"

"I'll tell you what I want you to do," said Max.

"What's that, Maxy?"

"Mind your own damned business, that's what, otherwise you'll get a thick ear."

"*Je m'en fous*," said Jean-Louis impudently, for this was virtually his slogan; as Max aimed a kick at him, he leapt aside with the agility of much practice, shouted out an obscenity and scuttled, giggling, down a side-turning that would bring him out at the Portelet-sur-Seine Junior School.

Max laughed, and continued on his way. But his laughter died as soon as it was born. He had come to the point where he could take no more; he knew it; the knowledge of it burned within him. He ran on to the platform and looked around him. The name of Portelet-sur-Seine was written in enormous, white lettering on the wall facing him. He stared at it as he had stared at it every morning and every evening for the past four years. He fought his way into the train and stood by the corridor window, lighting a cigarette.

There were, after all, a few who had escaped. They had married. They had made a new family unit of their own. They were the lucky ones. You could not go out into the jungle world alone, but you could go if there were someone beside you, someone to love and be loved. You could begin again. You could forget death, and concentrate on living.

A man, making his way along the corridor, knocked against him and, with a glance at the handsome, gangster face, apologised.

"That's all right," said Max mechanically, and suddenly and unexpectedly smiled. He would not normally have been so civil, but there was a strange peace spreading inside him, for the miracle had happened, the barbed wire was lifting; for the first time in the long, bitter years, he saw the path that led to freedom and the companion who would tread it with him.

The man was surprised, but Max no longer saw him. He leant his forehead against the cold window-pane. He knew now what had happened to him; he was in love, utterly and completely in love. For that moment his face was as defenceless, as young, as astonished as Deirdre's might have been.

When he stepped on to the platform at St. Lazare, he was still smiling.

*　　*　　*

"Well, Inspector?" said M. Wolff. He had come out to buy cigarettes. It was another beautiful day. He blinked a little in the sunshine. It struck him that he was growing like a mole; it was seldom nowadays that he took the air, and he had not gone near the woods for over three years. For a wild, reckless moment, he thought he would abandon the Hostel and leap on to the nearest bus. But there were innumerable things to see to, his desk was littered with papers, and he had not even ordered today's supply of food or given directions to the kitchen staff. He sighed, and looked at Granier, who was undoubtedly as fettered as himself.

"Well, M. Wolff?" said Granier. "I gather your young man's back in the fold. He seemed quite above himself, last night, when I met him. But I somehow got the impression that he was happy. Don't you occasionally find the running of your Hostel a little difficult?"

"Just mention the times when it's easy," said M. Wolff crossly, fumbling with his packet of cigarettes.

"A great responsibility," said Granier. He was, M. Wolff perceived, in one of his heavier moods. There were great shadows under his eyes as if he had not had enough sleep. He said, "However, a miracle has just occurred."

"According to which church?"

"According to any church you may care to mention."

"If you are going to tell me that Max has just had a vision, I shall fight you to the last breath," said M. Wolff. "He does not believe in his own religion, much less the religion of one of our minor prophets." And he peered up at Granier, to make sure the point was taken.

Granier said, undisturbed, "Well, for a minor prophet, He didn't do so badly. He was a Jew after all, like yourself. Personally, I always think some of your own prophets are remarkably tiresome. They are the kind I should have had to arrest—Jeremiah, for instance. He has never been one of my favourite characters."

"Oh, if you're going to go doctrinal on me," said M. Wolff, "you'd better excuse me while I examine the Torah. But I suspect I should beat you, any day. Christians are mostly extraordinarily ill-informed about their own creed. Which reminds me, I have a charming story for you."

Granier glanced out of the corner of his eye at the clock. M. Wolff saw him, and continued relentlessly. "One

Sunday morning," he said, "during the worst deportations in Germany, the good Christians went to church. And the poor Jews followed them, thinking they would be safe in the House of God. The service begins. Then, with a great clash and clatter, the storm-troopers come in. '*Heil Hitler!* All Jews to leave immediately,' says the leader. And out they creep, in little huddles, like sheep herded into the slaughter-house. But not all. Not all. A few remain, kneeling, praying they might be overlooked. He cries again, 'All Jews to get out.' A few more go, then for the third time he roars, 'If this church is not cleared of Jews within the next minute, it will be burnt to the ground.' A pause, sir. Then Jesus on the Cross turns His head to the Virgin Mary, and says sadly, '*Ah, maminyu, kum! Lomir gehen.*' Which, freely translated from the Yiddish, means, Ah, mama, come on, let's get the hell out of here. As you so justly remarked, He was a Jew, too."

Granier who had listened to this with lowered eyes, said, "I was going to tell you a miracle. Another kind of miracle."

"Is Max following after a Christian?"

"Not as far as I know. But he passed M. Quiqueran, this morning, and did not say a word."

"*Mazeltov!*" said M. Wolff.

"I saw it with my own eyes. From my window. Quiqueran looked almost hurt. I wondered if Max was at long last growing up. Anni is devoted to him, and assumes that because he is kind to Patricia he would not harm a fly, but I have always regarded him as extremely dangerous. Of course, women go far too much by charm. But I must admit it was a great relief to me. And, I imagine, to Quiqueran."

"Even possibly to me," said M. Wolff. He studied the packet of cigarettes he was still holding. His face was doubtful, a little perturbed.

"I thought you'd be more pleased than that," said Granier in a jolly voice that was not usual to him. "After all, you know as well as I that Max has been heading for prison for some time. I'm afraid I've never been particularly sympathetic with Quiqueran, but he is as entitled to his personal safety as anyone else, and the moment has been approaching when I should have been forced to take the boy in charge. Now we can all relax a little. Perhaps he's found himself a girl-friend."

"Max is always finding himself girl-friends," said M. Wolff. "The girls like him very much indeed. They like him rather too much—" He raised his head. "Sometimes I wonder if anyone knows anything about anyone else. You'd think I'd know my own boys. I ought to, God knows. I've been with them since they came out of the camps. We have the same background. I know what they went through. I've nursed them through their crises, and I had a fine time with them, about a year after it was all over, when they went down, one after another, with raging fevers, and no doctor could say what was the matter. A kind of psychological reaction, I suppose. Anyway, there was all that, and a great deal more besides—and yet, you know, I don't know a damn thing about them. Not even that little devil, Jean-Louis, for all he's only ten years old. I have come to the conclusion, Inspector, that violent persecution has one universal effect on the victim. He learns how to be alone, and he must always be alone. All my boys are like that. They can't be away from each other, yet even with each other they are isolated. There are so many things they will never tell me. I could give you a character sketch of all of them, and I still know absolutely nothing."

"Oh, wait till they fall in love," said Granier. "Then they'll talk. Get it all out of their systems."

"I wouldn't know," said M. Wolff. He turned towards the Hostel. "Anni well? Patricia?"

Granier held forth on them for a moment. Then M. Wolff remarked, "If I were Quiqueran, I shouldn't be too sure it's all over. I don't think Max is of a very forgiving nature. Well, when you have to arrest him, come and tell me first—Look at that! Ah God, look at that!"

It was the crocodile of girls from the College. They were going to Paris to visit the Cathedral of Notre Dame. M. Wolff gazed at them delightedly, then raised his hand in salute to the pretty little fair girl at the end. "Enchanting," he said, "and such nonsense, such nonsense." Then, more seriously, "I sometimes wonder, Inspector, which is the most lost—Miss Pelham would kill me—her nice little girls or my not-so-nice little boys. Oh, but I mean that. My boys were thrown into barbarism, whether they liked it or not. Anthropologically speaking, they have regressed through three stages of civilisation. They are living anachronisms, but so are these charming and preposterous little creatures who are being brought up as Victorian misses, for all it happens to be the year 1949."

"It's a pity they can't link up together," said Granier, without thinking.

"God forbid!" said M. Wolff.

* * *

Deirdre spent the day in a happy confusion. Her feelings were on the whole uncomplicated. She was enchanted with Max, who was like no one she had ever met. He was exciting, he was provocative, he was unpredictable; when he kissed her, it was like no kiss she had ever experienced, bore no resemblance to the kisses she had from time to time received from hot, shy young men at hunt balls. Their white-gloved hands were always a little damp with what they politely called perspiration, they breathed rather heavily, and they smelt of moth balls and expensive shaving lotion. Their faces, neatly pinned down afterwards in Deirdre's drawing-book, were reddish moons, their mouths were usually open, and their eyes would swivel sideways in case some irate fox-hunting relative were surveying them. It was all very pleasant and quite exciting, but when it was done, it was done, and she had always returned home placidly and forgotten about them.

But this—Max was no more the hero of her imaginings than he was one of the muscular young men at the hunt balls, but the very thought of him quickened her body, and she longed passionately for the moment when she could see him again. Sitting in the Paris train, she doodled on the envelope of her mother's last letter—"I hope you are being a sensible girl, Dee dear, and don't forget, Daddy's spent a lot of money on you, and we are expecting you to work hard and not moon about too much—" and dark, derisive eyes, high cheek-bones, indented nostrils, sprang to life beneath her fingers as they had done last night when, before falling asleep, she had jotted him down. As Miss Pelham expounded on the history of Notre Dame, Deirdre stood there, hearing nothing but Max's quick, violent words, the inflexion of his voice when he teased her—*Tiens, tiens!*—the savagery that burst out of him from time to time. She looked at Miss Pelham in her silk suit, with the girls gathered attentively round her, and thought how dull she was compared with this young man who spoke as much with his hands as with his voice, who could convey every mood by this intonation, who swore at her, laughed at her, said in a whisper, *Je t'aime*.

Oh, magnificent, magnificent, thought Deirdre, how happy I am, how wonderful that this should happen to me. She furtively opened her handbag, and peered at the great knife which lay at the bottom of it. She was disconcerted when Nora's gruff, husky little voice said in her ear, "You look very enthralled, Deirdre O'Brien. Is this an outbreak of religious mania, or are you in love?"

Deirdre snapped her bag shut. She turned a blank gaze upon Nora, seeing her plump little face as all eyes and mouth, cleft, sensual mouth, defiant eyes with flyaway brows. She said, "Oh, I don't know. I was just thinking."

"Are you sure you don't know?" said Nora. Then she swung round, producing an expressionless smile as Miss Pelham advanced upon her.

And Deirdre then forgot about her, but Nora did not forget about Deirdre, and spent a great deal of rather profitless time wondering how on earth she had met her boy, who he was, and how surprising it was that so dumb a beauty had such guile in her. She began to feel quite a respect for her; this was the kind of achievement that she could appreciate.

The girls arrived back at the College by two o'clock, and spent the rest of the afternoon doing English and French homework. This to Deirdre was entirely useless, for she could not write well in either language; her English spelling was if anything rather worse than her French, and how could anyone be expected to concentrate on a stupid dictée, which began:

"Je ne sais pas qui elle est, monsieur le curé. Je viens de la trouver dans l'église; elle cherchait sa maman, que je pensais trouver chez vous—"

when all the time a voice, which did not belong to any clergyman, was saying, *Je t'aime, je t'aime.*

She actually wrote these shameless words down, and did a delightful little drawing of Max standing there astride, his jacket balanced on one shoulder—then she came to her senses, hastily folded the incriminating page, and put it in her handbag.

She remained in this dream all day, and Miss Pelham gave her a public scolding, because there was a great gap in her French dictation where it appeared she had not attempted to take the words down at all.

At a quarter to ten she slipped softly down the stairs. Nora heard her, and leant out of the window to watch her cross the Place du Triangle. She hoped that the young man would put in an appearance, but there was, to her great disappointment, no sign of him.

Deirdre was unaware of this. She was equally unaware that someone else had observed her, and was quietly following, a discreet distance away. She walked gaily along, swinging her handbag. She could not wear her best dress, because it was stained with pistachio ice-cream, but she had changed into an Irish green linen; she surveyed herself in the mirror before she left, and was delighted by her own loveliness; it was for Max, and Max would be delighted, too.

She took her time. She knew she was too early, but she could not bear to wait any longer. The life of the town mingled with the excitement within her, so that she hummed to herself as she strolled along. The humming was entirely tuneless, but it expressed her happiness; she was so very happy, she knew this was going to be a perfectly marvellous evening. The young men whom she passed whistled softly and wished her good-evening, but she neither heard nor saw them, only thought that in a brief while Max's arms would be round her, his mouth on hers.

At last she came to the river. She stood there, gazing out at the nightingale-studded woods beyond. Then she knelt down on the bank, and sat back on her heels. She stayed there, motionless. Her golden hair was blown back from her face, her eyes were rapt. One hand rested on her knees, the other held the clasp of her handbag.

The young men at the hunt balls all came from families in the district. They had all been to the right schools, one or two had managed to wriggle into the university, others were either in the Services or had high-up jobs in their fathers' business. They were none of them particularly intelligent, they all voted the same way, talked the same way, did the same things and could be correctly forecast in all their reactions.

And Max she could not place at all, except that she knew that he and the young men would not have a decent word to say to each other. He did not appear to have much money, and his clothes were of poor quality, though he wore them well. He had this strange number tattooed on his wrist, as if he were one of her father's cattle. He was a Jew, of course. She knew that from Miss Pelham. He had had a bad time during the war, but what that bad time might consist of she had no idea. He was quite extraordinarily good-looking, and he appeared to love her very much.

And what else? There must be so much more. Deirdre seldom bothered about people, except to draw them, but now the excitement stirred within her again. She glanced at her wrist-watch. It was five past ten. He should be here at any moment. She drew in her breath with a little shuddering sigh, and the handbag, coming open, fell to the grass at her side. She did not notice the flutter of white paper. She heard nothing, and when a thin shadow swooped over her and a bony hand appeared across her shoulder to grasp the page from her notebook, she turned a startled and affronted face on the intruder.

"You're quite an artist, mademoiselle," he said. Then, "Why, it's Max. I'd recognise him anywhere. What a clever little girl you are."

Deirdre stared up at M. Quiqueran. She had never spoken to him, but she knew him well enough. The girls used to make fun of him, for at the beginning he had stood there and stared at them, giving them furtive little smiles, obviously begging for them to speak to him.

"Dirty old man," Nora said scornfully. And once (when Miss Pelham was not there) she had marched up to him and demanded in a ringing voice, "Well? And what do you want? You ought to be ashamed of yourself at your age. It's the kind of thing people go to prison for."

Deirdre remembered this now. M. Quiqueran had gone

a dull, ugly red. He had walked away at once, in a stiff, jerking manner, rather as if he were a marionette whose strings were not being correctly pulled. He never came near the girls again. Nora must have mentioned the incident to Miss Pelham, for the girls were warned that he was not at all a desirable character; they were to report at once if he so much as looked at them.

This had not seemed particularly funny to her at the time. It seemed even less funny now. The river bank was deserted. The nearest houses were several hundred yards away and faced the road. There was no sign of Max.

A little movement of fear passed through her. Perhaps it was his smile, his fixed gaze. M. Quiqueran sat himself down on the grass beside her. There was scarcely an inch between them, and his proximity made her feel a little sick. Her drawing eye that saw so much, even when she herself saw so little, registered something strange, half-fearful, half-daring, in the look of him and, though nothing in her life had prepared her for such a situation, she sensed that something was very wrong; for once the double vision became one. A purely primitive fear gripped her, and she looked wildly across her shoulder, praying that she would see Max come striding towards her.

There was nothing to see. There was only the green grass, and the river flowing softly by.

She spoke at last. Her breathing was out of control, so the words were oddly punctuated. "Will you please go away," she said. "I wish to be left alone." And she turned her face from him, as if by shutting him from her sight, she could obliterate him altogether. That swift gesture was a mistake. The next instant his hand came down on hers. The touch was repulsive to her. She gave a little cry of disgust, and tried to pull her hand away.

His grasp tightened. He said in an arch, self-conscious voice, "I don't know what your Miss Pel-ham would say

to you, I really don't. Taking a lover like that. And one of
the Jew-boys—" Then he quoted in a sad, mocking way,
"*Je t'aime, je t'aime*—How pretty that sounds. Now what
would you do if I told Miss Pel-ham all about it, eh? Or
perhaps I should say, what would you do to stop me
telling her?"

She grew deathly still. Her face was white. She faced him,
her hand cold beneath his. She said not a word.

His other hand stole like some obscene and creeping
thing and fastened on her ankle. To Deirdre it was as if she
had fallen into the clutches of some octopus-like monster;
the hand was a tentacle and she had not the strength to
wrest it away. It made her feel ill, to the point of physical
sickness. The terror was rising to hysteria in her throat,
and it was all the worse because she could not understand
it; M. Quiqueran was disgusting, yet what he was doing was
not in itself so frightening.

Her free hand fumbled for the handbag, as if its hard,
homely touch could help her.

"You know," went on M. Quiqueran, his hungry eyes
roving over her, "I think I must give you some advice. I
don't know how long this has been going on, but I must
tell you in all fairness that Max Wrzonski is a very unsuitable
person for you to know. He's a bad lot. He's a Jew. Not
that I'm against Jews, of course, but really he's quite like
an animal. Those boys can't help it, actually, they're made
that way. They have no decency, no morals. Ask Inspector
Granier, if you don't believe me. Max has nearly been in
prison several times. He's got a wicked temper. I suppose, to be charitable, one must say that he's quite
unhinged. Psychopathic, if you know the word. He
actually carries a knife, like any gangster. Why, he's
threatened me with it—Me! I don't think you ought to see
him again. A nice, pretty girl like you doesn't have to take
a lover who's a thug and a lunatic and will certainly end on

the guillotine. I'm sure you agree with me, don't you?
Now I'm quite a different sort of person. I could show you
I know how to make a little girl happy."

Most of this she did not take in. She could not speak.
If she had but known it, one suggestion that Max was due
at any moment would have sent M. Quiqueran fleeing from
her like a hare. But she said nothing, and meanwhile the
hand was beginning to move slowly up her leg; it appalled
her so that all coherence was shocked out of her. But one
word rang in her mind. Knife. Knife, knife, knife.

Her hand slipped, half-unconsciously, inside her handbag.

M. Quiqueran might normally have been thinking of
Max, too, but the splendour of this conquest drove all
caution from him. He did not really mean any harm, but
this beautiful, terrified creature was too much for him to
resist. His hand moved stealthily, stroking, caressing. He
leant over her, so that his breath was on her face. He said
playfully, "Don't you want a little husband? *Tu ne veux pas
un petit mari?* You don't want to go with a dirty Jew. I,"
cried M. Quiqueran, unaware that this was his swan-
song, "would be kind to you. I like you very much. I
don't say that to many girls, I assure you. But I think
you're sweet."

And he stooped, in an ungainly movement, to kiss her.
His hand was on her knee. Strangely enough the threatened
kiss restored her to her senses. The other had been the
unknown, but a kiss she recognised well enough, and she
was not taking it from this utterly repulsive creature; it
would make the other enchanting kisses she had received
seem fouled and filthy. The dreadful paralysis left her.
The primitive instinct that had made her sink her teeth
in Max's thumb at last asserted itself. Deirdre was strong
and healthy, and her body was trained to swiftness, while
M. Quiqueran's was not. He was, besides, at a most awkward
angle. Nothing had prepared him for his victim's violent

reaction. All her disgust, all her pride in her own youthful body which was being so disgracefully insulted, combined to give her strength. She screamed out, "Max, Max!" She wrenched her hand away, and began to hit at him, wriggling beneath him so that he began to feel as if he were in an earthquake.

She did not realise that the battle was already won. Her cry for Max had been quite enough; the blows and kicks were in a way unnecessary. M. Quiqueran, receiving the weight of both her hands, one of which clutched the closed knife, tried frantically to scramble to his feet. He was no more efficient at seduction than at anything else. This scene was the last thing he wanted. His one idea now was to put as much distance between them as possible. Her cries were appallingly loud, and the thought that Max might suddenly appear beside him made him nearly faint with terror. Never was Don Juan so discomfited. Never was Don Juan so passionately anxious to let the lady be.

But, ironically, Deirdre would not let him go. She was by this time quite hysterical; she continued to slap and scratch and kick. It was the seducer who struggled to free himself; it was the victim who held him fast.

He fell suddenly on top of her, through no design of his own, but simply because a flailing blow had winded him. He fell, gasping and swearing. He almost smothered her. This last disgusting contact of his face against hers made her hand clench in revulsion; her fingers pressed the spring of the knife.

M. Quiqueran jerked himself up, but it was too late. The six inch blade shot into his chest. His body heaved in one last, violent spasm. Then he rolled on to the grass and lay still.

Deirdre managed at last to drag herself to her knees. She did not realise what she had done. The knife fell between them. She looked at it. Then her face grew as green as her dress. She began to retch helplessly, the tears of shock and reaction rolling down her face. Her appalled eyes fixed themselves on M. Quiqueran who lay there dead; she had never seen death before, but it was something she could not fail to recognise.

She was wild with terror. She thought she would go mad. Her head felt as if it were bursting. The river and the grass and the trees and the sky were whirling round her. She sobbed, "Oh, won't anyone help me? Oh, Max, Max, why don't you come?" And she raised a despairing face to the sky, her hands at her throat as if her panic were breaking her.

At her side, M. Quiqueran, who had never been silent, either to the Germans or anyone else, lay for the first time as still as the grave; his troubles were over, he would never be afraid again.

But Deirdre scarcely saw him. She did not even attempt to rearrange her clothes. Her dress was crumpled above her knees, a broken strap dangled from the arm-hole. Her face was ashen, and her hair streaked across it.

And it was in this state that Max first saw her.

*   *   *

He was furiously angry at being so late. He had dressed with the utmost care, and he carried with him a bunch of roses that he had bought in Paris and which had cost him a great deal more than he could afford. He brushed past Moishe, who made no comment, then swore silently as he saw M. Wolff in the hallway, plainly waiting to speak to him.

He said, "I want to apologise for yesterday."

Max longed to tell him to go to the devil. He knew M. Wolff very well, and he did not trust this sudden humility. The old man had always had a flair for nosing out what he was not supposed to know. He shot him a savage, wary look. He dared not do as he wanted, which was to push past him and run full-speed for the river. He said, rather sulkily, "Oh, it doesn't matter." He added, even more rudely, "*Je m'en fous.*"

"Like Jean-Louis," said M. Wolff, smiling. "They say that *s'en foutisme* is the disease of this age. It has certainly brought down an incredible number of French governments. But I really do apologise, Max. I'm sorry. I had no right to speak to you like that. We were both very tired. I hope I am forgiven. I'm glad to see you looking so full of spirits." He touched the roses. "Good luck. I hope she's nice. I won't wait up for you."

"Thank you," said Max, stiff-lipped, then a faint, bitter smile caught at his lips. The old so-and-so knew well enough that he had scarcely any jurisdiction over the boys in the Hostel, but he would raise hell and the devil if he knew that one of them was going out with a *schicksah* from the College opposite.

He added, with a deliberate patience, "May I go now?"

M. Wolff made him a little bow. "Of course, Max. *Amuse-toi bien.*"

"Thank you, sir."

That meant a delay of five minutes. But, as if this were not enough, he then had to meet Granier, out for his evening stroll—an amiable Granier who at once button-holed him. It only needs Quiqueran now, thought Max, or perhaps Miss Pelham, waiting for me to mend her fuses. But Miss Pelham was reading a tough American thriller in the privacy of her bedroom, and the meeting with M. Quiqueran was still to come.

Granier, looking less dyspeptic than usual, said jovially, "Well, Max? Anni's still pestering me to know when you're coming to supper."

"I don't know," said Max. In his impatience he could hardly stand still. She would be waiting for him. She might think he had changed his mind, decided not to come. Perhaps she was angry with him. Perhaps she was not waiting. Perhaps, when he came, she would not be there—

"Tomorrow, perhaps?"

"No, I don't think so. I—" He who was normally so swift of tongue, who had lied his way out of so many scrapes, could now think of nothing to say except, For God's sake, leave me alone, can't you see I have other and more important things to do? He said desperately, "I'm sorry, M. Granier, but—"

Granier fixed his eyes on the roses, much as M. Wolff had done. Max at that moment felt as if he were carrying in his arms a flowering forest. The consciousness of looking an abject fool made him do something that he had not done for longer than he could remember; he began to blush, and he knew that Granier had noticed. His temper flamed out. He shouted, "I've got an appointment. I have no time to waste in arguing with you."

And he turned his back on the Inspector, but not before noticing that amused grin that was spreading over his face. However, he was by now past caring. He began to run down the street, nearly banged into someone, dodged to avoid him, and knocked over a table outside a café, sending it spinning and deluging an enraged customer with a cup of very hot coffee.

He was to think afterwards—when he could think again—that it was fated. But at the time it seemed simply one of those damnable things that occasionally happen to all human beings, for no reason at all. By the time he had argued with the proprietor, apologised to the customer and bought him another cup of coffee, another precious fifteen minutes had been wasted.

And so by the time he arrived at the river bank he was over half an hour late.

Chapter Six

HE heard Deirdre calling his name. Her terror was unmistakable. He heard her frantic, hysterical crying. He ran towards her as he had never run in his life. He arrived panting, five hundred francs of rose-petals falling about him. He let the bunch drop to the ground. He did not at first see anything but her. Then he believed he must have gone mad. She was almost unrecognisable. The lovely, well-groomed little girl with the glossy hair and graceful movements that had so enchanted him was gone. Instead there tottered to meet him a maenad, distraught, tear-blubbered, with hair over her face, frantic eyes, and torn, disarranged clothes.

The sight stirred something in the depths of his memory, fathoms down where the horrors lay. In the warm air the atmosphere shivered and shifted. This was most dreadfully familiar. He had been here before. In that second past and present slipped into a fearful unity. The colour began to leave his face. He swallowed. He took a step towards her, holding out his arms. Then, as she stumbled into them, his eyes moved sideways, and he saw M. Quiqueran lying on the grass, his shirt stained and his eyes staring sightlessly at the sky.

He did not at first say a word. He saw that M. Quiqueran was dead. Death had been his familiar too long for him not to recognise it. He saw, too, the knife, his knife, lying in the grass. Deirdre was sobbing on his shoulder, calling out his name, muttering things in English that he could not understand. But he was scarcely listening to her words. He saw only her crumpled skirt, the broken strap, the bruised

135

hands. A slow, sick, murderous rage began to swell within him, so engulfing that it threatened to break his very guts asunder. Suddenly he pushed her back from him, gripping her arms. He said in a harsh, tight voice, "What did he do to you?"

She whispered, "Oh, Max, Max—"

"What did he do to you?" The breath shrilled from him. "Tell me. Tell me at once, do you hear me?"

And the vision from the past crashed down on him like a blow from a clenched fist, shoved the present aside, so that dead and living became one, so that everything keeled before him.

Only she had said nothing. She had only looked. She stood there, her hands dangling, her shamed, almost witless face averted. The tears were pouring down.

What did he do to you? He had said those words. He had spoken them in his shrill, boy's voice that had not yet broken. In that moment he had learnt the greatest anguish of all, the anguish of impotent hate. He knew it now again. He released Deirdre. He strode across the grass to stand over M. Quiqueran's body. If only there had been a little life left—enough to be humiliated, enough to feel pain. If by defiling the body he could have made it suffer, he would have done so. If by a gesture he could have committed this creature to eternal torment, he would have made it. He was burning with hatred, and it was all futile; he was helpless now as he had been helpless then.

They had taken her away, his little Chaja. He had never seen her again. She had been swallowed up like all the rest; she was only fourteen; this was the dirty ending of her life.

He rolled the spittle round in his mouth, and ejected it on to M. Quiqueran's body. *"Scheisser!"* he said, and then he nearly vomited, so violent was the revulsion within him.

He swung round on Deirdre. He looked at her, so it seemed to her tear-blurred eyes, with savage rage. He repeated in the same tight voice, "What did he do to you?"

She could only sob. The sobbing maddened him, and nearly broke his heart. He began to shake her, then, as she still would not answer, slapped her face.

This affront—for such a thing had never happened to her in her life—brought her back to coherence. She stared up at him indignantly, and whispered in a cracked, husky voice, "He was disgusting—"

"What did he do? Oh, for God's sake," shouted Max, "for dear God Almighty's sake, will you answer me!"

"He—he—" Her face grew slowly scarlet. "He stroked my leg and tried to kiss me—"

Max's voice came out with a slow, heavy quietness. "Is that all?"

"Isn't it enough?" She broke out crying again.

He held her now, but coldly, dispassionately, as if emotion were dead. She was long past knowing anything, but she could never have understood the amazement, the fear and—this she would have understood least of all—the bitter ironic laughter, that warred within him. His face had grown expressionless, only his eyes blazed, and they were fixed, not on Deirdre, but on M. Quiqueran.

M. Quiqueran had been afraid for a long time. Retribution had always been around the next corner. There were plenty, apart from Max himself, who would never forget that M. Quiqueran had smiled at the Bosches while others were being tortured to death in that little house beside the Mairie. They might have killed, in memory of those dying cries. He, too, might have killed, in memory of a sister defiled and murdered, in memory of a mountain of bones sprawling on the earth. But they had not killed. He had not killed. M. Quiqueran had been killed in the end by a foolish little girl from Ireland, killed for a straying hand, for an embrace that meant nothing.

Max said coolly at last, "Well, it doesn't matter." He gave her a grim smile. "He's dead. And about time, too."

"Did—did I kill him?"

"You did. You made a pretty good job of it, too. Quite professional." He continued to smile down into her sick face. The smile did not touch his eyes. "Now we'll have to see what is to be done about it. You can't very well hide a body, these days, but at least we might be able to postpone the finding of it, make it perhaps a little more difficult to recognise. You will go back to the College, and you will know nothing whatsoever about this. Did anyone see you together tonight?"

"I didn't mean to kill him."

"Did anyone see you together? Answer me, please. There's no time to waste."

"No, I—I don't think so—"

"That's all right, then. There is after all," said Max in a voice that appalled her, for it was so remote, so devoid of warmth, "absolutely nothing to connect the two of you together. You've never spoken to him before, have you?"

"Oh, Max, Max—"

"I asked you if you had ever spoken to him before."

"You're hurting me—"

"Look," he said, with a physical effort at self-control that contorted his face, "this—this *salaud* is dead. You stabbed him. He deserved it. To my way of thinking, it's not murder. If you'd chopped him into little pieces, it wouldn't have been murder. But Inspector Granier isn't going to take so charitable a point of view. He's a *flic*, after all. He's going to do his damndest to find out who did it. You might get away with it. You could say it was in self-defence. But whatever the verdict, there'll be a hell of a scandal— You don't want that, I think? Well, then, please pull yourself together and answer my questions. Have you and this—this *ordure* ever spoken together?"

"Of course not!"

The tone of outrage made him break into a brief, hysterical laugh. "You've never spoken to him," he said, staring at her, "yet you've killed him—"

"I didn't—" She was sobbing again. "I don't know how it happened. We were struggling and somehow— Oh Max, you're being so horrid to me, and I'm so frightened. I truly don't know what happened. I can't tell you—I think I just went out of my mind. I didn't know what to do with him, and he was being so revolting, pawing me like that, and—and—" She raised a fierce, accusing face to him. "You were late. It's all your fault. If you'd come when you said you would, this would never have happened. But I suppose you thought it fun to keep me waiting and—" Then, because his face frightened her, she began crying in real earnest, her hands feebly clutching at him. "Oh, don't look at me like that. Please don't. Don't be angry—I didn't mean it. Please be kind to me—" She began to stammer. "He asked me if I'd like a little husband—It was so horrible. Max, Max, Max—"

At this his face softened. He drew her close to him and began to gentle her. His chin rested on the top of her head. If he were seeing a magnificent dream being blown to shreds, he said nothing about it. The dream was gone, and he knew it, but he merely passed his hand across her shoulder blades, and pushed up the hair at the nape of her neck. Then, his hand motionless with the soft gold trickling through it, he said quietly, "Listen, my girl. You are all right. You are all right. You are all right, I tell you. Leave it to me. I'm used to this kind of thing. I've dealt with similar situations before. I'll look after you. Nobody's going to hurt you. In fact, nobody's going to have the faintest idea that you ever knew this gentleman. Stop crying. I'll see to everything. You've nothing to worry about." His hand stirred briefly. "If there's one thing I could take a degree in and pass with honours, it's telling lies to *flics*. I've told more lies to *flics* in my time—and got away with it—than you could ever imagine. It's my métier, so to speak. I swear it'll be all right. Granier won't get his dirty hands on you. Only—Now listen to me, Deirdre. Listen, darling. You must listen. And stop this howling. There's nothing to howl for. I know you've had a shock, but it's over now, and I'm here to look after you. You're not crying for this dirty pig, surely? If you hadn't killed him, I'd have done it for you. He deserves all he's got. And I hope he's in hell. I hope he stays in hell for ever and ever. But listen to me. Are you listening?"

"Yes, Max."

His brows flickered together. But he went on, in the same controlled voice, "We—I will do a little tidying up, and then you must go straight back."

Her hands fastened so fiercely on his that he flinched. She cried out, "I can't, I can't—"

"What do you mean, you can't?"

"I can't! Don't leave me. You mustn't leave me."

"My dearest child—"

"You mustn't!" Her voice soared up. "I'll go crazy if I'm alone. You must come back with me."

"Are you mad?"

"But don't you see, you must. You can't leave me alone now."

He was beginning to see that the situation would exercise all the wits he had. He pushed away from him his new-found youth; he was only two years older than Deirdre, but in that moment the distance in years between them might have been a couple of decades. For a second he set his teeth then, enfolding her in his arms, he balanced his foot on a hummock and cradled her on his raised knee. He spoke gently into the tangled hair, forcing laughter into his voice. "*Tiens, tiens!* Do I come back with you into your convent? And where, may I ask, am I supposed to sleep? In bed with you?"

To his utter consternation, she said, "Oh please, if you would. I can't be alone. I should always be seeing him. His face—I couldn't bear it." Her voice was rising again. "I tell you, I couldn't bear it. You must come. You must hold me—"

"Ah, shut up for God's sake," said Max, then with a desperate attempt at lightness, "You're talking nonsense. What do you imagine your Miss Pelham would say when she brings you your morning tea and finds two heads on the pillow? Do you suppose she'd offer me a cup, too?"

Even in her panic, this seemed to Deirdre a little unlikely. She did not answer, but she still burrowed her head into him, and he winced again; this time it was not from physical pain. He said steadily, "Now you're going to be a good girl, and stop all these hysterics. You'll leave everything to your Uncle Max. *D'ac?*"

"Y-yes."

"That's the stuff. Have you got a handkerchief?"

"Yes."

"Then give it me."

"It's in my handbag. Oh, don't leave me. Please, please don't leave me."

His jaw tautened. He said, "Now, you're just being silly, aren't you? Let go—" He tried to force her hands away, gently at first, then he lost patience and gave her a shove so that she fell back on the grass. He ignored her. He stepped over to her bag. He hesitated for a second, eyeing first the knife, then M. Quiqueran's body. He said at last, in a hard, abrupt voice, "Turn over."

"What do you mean?"

"Oh, stop asking me what—" He checked himself. "Will

you do what you're told? I want you to turn over. I want you to lie with your face in the grass. You're not to look until I tell you—Oh, for God's sake!" In a couple of strides he was beside her again. He seized her by the shoulders, twisted her round, thrusting her face into the ground. "Now, stay there," he commanded. His face was working a little. He added, "If you move, I'll hit you. I mean that."

She lay there where he had put her, her face buried in her arms. Her shoulders still heaved with sobs. But she obeyed him. She did not raise her head.

He picked up the knife. For a moment he balanced it on his palm, looking at it. At last, almost reluctantly, he stooped down to wash it in the river; he wiped it on the grass, then put it back into his pocket.

Then he stepped over to M. Quiqueran. There was a strange look on his face now, almost one of exultation. The danger snapped around him. The ghosts were at his side, exhorting him with bony grins. *Go on, boy. You've done it before. Do it again. You'll floor them, you always did.*

M. Quiqueran lay there. The blood had dried; it was only a dull, rusty patch on his shirt. His hands lay slackly beside him. His eyes were upturned to the velvet of the sky, so that only the whites were showing. His mouth was open in a humorous dismay. Max, with the briefest of glances at him, threw his jacket on to the grass and rolled up his sleeves. Then he gripped M. Quiqueran by the shoulders. His enemy was bigger than he, and the dead weight of the body made the sweat pour down Max's face, made the dark patches spring under his arm-pits and between his shoulder-blades. But he tugged and heaved, lugging the corpse nearer and nearer the river; at last he levered it with his foot, gave a final, tremendous shove, and it landed in the water with a splash like the aftermath of an explosion.

Deirdre listened to the splash. She still did not raise her

head, but her body stiffened and hunched together. She had stopped crying. She did not make a sound.

Max stood there, gasping, watching the body of his old enemy being carried downstream under the bridge. The current was not strong, and M. Quiqueran floated gently on his last journey, with an unwilling, bobbing movement as if he were not certain that he had Charon's fare. Only the immersion had released the gases within him, so that he belched, once, as if he were alive again, and this was so obscene and unexpected that Max, staring after him, suddenly heaved and turned his head aside.

The body was slowly borne round the bend. It might be discovered at any moment. Max wished he had been able to attach a stone to it. But there was nothing within sight, and time was short. If only the corpse would sink—But it floated obdurately, and at last Max could watch its progress no longer. He knelt down by the river and washed his face and hands, splashing the water over his body, not caring that his shirt, the beautiful shirt specially put on for this occasion, was soaked through.

The nightingales in the wood were still singing.

He took out Deirdre's handkerchief, and as he did so, saw the paper with his own image upon it, and the words: *Je t'aime, Je t'aime*. A grimace convulsed his face. He left the paper where it was. He came back to Deirdre and crouched down beside her. He turned her over, very gently, and raised her head on his arm. He stared down into the white, strained face, and the memory of the dream was unendurable so that he could only bow his head and touch her cheek with his. He held her against him. He did not speak. He looked for the moment as lost as she. His face was bewildered with suffering and grief. Then he said softly, "It's all right, sweetheart. I'm going to wipe your face for you, and blow your nose for you, and comb your pretty hair back, then, when you're tidy again, I'll take you back home."

"I feel so ill, Max."

"Of course you do. My poor darling. But it'll pass. I tell you what—I'll buy you a little bottle of brandy."

"It would make me sick."

"No, it won't. It'll do you all the good in the world. Now, blow—"

She obediently blew her nose into the handkerchief he held out to her, and her sob changed to an hysterical giggle. Then as he wiped away her tears, and began with surprising dexterity to arrange her hair, she whispered wretchedly, "Do you think it will be all right?"

"Of course. Don't you trust me?"

"Oh yes, I do. But it would be so awful if my mother found out. She'd never understand."

"Does she look like you, your mother?"

"A little, yes. Is yours like you?"

"She was. Very much so."

"Oh, of course she's dead. I'm so sorry."

"It doesn't matter. It was a long time ago."

They were speaking in whispers. There was no one to hear them. M. Quiqueran, who had meddled so often in what did not concern him, was out of sight. The weight of the water in his clothes had at last dragged him down; he surfaced occasionally but now the river held him fast. Yet still they whispered, she, too exhausted to do anything else, and he—perhaps he was struggling to preserve what might possibly be their last moment of peace together. The moonlight blanched their faces, and they huddled together, with the bunch of roses lying crushed and broken on the trampled grass a little way away from them.

Max's eyes fell on the roses. But he was so blinded that he did not see them for the danger they were. He was remembering how happy he had been when he bought them. It was going to be such a wonderful evening. There had been no premonition of disaster. And now the night was still about them. There was no sound except the gentle splashing of the water, and the monotonous song of the nightingales—a song that he was never going to be able to endure again, to the end of his life. It was a lover's night.

He heaved a deep sigh. He whispered to Deirdre who had closed her eyes, who lay back in his arms as if she were asleep, "Darling, we ought to go."

"No," she said, like a child unwillingly awakened, "no."

"Yes. We must. You've got to get back. You've got to look as if nothing had happened."

"I do wish you could stay with me, Max."

"Yes." He sighed again. "Yes, I wish I could."

"I wouldn't be afraid if your arms were round me."

He did not answer this directly. He raised his head and cried out in a voice where the grief and hysteria rang, "Why shouldn't we, after all? Why shouldn't we? You want me and I want you. We could do it properly. We could get married. But it's no good. It's never any damned good. In a little while, when all this has blown over, you'll go back to Ireland and you'll never think of me again."

"I'll never forget you."

"Won't you? In a year's time, if someone mentions my name, you'll say, 'Max Wrzonski? Who's that? Never heard of him.' That's what you'll say."

"Oh, that's just silly. How could I forget you?"

"You'll be surprised. Come now. I'll take you back. When we get to the Place, you must go alone. And listen. Tomorrow morning—"

"I don't know what I'll do tonight."

"I'll tell you what you'll do. You'll sleep. Like the—like a log. Believe me, you will. I know. One always does. But tomorrow morning, now. You know absolutely nothing of this. Nothing. Do you understand me? You know nothing about old Quiqueran, or me, or the river. Why should you? You were asleep in bed."

"But if they ask me—"

"You still know nothing. And they won't ask you. Why should they? Why should they imagine you had anything to do with it?"

"All right, Max."

"There's a good girl."

"You talk to me as if I were a baby."

"Well, you are, aren't you? A silly baby. A nice baby."

"Max."

"Well?"

"I'm so frightened."

"You've no need to be. I'll take care of everything for you. Give me your hand and I'll help you up."

She swayed a little when she was on her feet. She looked wan and pitiful. Max knew how strangely human beings could react, but even to him it seemed incredible that this child had killed; she looked young, vulnerable and innocent. He held her close for a moment. There was everything around them that was beautiful, but to him it was now hateful; the hatefulness of it, the bleak imperviousness, struck him like a knife. Catastrophe had swooped upon them, but no one and nothing cared. The nightingales would continue to sing if they both lay dead, the river would still flow, the woods would still be thick with trees.

"If only," he said to her bowed head, "people would leave us alone. Your Miss Pelham and *ce sacré* M. Wolff. They're old and finished. They both live in the past. She only bothers about her school, and he doesn't really care about anything but his dead wife and kids. Your Miss Pelham will say, Why do you let a dirty Jew make love to you, why do you go with a boy like that, what would your mother say. And he, he just stands there with his *tallith*, and tells long stories about the *Hakamin*, but he doesn't care, he would only say it was wrong, he'd never try to understand. They can neither of them see that it doesn't matter,

146

none of it matters. We're people, aren't we, like everyone else. We love each other, don't we? What's wrong with that? We only want to be left alone. We're not hurting anyone. Oh, God," cried Max, "it's all so unfair—"

He stared across the river. There was no sign of M. Quiqueran, who had once uttered the same words. He had floated downstream and entangled himself with some weeds. But the trail of death lay across the water, and its stench blew against Max's nostrils, so that he shuddered; his exhausted eyes blurred and the vision of barbed wire and bleak, black barracks beat again upon them.

He turned a bright, despairing gaze on Deirdre. "Do you know," he said, "they built nests for the birds on top of the barracks—the Bosches. They used to feed them. And we were starving. We were dying off like flies. But they fed the birds."

She did not understand what he was talking about. She did not attempt to answer him. There was something about him that frightened her, but she said, following her own line of thought, "You don't think my mother will find out, do you?" She raised her eyes to his, not seeing in them the defeat and irony that blazed in their haunted depths.

"Why the hell do I love you?" he said. Then, almost savagely, "I'll tell you something else. They had a band. It played military music, pom-pom music. You know the sort of thing. It was very jolly. They played it when people were driven into the gas-chambers. Can you understand that?"

"I don't know what you're talking about."

"Of course you don't."

"And I'm tired. Oh please, won't you take me home?"

"Come on then. Baby."

"I'm not a baby."

"You are."

Then the absurdity of this made them both smile, and

they began to walk slowly back into the town. This time they did not quarrel. Only for Max that journey had a bright, bitter edge to it, as if this might never happen again —and for her an extraordinary fear. To her chilled and exhausted mind it seemed as if a dark passageway had opened up before her, with dreadful, unmentionable things huddled at its end. She began to shiver and could not stop. Perhaps Max saw that passageway, too. When he spoke again, it was to say abruptly, "There's no one will live in that house there. Have you ever looked at the plaque?"

They were passing by the house next to the Mairie. It was a house like other houses, only it wore a derelict, un-inhabited air. It had the dusty, melancholy look of a place deserted by humanity. Deirdre, for the first time longing passionately for pretty chintz and pink lamp-shades, struggling to slide away from this constant battery on her emotions, raised her heavy eyes to the engraved square of metal above the door.

"To the memory of the loyal citizens of this town who died here for their country. *Vive la France!*"

She muttered stupidly, "People died here?"

"No," he said, "no. They didn't just die."

"That's what it says."

"I know." Then he saw how her body drooped, saw the white, unbelieving face, and she was so changed from the bright, gay little girl whom he had first met, that his love and pity swelled within him. He could not utter the dreadful things that were tumbling to his lips, could not loose upon her the evil that he had struggled for so long to push to the back of his mind. He whispered, his voice cracking a little, "You're very tired, aren't you, my darling?"

"Yes." Her mouth was beginning to tremble. "So tired."

"You'll soon be home. It's only a little way now. Come. Shall I carry you?"

"Oh, you're silly." The absurdity of this almost made her laugh. "You couldn't. I'm almost as big as you."

"I could pick you up and throw you in the air," he said. "You've no idea how strong I am. Feel!" And he tensed his biceps, then took her hand and placed it on his arm.

The touch of his wiry, young body stirred her. She did not laugh any more. She stroked his slender arm, while her unhappy eyes explored his face; her expression was bewildered as if she were struggling to understand the contradictions that made him what he was.

They reached the Place du Triangle. Deirdre stared about her. What had happened seemed now as if it could never have happened to her. She was dazed with fear and shock and exhaustion. Even when Max spoke to her, she only listened to him with half her mind.

"Remember," he was saying in a quick, urgent voice, "you know nothing. Nobody will dream of suspecting you. How could they? You must try to forget that the whole thing ever happened." Then, forgetting caution, he exclaimed in sudden anger, "Do you know, I believe you will do just that!"

She shook her head. It was as if she did not hear him. She muttered again, "I don't want to be alone. Don't leave me. Not just yet."

"It's midnight. You must go now. We'll meet tomorrow."

"Tomorrow?" She hesitated. "Oh, I don't know if I can. I—"

He interrupted her brutally. He did not raise his voice, but the tone was such that she drew back, staring at him. "So you're going to chuck me now, are you?" he said.

"No, no—"

"I've done my job, so now I can be kicked back into the gutter where no doubt you think I belong."

"Of course not. Only—"

"There's no 'only' about it. You are meeting me tomorrow. Is that clear? I've got to know if anyone's spoken to you about it. After all—" He was improvising now; he saw clearly enough that she did not want to come. "After all, old Granier's not a complete imbecile. Damn it, the man's an inspector. They wouldn't make him that for nothing. For all I know, somebody may have seen us, somebody who knows where we come from. It wouldn't take long to put two and two together."

"Oh no, no—"

Her fear sickened him, yet it gave him a certain savage pleasure, it drove him on. "Oh yes, my girl. Everyone in the town knows that old bastard couldn't keep his hands off a woman. Granier will certainly think there's a woman at the bottom of it, and he'll begin to consider what woman it could be—" Then he saw her horror-struck face. He was appalled by his own cruelty. He caught at her. He felt the unwillingness of her body, but he would not release her, only held her more tightly in his arms. He whispered, "I didn't mean that. Forgive me. I'm sorry, sweetheart. Nobody could possibly connect that old devil with you. You're all right. I'll see to that. And now you'd better go, hadn't you, before I say anything more."

She took him at his word, and more swiftly than he had expected. He knew that for all she dreaded being alone, she was thankful to be rid of him. She flew across the Place du Triangle, and he was left standing there, staring after her.

He stood there for a long time. Once he raised his hands to his face. They were sticky with sweat. They felt clammy and unpleasant against his cheeks. But he did not even realise that he was making the gesture. It seemed to him that something shocking and unforseeable was happening inside him. He felt sick and ill, so ill that it was like a presentiment of death. The food he had eaten at supper was twisting in his entrails like a bullet. The awful, phantasmagoric unreality was upon him again, so that he was no longer entirely in this world; it was as if one foot were on shore and the other on some moving thing going further and further away, so that it threatened to break him in two; security was toppling about him, and the spectres, stinking of death, were closing in on him, ghosts that refused to be laid.

What did he do to you?

He remembered the face even now. How he had prayed to meet that face again—A young face, stupid, with a vacant, astonished grin. A boy, who at home had perhaps been a decent boy, who was even now a little bewildered by what he had done. Perhaps he was dead. Perhaps he had never realised exactly what he had done—

What did he do to you?

But she had not answered. "You can say good-bye to her if you want to," they had said. "You won't see each other again."

He could see her eyes now, incredulous, ashamed, hurt to death. They were Deirdre's eyes. Only she was fourteen. They had got on well enough. She had always bossed him around. She was a bossy little girl, plump, dark, sure of herself, secretly devoted to her wild little brother, but determined to keep him in his place. She had always helped him out of scrapes and scolded him well for it afterwards.

And now she said not a word.

"Good-bye, Chaja," he said. "Look after yourself. *Zahn mehr gesint.*"

And still she said nothing, only the tears began to stream down her cheeks, as they were streaming down his.

"That'll do," they said. "Do you think we've got all day to waste while one little Jew-brat says good-bye to another?"

They dragged her away. She made no resistance. She did not look back at him. He shrieked after them, "One day I'll kill you for this," and a boot swung out at him, caught him in the face, broke half his teeth so that his mouth filled with blood, and he tumbled to the ground. But he did not cry out, only stared after Chaja, who still did not speak, and he tried to call after her, but the blood and teeth prevented him, so that he could only make gutterul, animal sounds, and they laughed at him.

He never saw her again.

And he had not been able to help her. That was what hurt so terribly even now. He had not been able to help her.

He had tried to make Chaja understand that it was nothing to be ashamed of, it was not her fault, the shame was not hers. But he was young and such a situation was beyond him; he could not think of the right things to say. And she was already away, poor little Chaja, she was past understanding.

But with Deirdre it was, thank God, different. Here there was something he could do. He knew that she was afraid of him, but he did not believe that her love for him was gone; he could still love her and help her; it was only a question of making her understand.

The touch on his arm made him swing round, white with rage. It was as if the young Nazi with his imbecile grin had come up to him. He lunged with his fist at an astounded Granier, who stepped swiftly back, exclaiming, "Good God, boy, what's the matter with you? Standing there in the middle of the Place, muttering to yourself like that. Do you know it's well after midnight? You ought to be in bed."

"Why aren't you in bed, yourself?" said Max with a snarl, "with your little wife?" The anger leapt to his voice again. "How often have I told you that I'll not be touched? Pawing me like some bloody queer—"

His own hysteria checked him. He grew silent. He could not control his breathing, which was like a piston, nor his heart knocking at the walls of his chest, bang-bang-bang, nor the tell-tale sweat now streaming off him, but he could grow silent. And silent he was, while the inner voice spoke grimly to him, saying, This won't do, you fool, this will not do, get a grip on yourself, for God's sake, or you are done for.

"Now, now," said Granier. He stared at the dark, haggard face, coldly outlined in the flare of the street lamp. He said again, "Now, now. There's no need to speak to me like that. All right. You mustn't be touched. I'll try to remember. It seems to me a poor state of things when a man can't touch his friend without being called names, but I'm sorry. I didn't know you were so sensitive. Are you feeling all right? You don't look very well."

"Of course I'm all right."

"Have you been drinking?"

"I have not."

"There's no need to shout, is there?" Granier's eyes, perturbed yet beginning to glint with a professional light, roamed the boy's face. He said, his voice very gentle, "What's the matter, Max? You're not in any trouble, are you?"

Max replied with the utmost calmness. His face was blandly smiling. Both the calm tones and the smile aroused Granier's suspicions, but this he did not know. He said, "No, sir. Not as far as I know. Haven't you got your quota of arrests for this month? Has the prefecture sent you a dirty little note, informing you that the jail is too empty?" Then, because he knew that this was dreadfully wrong, that he was playing the hand atrociously, he steadied himself with an effort that nearly tore him apart, and continued in a quiet, reasonable voice, "Actually, I was in bed. Only I had to come out for a breath of air. You know, I suddenly felt quite dizzy. It's so infernally hot. When it's like this, it somehow—*oh merde, alors,* this sounds so damned neurotic, but it takes me back. I begin to think of things again. The camp. And what happened to my family. I know it's ridiculous, but sometimes it happens, even now."

Granier said after a pause, "Do you know, that's the first time in the whole of—I hope I'm not presuming—our friendship that you've mentioned the camp to me. I'm glad. I've always felt it would be a good thing if you could talk it out. It's not right to let things stew inside you."

Hell, hell, hell, Max's inner voice was saying; his normal voice replied coolly, "Oh, what's the point in going back? It's not even interesting. I only mentioned it because— oh, I don't know. I tell you, it's the heat. Forget it, Inspector. I've more or less forgotten it myself. There's nothing to talk out. And now I'll take your advice and go back to bed." He looked up impudently at Granier. "Good hunting, sir."

He strolled off and, as he moved, he sang:

"Ah, ah, ah, ah, putain de toi,
Ah, ah, ah, pauvre de moi!"

Granier hissed at him, "Shut up, Max. You're waking the whole neighbourhood."

"I'm sorry, Inspector. I'm so sorry. Good-morning." And he swung into the Hostel.

He went towards the kitchen. His mouth was dry. He felt a desperate craving for a glass of clean, cold milk. He saw that the light was on. He came in and looked up at Moishe, who was sitting on the edge of the table, eating a hunk of bread and butter.

He knew that Moishe had a girl in the town, and often came back in the small hours. M. Wolff knew this, too, but preferred to ignore it. "I am not," he once remarked, "a custodian of morals. Anyway, it's far healthier. And it's none of my business."

Max nodded at him, then opened the cupboard to take out a bottle of milk. He poured half of it into a tumbler. His eyes met Moishe's over the rim. They looked at each other in silence. In the old days, they had often looked at each other in such a way, without speaking. The invisible, unbreakable wire tugged between them as it had done then; the message came clearly: *All right, I know nothing.*

Moishe said, his mouth full, "Been out for a walk?"

"Uhuh," said Max. "I found I couldn't stay in bed. Too infernally hot. I stuck it out till about midnight then I thought that as I couldn't sleep, I might as well put my clothes on again and take a stroll. Feels like a storm to me."

Moishe said calmly, "I thought I heard you tramping about." He stuffed the last piece of bread into his mouth, and rose to his feet. The great bulk of him seemed to fill the kitchen. It dwarfed Max so that he dwindled into a lean, dark shadow. "Well," he said, "I'm going to bed." He did not say good-night. Only he paused at the door to look at Max again. The wire tugged once more.

All right, I know nothing.

And presently Max followed him. It was half past two in the morning.

*   *   *

Portelet-sur-Seine knew all about M. Quiqueran when it awakened to the day's work. Nobody talked about anything else. Ironically enough, Granier, still sleeping, was almost the last person to learn the news.

The body had been discovered at three o'clock. It slithered on the slimy weeds and drifted into the shallows; there it lay, tethered by the green, clinging ropes, to be discovered by a drunk who was struck cold-sober by the ugly sight, and who ran along the path, shouting and cursing, until an angry, pyjama'd householder emerged, demanding furiously what was the matter. A call was put through, and presently uniformed men appeared to lug M. Quiqueran out of the Seine and carry him into the town morgue. A great knife wound was found in his chest. There was no trace of the weapon. It was all very dramatic, and there could be no doubt that it was murder.

The boys of the Hostel were discussing it over their coffee. Max, shrugging his shoulders, said simply, "About time, too." He looked tired as if he had not slept. But he was entirely in control of himself. The hand that carried the cup to his lips was steady; he chewed his *tartine* in a calm, rhythmic manner.

"He was almost cut in two," said Jean-Louis. "It was a terrific wound. There was blood all over the place."

"I suppose the river ran red with it," said Max.

"Well, it was all over the bank, anyway. He must have been going out with some woman. There was a huge bunch of roses on the grass. Fancy old Quiqueran buying roses. Anyway," said Jean-Louis, with the utmost heartiness, and plainly enjoying it all very much, "they'll do for his grave. I shouldn't think many people will send him flowers."

Max's hand, engaged in cutting himself another slice of bread, was for one second motionless. He did not look up, but he sensed the same immobility in Moishe, who was near him. The wire was tugging like mad. Then he finished cutting the slice, and calmly proceeded to butter it. There was nothing in his face to reveal the consternation and dismay within him. This was what happened when one's emotions got out of control—He had been entirely concentrating on protecting Deirdre. It was she, after all, who had killed Quiqueran. By a process of what now seemed to him insane logic, he had believed that she was the one in danger. The naïveté of this assumption was now painfully obvious. All that he had said to console her was true. No one would suspect her. How could they? It was preposterous to imagine that one of Miss Pelham's English girls should possess a knife, much less use it.

And suddenly Max, forgetting the boys around him, began to laugh. God Almighty, good God Almighty—

That old bastard, Quiqueran, had never had much sense of humour, but surely his corpse must now be rocking round the morgue. This was almost too good to be true. Who was his enemy? Max. Who had always threatened him? Max. And who, by the strangest stroke of providence, had not killed him? Max. And who was now perhaps going to be accused of his murder?

Max stopped laughing. Moishe's voice came over his shoulder. The room was very still. The other boys were all looking at him. Moishe said, "Well, I'll be in this evening. Why don't you come to the pictures with me, Max? It's not good for you to stay in so much."

"I'll think about it," said Max.

As he turned to the door, he saw them all clearly. They were all avoiding his eyes. Their heads were averted. But a power came out of them, a power of extended hands, hands that already formed a circle around him. A bewildered yet bitter smile caught at his lips. He did not know them. They did not know him. They were enclosed in the dark of a shared horror; within that horror's shade they lived their separate lives. He did not know if Nathan had a girl-friend, what were Baruch's politics, where Chaim's interests lay. He did not like them particularly; perhaps they did not like him. They swore at each other twenty times a day; like him, they passionately longed to be free of the intolerable, silent bondage.

And now there had come out to him something strange, impersonal and immensely strong. It was not love. It was not even entirely for him. It was as if a man had laid his hand on something burning; he would at once snatch it away and put on something to ease the smart. For each of them a hand was burning; for each of them that hand must be tended, for in its suffering they all suffered, in its danger they must all be afraid.

He gave them a look, these dispassionate friends of his,

then, without another word, went out. In the street he looked up at Rosedene College. He looked up at Deirdre's window. His mouth briefly set. Then he set off for the station, just as a sleepy, bad-tempered Granier was taking an urgent call from the prefecture.

*　　*　　*

"It's very unfortunate," said Miss Pelham, with her usual gift of understatement. "It's the kind of thing that upsets parents so much. They always assume that if there's one murder, there's bound to be another. The fact that it's a purely local matter will never strike them for a minute." She was speaking to one of her colleagues. The milkman had already told the cook, the cook had told the house-keeper, and Miss Pelham had learnt the news some ten minutes later.

"Of course," she went on, "he was a quite disgusting little man. Not that one sympathises with murder, but still— He collaborated, you know, and he was always trying to talk to the girls, and winking and leering at them. I'm not at all surprised this has happened, but I do wish he'd got himself murdered somewhere else." She saw her colleague's hastily suppressed look of surprise, and added quickly, "I'm not condoning murder, of course, but really, we can't afford to get mixed up in that kind of thing. I think I shall have to talk to the girls about it. I'd rather they heard about it from me. After all, the whole town will be talking of nothing else."

She came into the dining-room a quarter of an hour later. She studied her charges as they devoured their bacon and eggs. English breakfasts were included in the curriculum. Miss Pelham firmly believed in preserving the atmosphere of the home country. A visiting relative—an uncle who had lived abroad and had developed an unhappy continental sense of humour—had once quoted softly at her, "There's

one corner of a foreign field That is for ever England".
She had acknowledged this with a wintry smile. She did
not find it amusing. These, after all, were English girls.
Some of them, no doubt, would marry into the diplomatic
service and live abroad; all of them would become in some
ways cosmopolitan. But it seemed only right to her that
here they should live English lives, eat English food and
live in the correct English atmosphere. The unhappy M.
Quiqueran's sudden exit was in its way a confirmation of
her theory; it showed where foreign extravagance could lead.

As she looked at her pupils, a faint pride glowed within
her that not even the ugly news could extinguish. They
were all so very charming. Her eyes roamed from Deirdre's
shining golden head to Nora's dark curls, from brown
pony-tail to red chignon. Some of them had been difficult,
but they were all settling down nicely, even Nora—and
soon she would be turning the pages of the *Sketch* and
Tatler, and be able to say proudly, That was one of my
pupils, you know.

She said in her pleasantly modulated voice, "Will you
listen to me, please? I have just heard some rather distressing
news and, as you know, I always prefer to tell you these
things myself. I know you would never listen to gossip,
but people do talk so, and I'm afraid you're going to hear
about it whether you want to or not."

She paused. The faces upturned to hers expressed only
the mildest interest, which was as it should be. Nasty men
like M. Quiqueran should never cross these well-regulated
lives. She said, lowering her voice a fraction, for the dead
after all were the dead, however unpleasant, "You all
know M. Quiqueran who runs the Syndicat over the way.
Well, I am sorry to say he is dead. His body was found in
the river this morning. It's very sad, but of course it's
nothing to do with us, and I shall expect you to carry on
with your classes as usual."

"Did someone bump him off, Miss Pelham?" inquired Nora.

Miss Pelham's brows met a little. It was typical that Nora should be the only one to make such a vulgar remark. She opened her remark to rebuke this lack of breeding, but Nora added cheerfully, "Beastly little man. Always pinching and leering—"

"Nora, my dear!"

"Sorry, Miss Pelham. Shouldn't I have said that?"

Miss Pelham, if she had cared to analyse her thoughts, would have found herself, at that moment, thankful for M. Quiqueran's death. But she did not believe in analysis of any kind and, with a silent resolve to speak to Nora at some later date, she said composedly, "I don't think one should speak ill of the dead, my dear. I agree with you that he was sometimes a little gross and impertinent, but now the poor man has passed over, we must just try to forget about him. It is after all a great tragedy for his wife and children. And remember that Christian charity is a quality we should all cultivate."

"Yes, Miss Pelham," said Nora, and flickered an eyelid at her neighbour.

Miss Pelham watched them as they streamed out of the dining-room. They all moved with far more elegance than when they had first come. They no longer rushed and scrambled like young puppies. Then she exclaimed, "Deirdre! You're looking very pale." She put a hand under the girl's chin and tilted her face to the light. "I don't like to see you without your pretty colour. Is anything the matter? Are you feeling all right?"

"I'm a bit tired," said Deirdre. She looked to Miss Pelham's keen eyes rather more than a bit tired. There was no expression in her face. Her eyes shifted before Miss Pelham's gaze.

"I hope this news didn't upset you. I know these things

are very shocking, but no one can lead a completely sheltered life, and I'm afraid there are a great many dreadful things in this world. You just have to say to yourself firmly that you're not going to be upset by them. You mustn't take things too personally, you know. After all, this is nothing remotely to do with you. I don't suppose you've so much as exchanged a word with this unfortunate man." Miss Pelham at this point gave Deirdre a half-smile. "I cannot pretend that I approve of Nora's vulgar remark, but it must be admitted that he was a very undesirable character and, though I must not say I'm glad he's dead, I cannot honestly say I'm sorry either." Her smile turned to a gentle laugh. "I expect that shocks you a little."

"No. Oh no." The grey eyes lifted. "Miss Pelham—"

"Yes, my dear?"

"I want to go home."

Miss Pelham looked into the lovely, distraught face, saw the tears already brightening the eyes. She was not unused to this kind of thing. It happened regularly. It was natural enough that these girls, who came from carefully sheltered homes, should feel homesick. She said firmly, "I think you'd better come into my study, and then you can tell me all about it "

Deirdre said again, when Miss Pelham had settled her by the window, "Please, I must go home."

"Tell me why. You can speak quite frankly. Are you unhappy with us?"

"No. Only—"

"Only you're homesick. Of course. I understand perfectly. You mayn't believe this, but sometimes I'm homesick, myself. Only the other day, I looked across the Place, with the hot sun shining and everything so glaring, and I thought it would be so nice to look at English fields instead, even if the rain were pouring down. Only for you it's the Irish moors, isn't it?"

"Yes." The tears were beginning to fall in torrents, for indeed her unhappiness and confusion were quite unbearable.

"And little—what is he called now?—Dusty."

"Rusty. Oh, please, please let me go home." And Deirdre burst out crying in good earnest, as Miss Pelham wanted her to do, for she knew that a good cry was sometimes the best tonic in the world. But it was not the glaring streets, nor the blazing sun, nor even the dreadful things that she had done. It was the oppression of a violence such as she had never imagined, the realisation of horrors, all the worse because she did not understand them. Humans branded like animals. Birds nesting on barracks, and bands playing while people died. The violence that she herself had committed was already blurring in her mind. It was not quite possible. It was already unreal, a queasy memory of an unclean hand, a foul-breathed mouth close to hers, a creeping voice whispering dirtiness to her.

M. Quiqueran was dead. It was surely nothing to do with her. It was not her fault. It couldn't be. It was just an accident. Nobody could believe she had done it. Max had promised her that. The dark, bitter face flared before her eyes. The emotion that spilled out of him was a burden that her shoulders were never meant to bear. It was as if he were forcing a decision upon her, compelling her by the violence of his personality to follow him, even when she was so afraid. Oh, it was not the bright streets, it was something far worse, a long dark passage leading into hell, and it seemed that Max must urge her along it, dragging her with him, shackling her to him with his love, compelling her to want him when she was desperate to be away, with God knows what horrors cast upon her, whether she wished it or not.

At that moment she longed with a sick longing for the Wicklow hills, the clean, cool air, and simple people who said things that she could understand, yet at the same time her need for Max was such that she thought she would cry aloud with it.

Miss Pelham was speaking, the calm voice cutting through the storm, a cool, disinfected voice, speaking sanity and reason and common sense. Miss Pelham would never talk of gas-chambers and people dying, even if she knew of such things. Miss Pelham would never permit herself to dream of a wild, handsome boy who could be so tender, and then roll a dead body into the river. Miss Pelham had certainly never lain on a bank with a furious young man who, instead of kissing her, delivered a fierce lecture on what could happen to young women when they were foolish. Miss Pelham would never in a hundred years understand this whirlpool of violence, emotion, longing and revulsion, and Deirdre could not fully understand it either, any more than she could understand the conflict within herself, the need and the rejection that warred so pitilessly within her.

Miss Pelham was saying, "I'm not meaning to sound unsympathetic, my dear, but I am going to ask you to stick it out. You'll find it easier than you imagine. In a few days, perhaps even in a few hours, this will pass. You've never been away from home before, have you?"

Deirdre shook her head. She could not speak.

"I thought you hadn't. I'm so glad you've spoken out about it. I've noticed for some time that something was wrong, but I didn't want to force your confidence. Now you've confided in me, I feel we really understand each other."

Deirdre raised her eyes briefly, then looked down at her folded hands. There was no irony in her character, but it seemed strange to her that Miss Pelham should speak so of understanding when there was all the world between them. She wondered what would happen if she revealed what was in her mind. *I put a knife in him. It was Max's knife. I have been meeting Max at night. I'm supposed to meet him again today. He talks of the most dreadful things and he makes love to me and I like it, but I'm frightened of him, yet somehow I can't bear to be away from him, and I know I would do anything he asked me to do.*

She said, "Yes, Miss Pelham."

"I never like to press for confidences," said Miss Pelham. She was feeling relieved and happy. At long last she had made headway with this odd, beautiful little girl. ("They always come to you," she was to write to her sister, that evening, "but you mustn't force them. You have to be patient and wait.") She said cheerfully, "I've an idea you'd like a day off from your lessons. I should go for a nice, long walk, if I were you. It's a beautiful day." She smiled as she spoke. "I wouldn't say that to everybody, you know, but I feel I can trust you. Why not take a stroll by the river? That'll blow these silly old cobwebs away. And then early to bed. Tomorrow you'll feel quite differently about everything. Is that all right?"

"Yes, thank you."

"Very well, my dear." She rose to her feet. "And don't forget—if anything worries you, come to me. After all, that's what I'm here for, isn't it?"

"Yes, Miss Pelham."

The charming little room was shut out by the closing of the door. A charming, neat, tidy little room, so artistically furnished, with the great bowl of roses on the desk. There had been other roses, their petals scattered on the grass; there had been blood, too, and dreadful sounds, sweating, straining, grunting sounds. And then the splash—

It's all right, sweetheart.

But it was not all right. Perhaps it would never be all right again. I cannot bear it, said the voice in Deirdre's mind, as she walked slowly up the stairs. She could hear the

Paris train in the distance. The wheels took up the refrain: I-cannot-bear-it, I-cannot-bear-it.

She came into her room. She sat down at her desk. She pulled out the notebook and began at once to draw, as if her life depended on it. It was as if something had taken possession of her, something outside herself.

The images flew into life, and presently as the other self absorbed her, page after page was covered with wild, dark faces, urgent hands, and strange, handsome bird of prey profiles.

Only once, in the middle of these, there dropped a hideous thing, a gargoyle of a face, with upturned eyes and loosely open mouth. And from it came a trail of rose-petals, with a knife blade through the last.

The girls were in the classroom below. They were reading a play. Their voices carried faintly to her, going up, going down—up for comedy, down for tragedy, in a kind of chromatic passion. But Deirdre, her yellow hair falling forward, did not heed them, only spilled comedy and tragedy out of her pencil lead, covering page after page, eased a little as if the poison were spewing out of her system. She did not register what she was drawing, not even the representation of M. Quiqueran's dead face. Only at the end she drew something so strange that she at last realised what she was doing; she stopped to stare down at it.

There was a row of black chimneys. The smoke belched out of them, like thick, greasy locks of hair. Beneath was a small square like a flag, and on it was written, "*Vive la France*".

She gazed at this for a long time, half bewildered, half appalled. It made no sense to her, but it hurt her because it was frightening and obscene. Then she could endure the sight of it no longer, for it was so vivid to her that she could almost smell the smoke, and the smell made her feel sick.

She slammed the notebook shut, and put it carefully away. Then she lay down on the bed, and did as Max had once bidden her: she rolled over on to her face, so that her head was resting on her folded arms. The golden hair spilled over the pillows. And there she lay, very still, with the breeze from the open window blowing in upon her.

Chapter Seven

INSPECTOR GRANIER waited for Max to come back from Paris. He was looking heavy and pallid. His stomach was causing him a great deal of pain. "If you're not careful," the doctor had once said to him, "you'll land yourself with a duodenal. Why can't you take things more calmly?" Granier had replied sourly, "Why can't the sun stop shining, why can't the rain stop falling?" He added, "And why can't you stop talking nonsense? When you doctors learn how to cut worry out of a person, then you'll have done something worth while."

The doctor, shrugging, had retorted, "Well, don't blame me if you go down sick."

Anni was saying much the same now, only she did not shrug her shoulders. She loved her husband very much, and the remark was provoked more by distress than by exasperation. She glared now at his untouched plate. "Aren't you going to eat any lunch at all?" she said, removing a knife from Patricia's clutches. "You'll only make yourself ill. What's the matter? Surely you can tell me."

"Oh, it's just that I have a hell of a lot to do," he said. His eyes turned briefly to the knife that Anni had set back on the table, well out of the baby's reach. He winced involuntarily, as the pain jabbed through him, and Anni, seeing this, spoke more shrewishly than ever.

"Oh, you just don't care," she said. "You'll end by killing yourself, and what do you suppose will happen to me then?"

"They pay you a pension," said Granier.

"Oh! I don't know how I put up with you—Do you

want some bicarbonate? Of course, you'd feel much better if you ate, but I suppose it's simply no good talking to you."

"Give me a glass of wine." He saw her face and suddenly smiled. The smile was unexpectedly charming. "Please," he said, adding, "You ought never to have married a policeman. You'd better make sure that Patricia has more sense."

"Patricia has more sense that the pair of us put together." She picked the baby up, remarking reproachfully, "No, darling. Knives are not nice things to play with—" She looked over her shoulder at Granier. She knew that he preferred not to discuss his work with her, but her own last remark reminded her of something, and her curiosity was too strong for her. "It's that old Quiqueran, isn't it?" she said.

He nodded. He did not look at her, only drank a little of the wine.

Her face changed. Still holding Patricia in her arms, she took a step towards him. "Oh, Jean," she said, "it's not Max, is it?"

"Look," he said roughly, the wine spilling as he set his glass down, "I haven't the faintest idea who it was. If I had, I wouldn't be sitting here. It might be anyone. The old devil must have had more enemies than anyone else in town. Do you know, Anni, it's an odd thing, public opinion. Nobody can pretend that Quiqueran was an asset to the community. I daresay there have been plenty worse, but let's face it, he was a louse, and though God presumably knew what He was about when He created lice, I personally could do without them. Yet, now the old so-and-so's dead, the same people who've been blackguarding him for years are beginning to say what a shame it is, and how disgraceful that the police let murders be committed like that. It's those Jewish boys that did it. That's what they're saying. I've heard it, at least half a dozen times already. And he hasn't been dead twenty-four hours—You see, even you asked if it was Max."

"Well," cried Anni, "it's natural enough. Max has been threatening him for so long. And I know you've been worried about it. But I just don't believe he would do such a thing. I don't think anyone else believes it either. People just want a scapegoat. Those boys are all foreign. It's so much nicer if you can pin the blame on a foreigner."

"Why don't they pick on the little English girls then?"

"Oh, be yourself. Those silly little geese couldn't hurt a fly. But I think it's a shame to malign those charming boys. They all stop to speak to Patricia."

"I'm afraid that wouldn't carry much weight in a court of law," said Granier. He brought himself heavily to his feet. One hand went apprehensively to his side. "I've got to go and see Wolff. I tell you this, Anni—I'm not looking forward to it at all. Why couldn't that old bastard die quietly in his bed, instead of causing so much trouble?"

And this, of course—though she had expressed it in a more refined manner—was precisely what Miss Pelham had said, earlier in the day.

*   *   *

Granier did not go across to the Hostel until the boys were officially back from work. He rang M. Wolff and asked him to keep them in until he had seen them. He spent an unpleasant afternoon in the morgue, awaiting the findings of the post-mortem. M. Quiqueran had died of a wound in the chest, made by a sharp-pointed instrument.

"There was considerable force behind the blow," said the police doctor. "It penetrated the third intercostal space. A direct puncture of the heart. It's quite a professional job."

"Could it have been done with a flick-knife?" demanded Granier.

169

"Yes. That would account for the deep penetration. You've not found the weapon?"

"No. We know where it was done, because the river bank's all trodden down, and it was easy to see where the body was lugged into the river, but I don't think we'll ever see the weapon again. We cannot, after all, dredge the entire Seine."

He was thinking that the murderer perhaps worked in Paris, and could easily throw the knife into the broader reaches of the river. He glanced once more at the sad remnants of M. Quiqueran, now dismembered and bottled: usually this kind of thing in no way touched him, but now it made his gorge rise, and the smell of formalin seemed absorbed into his system. He had explained to Anni, on one of the rare occasions when he was discussing his work, that it was all entirely impersonal. "If I let it become personal," he said, "it would be utterly unbearable. But you learn these things. After all, you're a kindhearted girl— it's not in you to harm an animal, much less kill it. Yet you eat your mutton for dinner without a qualm."

And now it was all too personal, for he was growing more and more convinced that Max was the murderer. There was a pile of withered rose-petals neatly put into a plastic container; the container lay on his desk in the prefecture. Granier found the sight of those rose-petals—a potpourri that a sentimental old maid might keep on her mantelpiece— more disturbing than the butcher's sight he had just seen; the dusty scent that came from them was worse than the formalin.

It was all so obvious that it worried him. It seemed almost too simple, yet that, despite the ingenuity of thriller writers, was how police investigation usually proved to be. The obvious suspect was nearly always the right one. He tried to picture how it could have happened. Max had gone off to meet his girl. Granier could see him now with the bunch of roses in his hand. He had blushed, poor kid. Poor kid! The poor kid had been dangerous from his cradle onwards; had not everyone prophesied that there would be just such an ending? Well, all right then. He had met his girl. They had presumably made love on the river bank, and Quiqueran—perhaps Quiqueran had played the role of peeping Tom. It would be enough, more than enough. Max would leap out at him. It might, it just possibly might have been an accident.

"I wonder who the girl is," said Granier aloud, and scribbled a note on his pad to remind him to make inquiries.

Then he set off for the Hostel.

He had always been on good terms with the boys. He knew them all, and he knew their histories. In the first hard days of their arrival, there had been interminable problems with passports, visas and work permits. His table had been covered with those incredible stateless papers, green things that unfolded like a fan. He had taken it all good-naturedly, turned a blind eye occasionally; he had never bullied, he had accepted occasional hysteria, he had kept his temper.

And, as if this were symbolic, the first thing that met his gaze, as he came up to the Hostel, was the chalked scrawl across the wall: *Juif, go home!* It shocked him more than he would have believed possible. It was as if he were suddenly returned to those sad, barbaric years when race was a capital crime, when humanity was something that it was safer to ignore. The strange compound of English and French added horror; it made the sentiment more universal.

He set foot inside the Hostel, and knew that the war had returned, indeed. He met at once the combined, cold, hostile stare of the fifteen aliens who had once, so he believed, been his friends. A few had not yet returned. He looked from face to face. Max was not there. He looked at them again, with a grimness that hid despair. He did not attempt to smile; a smile would be an insult. He knew that for them the

swastika was branded on his arm, and a futile rage, provoked
largely by lack of food, filled him. He wanted to shout,
Haven't I always been friendly to you? Haven't I always
helped you? Have I ever done you any harm? But instead
he swung round on M. Wolff, who stood there, looking
steadfastly at him; his face was impassive except for his eyes
which were sick and afraid.

He said, without preamble, "You know why I am here.
M. Quiqueran was murdered last night. I have reason to
believe that one of you may be able to help me in my
inquiries. Which of you carries a knife?"

He was utterly unprepared for the response. Hand after
hand went to trouser pockets. As fine an array of lethal
weapons as any militia could desire was immediately
paraded before him. It seemed that they all carried knives.
Mostly they were pen-knives, but there were three of a more
dangerous kind; one of these belonged to the German
boy, Moishe.

Granier, taken aback, made to look a fool, blustered to
cover up his confusion. He snapped at M. Wolff, "What is
this? An army? Did you know that all your boys were
armed?"

"I hadn't the faintest idea," said M. Wolff calmly. "I
should, however, like to point out, Inspector, that most
boys, all over the world, do carry knives. They are after all
useful for cutting the string on parcels, sharpening pencils,
and so on. Knives can be used for other purposes than
murder."

"There is one knife that was used for that purpose only,
sir."

"So I understand. But not necessarily one of these."

"Where is Max Wrzonski?" said Granier, ignoring this.
He sensed an immediate reaction in the boys facing him.
They were in physical fact lounging about the room, some
of them balanced on the edge of tables or the arms of chairs,

but he began to feel as if he were surrounded; the sweat pricked beneath his collar.

"He's not back yet, Inspector." M. Wolff added in a detached tone, "You'll forgive my saying this—naturally I am not unaware of your suspicions—but Max left for work early this morning, and had no reason to know that this interrogation would take place. If you find his absence sinister, I can only say that he may be doing nothing more illegal than going to a cinema, or taking his girl-friend out for a drink. I don't put any restrictions on my boys. They are free to come and go as they please. They all work and they all earn. They are not children. They do not have to live here. This is a Hostel, not a school."

Granier turned to the boys. He said, "Do any of you know where Max is?"

They shrugged. It was a gesture he employed himself, but he had once said to Anni that a shrug in Jewish needed a dictionary to interpret it. Those shrugs were eloquent; the boys glanced at each other with a kind of derisive contempt, as if the question were an absurd one.

Granier, gathering his official dignity about him as well as he could, said curtly to M. Wolff, "I should like to interview them all separately, please."

They came. Baruch. Nathan. Moishe. Jacob. Their names stepped straight from the Old Testament, and the waters of Kinereth, Lake Galilee, stirred in their strange music. Only instead of fierce, bearded prophets in white robes, these were grave-faced young men with secret eyes, and the iron-blue number branded on their wrists. Some of them wore kappels, but mostly they did not. Their French was fluent, with a trace of accent—Polish, Czech or German. They were like all the other boys who strolled the streets outside, yet they were as alien as the salt water of the Red Sea they had once triumphantly crossed. Granier, asking them sharp, impersonal questions, felt like Pharaoh's overseer, with the whip in his hand; he grew painfully aware, as others had done before him, of the stark invincibility of the conquered.

And they all knew nothing. Of course they knew nothing. He could have answered for them. No, they had not seen Max. Max? *Mais non*—He had probably been in his room. He liked to stay there and read. They gave the impression that this was an amiable but habitual eccentricity. He read poetry. Poetry! I ask you. *Un peu toqué, quoi! Mais Max, tu sais, il est toujours comme ça, il s'en fout.* Lower lips jutted out. Shoulders raised. Eyebrows shooting in all directions. Hands outspread. Voices sinking, then soaring to falsetto. *Mais voyons, monsieur, Max, c'est un drôle de type—*

Granier could have replied vulgarly, You're telling me! He eyed them, made almost dizzy by the waving, weaving hands. It was quite remarkable how little they all knew, even Jean-Louis who was so cheeky that he all but put him across his knee. "Did you work with the Bosches?" Jean-Louis asked, his eyes bright with such malice that it was hard to believe he was only ten years old, then when Granier, stung, denied this furiously—"But I thought all *flics* worked with the Bosches!"

He left Moishe to the last. Moishe, he knew, was Max's closest friend. He hoped that by keeping him waiting he could sap his nerve, but as soon as he saw that large imperturbable figure, he knew he had lost. He supposed afterwards that he had been foolish to imagine he could ever achieve victory.

Moishe came in, an enormous, heavily built boy, with hands like hams. The face he turned on Granier was gentle and kind. There was none of the suppressed mockery or defiance that had been so plain in the others. He sat down calmly, stretching out his long legs, and lit a cigarette, after offering his interrogator one. He looked exactly what he was—a farmer's son from southern Germany. There was about him an extraordinary air of honesty, competence and reliability. If I, thought Granier, were an employer, I'd take this boy on after one look at him. And then he thought quite irrelevantly that if Patricia, in twenty years' time, brought this young man back as her future husband, he would be utterly delighted.

He surveyed Moishe now, and was not delighted at all. He wondered what the Nazis had made of him. They must have found him a little disconcerting. Granier was finding him a little disconcerting, too.

He said warily, "I understand Max was in yesterday."

"Not the whole evening."

"Oh? Why? Were you out with him?"

"No."

"Then how do you know?"

"I met him on his way out. To the war memorial."

"To the—!"

"Yes, sir. To put flowers by our side—the Jewish side. Yesterday was the anniversary of his parents' death. Or rather the day when he last had news of them."

Granier stared at him. He was so completely taken aback that for a moment he had nothing to say. This he had not expected. He glowered at Moishe, who returned the look with an amiable, detached smile. He said at last in a choked voice, "Do you really expect me to believe this?"

"I'm sorry, M. Granier. It's true. I don't suppose he'd care much for my telling you, but still—The flowers are still there. You can look. His parents escaped from Poland, you know. They came here and were deported by the Nazis. His sister—"

"Yes, yes, I know. All right, then. He went to the war memorial. And then he came back. What time?"

"Oh, I've no idea. I didn't think to look. But he went out again, very late. He was restless. I think he was rather upset. The occasion, of course—"

"How do you know all this?"

"I met him in the kitchen. I came down for a snack. I was hungry. He'd just come in."

"How do you know he wasn't out the whole evening?"

"Because we played a game of chess together. To calm his nerves. He's very nervy, you know, and—"

"When did you finish the game?"

"I can't give you the exact time. Late. About midnight, I suppose. One doesn't normally look at the clock. I'm sorry."

"I suppose," said Granier, after a pause, "you didn't kill Quiqueran, yourself?"

"No, sir. He wasn't worth the trouble."

"And you believe Max didn't kill him, either?"

"Well, he couldn't have done, could he? I think in certain circumstances he might. But as it is, he didn't."

"I don't believe a word you're saying," said Granier.

Moishe gave a faint shrug. There was no insolence in the gesture. It merely signified resignation. There was nothing worth arguing about.

"And you've nothing else to tell me?"

"I can't think of anything, sir."

"All right. You can go."

He watched the mountain lumbering out. He thought with a sudden, half-rueful triumph, Pharaoh must have had absolute hell with him! War memorial, indeed. Flowers for his parents. That was a new one. He wondered which of them had thought it up. Max, probably. It bore the hallmark of his sardonic mind. They must have met in Paris—

He looked up as M. Wolff came in. He thought the old man looked very old, indeed, almost as old as he felt, himself. He said, "Well, I'll be going."

"I'll see you to the door," said M. Wolff.

They stood in the doorway and looked at each other, in mutual enmity and understanding. In their eyes was the same fear, the same regret. Then Granier became the

Inspector again. "I want to see Max when he comes back," he said. "I don't care how late it is. I've got to see him. I shall be at home. Tell him to walk straight in. The door won't be latched."

He could not prevent himself from walking to the war memorial. It was at the other end of the town, and took him half an hour to go there and back, but nonetheless, despite his exhaustion, he had to go. He stood by the memorial, staring at it. At the foot of the plaque for the massacred Jews was a bunch of red roses. It was quite withered. It had obviously been there for at least twenty-four hours.

He suddenly remembered, as he stood there, how once, a long time ago, Moishe had told him how he and a friend had found the means of getting out of the camp to beg food from the farms around. "When we came back," Moishe said, "we used to unfasten our trousers and make as if we were buttoning them up again, so that if we met a guard we could say we had been to the latrine."

It was after all a variation of the same trick. Granier surveyed the withered roses with a bitter smile. Then he walked slowly home. A curious, sad anger filled him; he was an honest man and he knew that there was nothing he would have liked better than to let the matter go. But he knew he must continue; justice was justice, and a murderer must not escape.

He was now entirely certain that Max had killed M. Quiqueran.

*   *   *

Max was not in Paris. He returned to Portelet-sur-Seine by a much later train than his usual one, and spent most of the evening eating a meal at Madame Dupont's. He knew that Granier would be at the Hostel. He was not trying to avoid the interview. This, he knew very well, was bound to come, sooner or later. He was merely determined at all costs to see Deirdre that evening, and he was terrified lest the Inspector might delay him or even shut him up.

He sat there now, over his supper. He scarcely knew what he was eating. He looked fierce and haggard, and he ate untidily, cramming the food into his mouth as if it were something of no importance.

Madame Dupont said, "I'm sorry, M. Max."

"All right," said Max.

"It's as much as my licence is worth. Can't you take your young lady into an hotel?"

"She's not that sort of young lady."

Madame Dupont, looking unhappy and studying his bleak countenance, said, "I can't afford trouble with the police. The Inspector's bound to come looking for you. They say he says you did it."

"They say he says!"

"I wouldn't blame you. That Quiqueran was a pig if ever there was one. Do you know, he recommended my nice rooms to two German officers? He brought them round here, becking and smiling. 'Captain,' he was saying, with a great, silly grin all over his face, 'Captain—' And do you know what they said to him? Do you know, M. Max?"

"No, I don't," said Max.

"*Heraus!* That's what they said." She imitated as well as she could the bullying shout, and Max gave a half-laugh. "*Heraus!* And then they kicked him out. But literally."

"Serve the b— right."

"That's what I said, M. Max. Only it wasn't fun for me, you know, left there with two Bosche pigs on my hands. But I got rid of them."

"I bet you did!" Then, interested despite himself, "How?"

"I said there was no *water*. I locked it up and threw away the key. It was very inconvenient for me, but the Bosches couldn't take it. They like their comforts. They swore a

great deal, and pinched a few things, but they left. I hope
they took it out of old Quiqueran. Did you use a knife on
him, M. Max?"

"I tell you, I didn't kill him. I don't know why I didn't,
but I didn't, and that's all there is to it."

"I wouldn't blame you at all," said Madame Dupont
again. "He was never any good. He never saw his wife,
except to give her another child, and then he just left her
to get on with it. He was always talking about his women,
but I'm sure he never had any. He said he had *rayonnements
aux doigts*, and the women fell for him like mad, but that
was all in his mind. Who'd want to sleep with a bundle of
bones like that? If there's anything I can do for you, M.
Max, you've only to ask me. Except," she added hastily,
for she was a practical woman, "bringing the young lady
here. I'm very sorry. I—"

"All right, all right." Max rose to his feet, and rummaged
in his pocket.

"Oh, never mind," she said, "never mind. You haven't
eaten enough to keep a flea alive. I don't want your money.
You ought to eat more, M. Max. You look half-starved."

"I eat plenty. Don't be silly. How much do I owe you?"

"Nothing. If you mention it again, I shall be very
offended."

He raised his hands. "Have it your own way, auntie. I
thought you ran a café, not a charity. But I won't argue
with you."

"If there's anything I can do for you—"

"Well, there is." He paused to look back at her. "You've
never seen the young lady, either here or with me or
anywhere else. You've never seen her at all."

"I've never seen her at all," said Madame Dupont, with
a sigh.

"That's fine." Then he saluted her in the impudent fashion
that was his, and made his way towards the Place du

Triangle. It was nearly ten o'clock. He moved swiftly and silently, keeping to the shadows. He moved as the hunted move, and once again the past caught at his heels; he half expected, at each sound of footsteps, to see a couple of German military police advance upon him. His hand went instinctively to his pocket, but came out empty; the knife, as Granier had foreseen, lay deep in the deepest part of the Seine, and would lie there, a rusted thing of steel until the end of time.

He waited at the corner of the Place du Triangle, flattened against the wall. The lights were on in Granier's study; they were on in the Hostel. They would be waiting for him. Let them wait. He stayed very still. It would have needed sharp eyes to see him, for he did not even light a cigarette. His face was turned to the front entrance of Rosedene College. There was a savage, compelling, despairing anger in his gaze. His whole mind and body were concentrated on one thing only. He did not think now of his own predicament. He did not think that soon the freedom he had spent his whole life fighting for might be for ever taken from him. He was only thinking, She must come, she must come. For a second his head went back against the wall, revealing the strong, bared throat. His hands were set flat against the stone. He looked as if he were in anguish, facing a firing squad.

Deirdre, he said silently, then repeated her name over and over again. Deirdre, Deirdre, Deirdre. You must come. You're not getting away from me now. Come. Oh, come—

She came. She was very late. She knew she was being summoned. She tugged against the summons, tugged desperately, but it was too strong for her. White-faced and shaking, she crept out of her safe, pretty room, a sad little lamb for sacrifice, and stole down the stairs to set her fearful foot once again on the unknown shore.

She came. She shut the door very softly behind her. She did not at first see Max, whose hungry eyes were fixed upon her. She stood there and then, very wearily, put up her hands to push back the heavy hair. When he came noiselessly behind her, and touched her arm, she whirled round, her mouth open to scream. Then she remembered, and stared at him, silent.

Only as she saw him, it all changed again, like the pattern in a kaleidoscope, and she knew how she wanted him. She framed his name with her lips, not daring to speak it aloud, then leant against him for a second, her eyes closed, while his arms came round her, hands clasped at her breast. For the one moment they forgot the world around them; for that one second they pressed against each other, oblivious of everything but themselves, at peace.

Then he drew away. Only now they did not walk as they had once walked, easily and confidently, not caring who saw them. Once they had delighted in each other, looked at each other, talked and laughed. Now they stole silently along, aware of their guilt, moving back against the wall as people came near, choosing the quiet, back streets; their eyes were wide, their ears alert.

"I feel as if I were a fox with the hounds after me," whispered Deirdre, then, "Oh, Max, where are we going? Is it the river?" And she hoped this was so, for she did not like these narrow, ill-lit streets; she longed for the fresh air, the sound of the water, and the nightingales singing in the woods beyond.

He shook his head. He said curtly, "No. It can't be the river. Have some sense. They'll be looking for us there. I don't know—We must talk. I must know what they've said to you." Then he stopped dead, so that she, with her arm linked in his, was forced to stop, too. She could feel the tremors running through him. She stared at him. She saw that he was smiling, a slow, bitter smile, and the smile frightened her, for when he looked like that she could not understand him. He said softly, "There's only one place we can go. I'm sorry, but there's nowhere else. And we must be able to talk. You do see that, don't you?"

"Yes, but—"

"Come on, then. We haven't much time."

Back home the soft rain would be falling on the hills. The birds would be nesting in the ruins of the seven little churches, and the kings slept sweetly in the Righ-fearta Church on the banks of the lake. This was where she and Rusty walked in the summer evenings. Sometimes she would take the boat out and scramble up the cliffs to St. Kevin's bed, while Rusty ran, barking, along the grass, chasing imaginary rabbits. And there she would lie on the rocky ledge, looking out across the glen, with the moon making shadows on the water, and the clouds flowing softly across the sky.

Here, they were once again in Portelet's main street, and the air smelt of heat and dust. Max paused for a second under the shadow of the Mairie. Then he pulled Deirdre back, to the small, square building that lay beside it.

She looked up once. Her gaze swam to the placque, and the words, *Vive la France*, rose before her eyes. The youth and life within her rebelled, and she began, quite indignantly, "But Max—" Only he paid her no attention; he drew her after him into the small yard that separated the two buildings. It smelt unclean. He whispered, "There's a side entrance. The door's broken. No one bothers about it. No one ever comes here, especially at night. Not even Granier."

The slats of the door were smashed. Max put his hand inside, and turned the handle.

They stepped inside. They were instantly in a half-light. The reflection through the barred windows of the street lamps and the cafés danced about them so it was as if they moved in the beam of a muted torch. They moved, driven by some incomprehensible instinct, from room to room. Everywhere it was empty. There was nothing. The furniture had long ago been looted. There was nothing left of the ancient cruelty, no hideous implements, no physical trace of suffering. There was only emptiness and the ghosts. Their footsteps echoed on the flags, so that although they moved softly, they sounded like an advancing army; their whispered voices echoed after them.

Max said clearly, as if this were something he had to say, "This was the Nazi police headquarters. Didn't I tell you? This is where they interrogated people. The cells are underneath. I'll show you—"

"No," she said loudly, "No. I don't want to see them."

The echo caught her words. *I don't want to see them.* And, as she stared, half-fearfully, half-angrily, about her, the other echoes came to her ears, the echoes of voices castrated by fear and intolerable pain, voices of men uttering thin, weak cries such as they had once emitted when they issued from their mother's womb.

"I was here once."

"You?"

She swung round to look at him. They moved a little way away from each other. The lamp of a passing headlight caught Max full on, so that he flared into her view. He was as she had never yet seen him. He was in his working clothes. The dark stubble was already shadowing his chin. The check shirt, open at the neck, was stained; she could smell the sweat on him. Yet the face that stared into hers was terribly alive with longing and with pain. The danger of him and his beauty stirred her so that she forgot how afraid she had been; the vision of the soft green hills and the deep lake faded. She gave him a faint little smile. Her hands moved out towards him.

He took them. They stood there as if they were plighting

their troth. He said in an angry voice, "I shouldn't have brought you here. But what else was I to do?"

She said, "Did they hurt you very much?"

"Oh!" The shoulders raised. He still gripped her hands. He laughed. "They beat me a little. It was nothing."

"They beat you?"

"Of course. What do you think they brought me here for? Don't you believe me? You can feel, if you like."

And before she knew what he was about, his grasp tightened on her hand, raised it and shoved it down his shirt. "There," he said. His face wore an odd look, half defiant, half ashamed.

She moved her unwilling fingers. She could feel the rough patches of skin on his back where the scar tissue had healed. She wanted to withdraw her hand, but she could not; her fingers still lingered fearfully, caressingly, then a sob of pity and horror rose in her throat, and he at once opened the eyes he had shut so tightly, caught her to him and began to kiss her.

"Ah, good God," he said, "there's nothing to snivel about. It doesn't matter. It was a long time ago. I don't even really remember. There were other things so much worse." The softness of the mouth beneath his was cracking his self-control, "So very much worse—They took my parents away, you know. And then my sister. We said good-bye, but she didn't know any longer what she was saying." His voice rose. "I felt so damnably lost. So alone—"

The echo seemed to catch the words again. *So lost. So alone*.

"Don't cry," he said. "Oh, my darling, don't cry."

"But why did they treat you like that? What had you done?"

"I'm a Jew."

"But I know that." Her mother sometimes spoke contemptuously of those Dublin Jews. Once one of them had come to a party. Deirdre had not been introduced to him. She did not remember him at all, but apparently he was rather vulgar. "Vulgar" was her mother's worst term of opprobrium. To be vulgar was to be at the bottom of the social scale. She drew back a little to examine the face above hers. There was nothing vulgar in that face. It was wild and fierce and desperate, but it was beautiful, and it stirred her as the amiable young faces of her dancing partners had never done. The cheap, check shirt, marked round the collar and under the arms, did not seem to belong to the spruced-up young man who had escorted her to the river, but it toughened him, made him more alien, and this, coupled with the vulnerable eyes, filled her with a confusion that brought the spontaneous words bursting from her lips.

"I don't care," she said, defying the whole of County Wicklow, defying her mother, defying the world that had bred her, "What does it matter?"

He burst into a half-hysterical laugh.

She repeated loudly, "Well, why should it? If you weren't a Jew, you wouldn't be any different. I should still like you." And on an impulse that she herself did not understand, she caught at his hand and touched with her lips the number branded on his wrist.

He snatched it from her. He swore at her, shouting, "Don't you ever dare do that again. Do you hear me? I won't have it."

She said, indignantly, "What have I done now? You're always shouting at me. I didn't mean any harm. Oh, really," she exclaimed, turning a little away from him, "you are quite impossible. I don't understand you at all."

"I know. I didn't mean to shout." He had her hands again. His face had changed expression. The words began to pour out of him. "I know you don't understand. How could you? But I want you to. You must. I want you to listen to me. I want to tell you everything, I want to explain."

185

He sensed her withdrawal, but now he could not stop. "Surely you can listen," he said. "After all, I've never talked like this to anyone in my life. Anyone. Only with you and me there mustn't be any secrets. I want to know all about you, all, all—down to the smallest thing. And I want you to know all about me. After all, when people love each other they don't want to hide anything. Do they? Do they?"

"I don't know." It was a fading, far-away voice. They stood in the middle of the gaunt, ugly, empty room. They had forgotten about M. Quiqueran and Granier. They were only aware of each other. Only the voices of the long-since dead were crying again, and now the long, dark road of her nightmare was clear, winding its stony path to Golgotha, with black gravestones dotted at the side. Before her were the bony faces with vast eye-sockets, the shadow of barbed wire pencilled across them, the smoking chimneys, the end of civilisation for torturer and tortured, its zero hour.

She lay back in his arms. Rusty was miles away. The green grass was blackened and scorched, the lake water was tainted, scummed with filth. Outside, people were talking, laughing, disputing. The cafés were filled with men and women relaxing after their day's work. But Deirdre and Max heard none of it. Around them was a dry rustling as of wings, the rustling of rags blown in the wind, the rustling of bones with no flesh to sheathe them, the rustling of a myriad voices from a myriad ghosts, wrapping their arms across them in this premature day of judgment; their gat-toothed, skeleton grins widened, for now they were all bound together, Jew and Christian, traitor and saint, hero and coward, in the undenominational bond of suffering.

And through it came his voice, violent, vibrant, a little shrill, saying unmentionable things, speaking the unspeakable, opening up the charnel house, dragging her into it with him.

"*We are going East.*

A scrap of paper, thrown from one of the covered trucks, landing on the hard earth, miraculously delivered. The last I heard from them. I don't even know where they are buried. It was their final message to me. Yet you know, yet you know, I have never been so aware of beauty. Another dawn. Another summer sky. It might always be the last. Every minute might be the last. I was so proud to have achieved the state of being still alive. It was life itself was the miracle. The sky has never again been so blue, the sun has never again been so golden and so warm. When I had typhus—that was in Gurs, that was before they deported me to Auschwitz. The camp doctor came to see me. '*Tu vas crever,*' he said. *Tu vas crever!* As if I were an animal. But I was an animal. I was lousy and shaven and filthy—So filthy. The smell, the stench. Even now I'm sick if I go to a swimming bath. It's the chlorine. But I didn't die. My parents died, my sister died, but I didn't die. When the Russians rescued us, they weren't so gentle with the guards as the English and Americans were. They used to beat them. I found a gap in the fencing so that I could watch and listen. I liked that. I liked to hear them howl. They had made me howl in my time.

"Only when I said good-bye to Chaja—my sister, you know. We cried so. We couldn't speak for crying. I have never really cried since. I think all my tears were done. She was so ashamed. You see, she didn't understand. I used to dream of finding *him* again. Perhaps there was more than one. They were like that. I shall never know. But I used to think of what I would do to him if I ever had the chance, oh God, oh God, the things I would have done—She was fourteen. Three years younger than you.

"There were the blue wagons. They were for taking people to the gas-chambers. We all knew what they were. At the beginning the Germans pretended they were escorting us to a public bath. They gave us a towel and a piece of soap. But after a time they didn't bother.

"We used to see great piles of mutilated corpses, with the hair stripped from their heads, the gold fillings snatched from their teeth. But after a while we hardly noticed. We didn't mind death any more. It was too common. It was life that was astonishing.

"Only I would like to know where my parents are buried. And my aunts and uncles and cousins. There were a lot of us. Some stayed in Poland. Some came with us to France. It didn't make much difference in the end. We thought we were quite safe. And now they're all dead. Isn't it strange to think that never, never, in their wildest dreams can they have imagined what would happen to them? Their last words to me were, *We are going East*."

The quick, vibrant voice fell silent. The last words shivered on the air.

We are going East.

Deirdre stirred in his arms. Her face, with the tears wet on it, was upturned to his. She wanted to cry out, Why do you tell me these terrible things, why do you have to hurt me so? But she did not, because his pain was so infinitely greater than hers; in a primitive desire to comfort and be comforted, she drew his head down to hers, and they huddled together like young animals, kissing, muttering endearments, sobbing a little, moving together, until Deirdre lost her balance and stumbled; she fell to the floor, with his arm outswooped to protect her from the stone flags; he came down on to his knees at her side.

She did not move from the shelter of his arm. She closed her eyes. There was no resistance left in her. She was dazed with pity and shock and longing. She would not say No; she would not even think of saying it. He knew that well enough. The battle within him revealed itself in the twisted, haggard lines of his face; suddenly it looked ravaged and old. He jumped to his feet. He said in a harsh voice, "Get up. You'll only catch cold if you lie there." Then he shouted at her, "Get up, damn you. What do you think I am? Don't you think I'm human? You are the most idiotic girl I've ever met."

This entirely bewildered her. She felt as if he had struck her across the face. This transition from gentleness to violence was more than she could take. She could not understand him at all. Her temper began to stir within her; her face grew sulky. She let herself be jerked up. She stared at him resentfully.

He said in the same harsh voice, "You never told me what Granier said to you."

"You haven't given me much chance. You like to do all the talking."

"Well, I'm giving you the chance now, aren't I? What did he say?"

"Who?"

He began to shake her, checked himself, and said more quietly, "The Police Inspector. Hasn't he spoken to you at all?"

"No, he has not." She answered him like a naughty child.

He gave her a look. Suddenly he was spoiling for a fight. He longed to beat her. He hated her for her beauty, her childishness, the innocence that he must not touch. He said in a voice calculated to sting, "You're damn lucky. You're luckier than you deserve. I'll tell you something funny. It'll make you laugh. He doesn't think you did it. He doesn't think about you at all. Do you know whom he suspects?" As she did not answer, he jabbed a finger into his chest. "Me! Me! I think what decided him was those roses. I bought you some, you know. You didn't even notice them, of course. I expect you get bored with people bringing you flowers. But old Granier saw me carrying them, and like the bloody fool I am, I went and left them on the bank. I've tried to cover up, but he's fly, old Granier, and he's had his eye on me for a long time. I expect you're relieved, aren't you? You're safe now." He added, "Provided, of course, that I hold my tongue."

She said nothing. She looked so sullen that he could hardly keep his hands off her, yet at the same time, even in her sulks, she was so beautiful that she brought a lump into his throat.

He said, "Thank you for being so concerned for me. It's most gratifying. I suppose no one's even mentioned the matter to a little angel like you?"

"Oh yes," she said, "Miss Pelham did."

"In the most ladylike way, I hope. What did she say? That dear old Quiqueran, God rest his soul, has passed away, snuffed it, gone to his Maker? Well? What did she say?"

She cried out, "I'm not going to answer you. I don't see why I should. I think you're a bit mad. You tell me all those shocking things, and now you speak to me in this way. You're terribly rude. You've no manners at all."

"Oh, I'm just a common boy," he said. His voice was dangerous, his smile even more so. Only his eyes were bright with despair, but this she did not see. He said, "You're being very haughty with me suddenly, aren't you? I suppose someone as rude as myself is rather distasteful to a lady like yourself. Only you weren't quite so haughty yesterday, were you? You were willing to howl in my arms, and let me take the responsibility for the knife you jabbed into the old bastard's belly—"

"Oh!" she turned blindly away, but he seized her arm in a grip that bruised her.

"Oh no, you don't," he said between his teeth, "Oh no, you don't, my girl. What size fool do you take me for? I suppose you'd like to run away and never see me again.

Back to Mummy and that blasted little dog you are so fond of. You'll leave me to face the music. Just like that. After all, I don't matter. I'm not a dog. I'm just a man. I'm a flirt, someone to play around with for an hour or so. Now you've finished with me, I can just go to hell."

He paused. He saw the sudden fright on her face. A look of incredulity came into his own. He exclaimed in a voice rough with anger, "By God, I believe—You are meaning to run away. You are! Oh, don't try to get away from me. We're going to talk this out, you and I. So you're double-crossing me, are you? I shouldn't be surprised if you actually asked the dragon to let you go home—" Her terrified look, her struggles to get away from him, answered him clearly. His face went white. His temper burst into flame. "You bitch! You damned bitch!" He swung out his arm to hit her for the second time in their acquaintance, and for the second time let it swing harmlessly to his side. She began to sob violently, but he paid no attention. He said, "So you're just leaving me to it. How charming of you. Leaving me to face a murder charge, for a murder that you committed. It doesn't matter if I'm thrown into jail. It doesn't matter if I'm guillotined. You don't give a damn for me, do you? As long as I get you out of your own stinking mess. But you've sized me up wrong, my dear. I'm not such a fool as you take me for. I'm not sacrificing myself for anyone. I've had enough martyrdom, thank you. You are staying here, and don't imagine you're not. You're in this up to the neck, and if you walk out on me now the neck may be all that's left to you. Murder's murder, you know." Her shocked face stirred him to the final brutality. "After all, I've only your word for it that the old devil tried to rape you. Perhaps he wasn't entirely uninvited. God knows, you're silly enough for anything."

She managed to jerk her arm away. She ran wildly for the door. She was crying hysterically.

He shouted after her, "*Garce!*"

Something stopped her. Perhaps it was the memory of what he had told her. Perhaps it was the memory of soft words, kisses, kindly hands. She hesitated, at the doorway. The colour began slowly to flood into her face. For the first time in the whole of her life a dim, adult awareness came upon her. She stood still. She hung her head.

Then he moved towards her. He said quietly, "I suppose you'll never speak to me again. I suppose you won't believe me if I say I really didn't mean it." He did not come close. He looked at her, then, as she said nothing, he went on, "Go home if you want to. Why not? I'll see that it's all right. I don't care what they do to me. I won't let anyone harm you, ever. I promise."

"But I don't want to go home," said Deirdre in an almost inaudible voice. Then the next instant his arms were round her again, and they were clinging together, as if for survival. She whispered, "Why do we quarrel like this? I don't want to quarrel with you. I can't bear it."

He gave her a helpless, half-ironic look. His shoulders raised. "It happens," he said. "It just happens that way. Do you think I really want to hurt you?" He laid his cheek against her hair. He said, "Why don't we go away together? This is no world for anyone. It calls itself civilised, but it's a lousy, rotten world. People hate each other and torture each other and kill each other. We could find somewhere away from everything, and we'd have each other and lots of children, and the rest of the world could just kill itself off, we wouldn't even notice."

She said, feeling very old, "I don't think that would be very practical. We wouldn't have any money."

He began to laugh. His laugh was a little hysterical. She noticed suddenly that he had grown very thin; he had always been gaunt, but now the flesh seemed pared down to the bones. "Oh," he said, "I'll find myself a job, and earn lots and lots of money. You shall have lots of nice clothes, and a radio and a television set, and I'll come home every evening, and we'll go to bed together and make love. Would that suit you?"

"I think that would be very nice," said Deirdre, and wondered why he continued to laugh. But his kisses comforted her, and now he no longer shouted at her, nor did he speak of horrors. The languor of exhaustion was upon her, and for that little moment in time she was willing to accept his sad, silly island, and imagine a little garden of Eden tucked away in the southern seas.

They were both very tired. At last they put their arms round each other's waist and walked slowly back to the Place du Triangle. Max said, when they were nearly home, "Will you meet me again?" His face twisted into a mockery of a smile, "Shall I say that I must report on what Granier says to me? Or shall I pretend that I must have your news? It isn't that. I just want to see you again. I just have to see you again. I must kiss you again, many, many times. I won't shout at you. I'm sorry I lost my temper. Have you forgiven me?"

She was moved enough to stop, to open her arms to him. But he checked her. "Not here," he said. "It's not safe. We shouldn't really walk about in the street together. Only I can't bear to let you go. I can't bear to have you out of my sight. Will you come tomorrow, darling?"

"Yes. Of course."

"I suppose it will have to be that abominable place. But I tell you what. We'll meet where we met the first time. We'll risk it. I wouldn't want you to wait in that house alone. Do you mind it very much?"

She minded very much indeed, partly because she sensed the effect it had on him. But, swamped in her tenderness for him, in this strange, unwilling longing for him, she said,

"It doesn't matter. Only you won't tell me all those dreadful things again, will you?"

He stared at her, in love and irony and despair. Perhaps in that moment he saw the world that divided them, must always divide them. Perhaps it struck him that she seemed not to have the faintest understanding of the serious danger he was in, on her account. Perhaps, with the eyes that had seen so much, he saw that a kiss was the frailest of links. It was as if they stood on different icebergs; soon the sea must flow irrevocably between them and not even their finger-tips would touch. But he ignored his own suffering because she ignored it. He said gently, "No. I'll never mention them again." The curious, twisted smile flickered across his ravaged face. "Poor little Deirdre. Poor little girl. You got rather more than you asked for when you took me on, didn't you?"

She said unexpectedly, "I think perhaps it's poor little Max."

He gave a little exclamation of surprise. Then he smiled again. "Perhaps it is, at that. Never mind. Poor little Max is used to looking after himself. Good-night, my dear, dear darling. Don't let the dragon catch you."

"Oh, mayn't I—Won't you even kiss me good-night?"

He closed his eyes for a second. He looked quickly around him. There was no one in sight. He said sharply, "You ought to have a keeper." He kissed her briefly and hard. He said, "Now get along with you, and don't let's have any more of this nonsense." And spluttering faintly as she raised an affronted face to him, he turned her about without ceremony, gave her a slap and pushed her on her way.

He did not follow her, until he was sure she must be back in the College. Then with a bitter smile still lingering, he lit himself a cigarette and set off for the Hostel.

Chapter Eight

M. WOLFF was waiting for him. He was sitting on one of the hard-backed chairs he had complained about to the American ladies. His legs were crossed. He wore his glasses, and looked severe and formidable, as was his way when unhappy and distraught. He was studying an Israeli paper. He scarcely glanced up as Max came in. He tapped ominously on the front page, and turned the paper round so that Max could see it. "Do you see this?" he said.

"I don't read Hebrew," said Max.

"Then you ought to be ashamed of yourself. If you came to *schule* more often—The Americans have just built a new hospital. And we haven't got one lousy armchair." He rose to his feet. "Max."

Max looked at him.

M. Wolff came up to him. He took off his glasses, wiped them, put them on his nose again. He cleared his throat. "Max."

Max waited.

"What the hell have you been up to?"

"Nothing in particular. Why?"

"Oh, don't try to be funny. Granier wants to see you. Now."

"Oh? What am I supposed to have done?"

"That's what I'd like to know." M. Wolff began to swear softly to himself. Then he burst out, "You heard the news this morning, of course. About old Quiqueran."

"Yes, I did."

"Did you kill him?"

"No, I did not."

M. Wolff was silent for a moment, then he said, "Granier's convinced you did."

"I suppose it's natural enough."

"Look, boy—He's been round here, this evening. He's been asking us all questions. I don't know what the result is. But you realise that if you did do it, I can't cover up for you. I've done my best up till now, and in all fairness to myself, I must confess that there have been some awkward moments. You go your own way, don't you, Max? You've never been one of the easiest to handle. But this—All right. You didn't do it. I hope to God you're speaking the truth. Whether you are or not, Granier's gunning for you like hell. I don't think he likes it any more than I do. He's always been fond of you. So have I, though the reason for it escapes me, for a more ungrateful young scoundrel I've never met. But he's a policeman, and he's an honest man. He won't let sentimentality stand in his way. I don't know what there is in the way of proof, but I do know one thing and—though I've no right to say this, whatsoever—I suggest you do some pretty fast thinking on it. You went out last night with a bunch of roses. I saw you. So did Granier. And there was a bunch of roses lying on the river-bank, with the grass all scuffed up beside it. That's all. I'm damned," said M. Wolff explosively, "if this doesn't make me an accessory after the fact, or something. Anyway, I hope you have the answer."

"I have," said Max smoothly.

"I hope it's convincing."

"It is. It also happens to be the truth."

M. Wolff eyed him, without answering. Then he said, "As you didn't do the killing, have you any idea who did?"

"Not the faintest."

"Well, you'd better go and get it over. He'll wait up all night for you. I've never thought him particularly bright, but no one can deny that he works."

"He's not a fool."

"Perhaps that's a pity—This is a hell of a business. Do you want a drink?"

Max hesitated. He wanted a drink badly. He said at last, "I think I'd better not. It might give the wrong impression."

"I expect you'll need it when you come back," said M. Wolff grimly. "You'll find a bottle of wine on my desk. If you do come back, that is." He looked at Max again. His face was suddenly furrowed with anger and grief. "If you did do it," he said, "I wash my hands of you. I won't lift a finger to help you. There's no excuse for murder, none at all. You ought to know that better than most. God knows, you've seen enough of it, and so have I." Then he said, "Good luck. I hope you floor him. I hope he simply doesn't know what hit him."

At this Max laughed. "Thank you," he said, "I'll do my best."

*   *   *

Granier waited. His stomach was murdering him, and so was his wife. He had scarcely been able to eat any dinner, and this to Anni had been the final blow; as a result, Patricia, normally the most cheerful of babies, had howled herself scarlet in the face, and continued to howl for nearly an hour after she had been put to bed.

"You're just trying to pin it on him," said Anni. She was standing there, arms akimbo, like any nagging virago. "You must have a victim. What proof have you? He talked big. All right. Boys do."

"He talked murder. Oh, for God's sake," snapped Granier, "why don't you mind your own business? This is nothing to do with you. It's only that you happen to know the boy personally. If you didn't, you wouldn't care a rap if I were pinning on him every crime in the calendar.

And can't you stop that confounded child yelling? It's driving me nearly mad."

"You talk of your own daughter in that way—" Then she saw his face, and her own changed. She came up to him and wound her arm round his shoulders. "Oh, Jean, I'm sorry. I suppose you're quite right. Only it's all so dreadful. When you think of what he's suffered—"

He patted her cheek in an absent-minded way. He said, "You can't always make an excuse of past suffering. It's too easy. Anyway, I may be imagining things. I'll know better when I've seen him." He looked up at her and gave her a wry smile. "Don't you see that I'm fighting my own sentimentality as much as yours? Do you really imagine I'm enjoying this? Now go away, there's a good girl, and stop worrying. You really think me a monster, don't you?"

"Of course I don't. You know I don't."

"After all, you might have married the public executioner, and that would have been even more complicated. Incidentally—and I find this extremely depressing—the whole town, who always disliked Quiqueran when he was alive, are now talking about him as if he were a model citizen, and saying all this comes from letting the Jews in. There's no logic in any of us, and that goes for you and me."

"But that's ridiculous."

"Of course it's ridiculous. Go and make me some coffee. I shan't be in bed till the small hours."

*   *   *

When Max came, it was nearly midnight.

He paused in the doorway. Granier, who was sitting at his desk, raised his head to look at him. He was a little astonished at what he saw. His eyebrows momentarily met. He had expected defiance, derision, anger, or perhaps sheer exhaustion. But Max revealed none of these. There was instead a strange air of exaltation to him as if he, who had run the gamut of danger so many times in his brief life, were rejoicing in this renewal of the bitter past. It was as if he welcomed his familiar, the imminent death that had tapped him on the shoulder, thrust its bony jowl into his and called him brother. There were shadows under his eyes, but the eyes themselves shone, the mouth smiled, the body was tense with anticipation.

Granier thought, He did it all right. And he's convinced he's going to get away with it. He said pleasantly, "Sit down, Max. I've been trying to get you all evening. I'll be as brief as I can."

Max sat down. His eyes never left Granier's face. There was no fear in them. In the small house next to the Mairie, he had also been invited to sit down. They had been perfectly civil to him. At first. Later, it was different. Only then the fear had lain like a weight within him. But now he was not afraid, only his skin pricked in anticipation, his muscles tensed as if he were waiting for a physical attack. He said nothing, but he accepted the cigarette that Granier offered him. His eyes narrowed a little in the bright light of the long-armed lamp that stood on the desk. It was directed at his face. Granier behind it was half in shadow.

Granier said quietly, "You know, of course, why I want to see you. I thought it would be better to talk things over here than in the prefecture."

"More friendly," suggested Max.

"Possibly. Well now—You've been out a long time this evening."

"Yes."

"Where have you been?"

"With a girl."

"I should like to have her name."

"Oh, I couldn't do that," said Max.

"Why not?" demanded Granier. "Too much the gentleman?"

"Of course." And the ruined, beautiful face broke for a second into an enchanting and most ungentlemanly smile.

Granier chose to ignore the smile. He said, "It wouldn't involve her in any way. It would be helpful to both of us. Come on now, Max. You know perfectly well I'm not interested in your sexual morals. You can sleep with half the girls in Portelet-sur-Seine for all I care. I just want to know her name."

"I'm afraid you'll have to want, Inspector. I'm not telling you."

Granier said with the sudden, unexpected flash that had made him what he was—it had astonished a great many people, from his superiors to the criminals who came up against him—"You're treating me like a Nazi commandant, aren't you?"

Max acknowledged this silently, with a faint quiver of his lips. But for the first time a wary look came into his eyes.

"Well, I'm not," said Granier a little angrily. His plain, heavy face was grey with fatigue and the pain that dragged incessantly at his inside. "If I were, I might get a little further with you. I see no reason for you to be so obstructive. Except possibly one, which you will certainly deny. I'm not offering to beat you up. Look. Look, boy." He saw the corners of Max's mouth faintly sucked in, but preferred to make no comment. "Quiqueran's dead. You know that. Stabbed with a knife. Where's your knife, by the way?"

"I don't have one, sir."

"Don't you? You did. You used to boast of it. Where is it? In the Seine?"

"I just don't have one."

"Well, never mind for the moment. All right, then. Quiqueran, as I said, is dead. And you, as there are dozens to witness, have been plaguing the life out of him ever since you've been here. There's scarcely a day passed when you haven't threatened him, told him you'd do him in, waved a knife at him. You used to scare the pants off the poor chap. I suppose, on an average, I received from him two or three complaints a week. I ought to have run you in for it. You were behaving like a gangster. Only I never really took it seriously. I thought it was just talk. I thought you were just bullying him. And in my heart, I suppose I felt he deserved to be bullied. Well, it's no longer just talk. He's dead. You can hardly be surprised if my immediate reaction is to think of you. Can you?"

"No," said Max. He had lowered his eyes now. The cigarette drooped from the corners of his mouth. His hands were in his pockets.

"I'm not making any accusation, mind. I'm just giving you the chance to clear yourself before the matter becomes official. I want to ask you some questions, and I should like you to answer them civilly. There's no point in being smart with me. You're not, after all, that young devil, Jean-Louis. Now. Where were you yesterday evening? Don't be smart, Max. I warn you. It won't do you any good. I want a full answer. You can take your time. There's no hurry. I'm not trying to rush you."

Max replied in an even voice, "I came back from work. I had my supper. Then I went out for an hour. I came back again, and played chess with a *copain*. Then I went out again for a breather. That's all. After that, I went to bed."

Granier looked down at the notes he had made of the interview with Moishe. It all tallied. But of course that was to be expected. "Who was this friend of yours?"

"Moishe. Moishe Goldschmidt."

"He was in the camp with you, wasn't he?"

"He was." The cigarette moved briefly.

"I see. You weren't out with a girl?"

"I've just told you."

"Yes, I know. You're sure you weren't out with a girl?"

For the first time, Max showed a faint discomposure.

Under the harsh light the sweat on his upper lip was plain
to see. He did not answer.

"I asked you if you were sure you weren't out with a girl.
Don't be too gentlemanly, Max. Your girl wouldn't like
you to be guillotined on her account. You've had a great
many girls in your time. You're quite a little Don Juan,
aren't you? I've heard tales—But as I say, I'm not a
moralist. And the girls have never lodged any complaints.
I believe you were out with a girl. I want to know who that
girl is, and where you took her. Perhaps you took her to
the river? There's some nice, soft, green grass there. It
would be comfortable. Romantic, too. Moon and nightingales singing—That's where you were, isn't it? With a big
bunch of roses in your hand. I hope she liked the roses.
They looked very expensive to me."

He smiled as he spoke, and the smile—or perhaps it was
the barrage of words—drove the colour from Max's face.
The look on him was as dangerous and ugly as the knife he
had once claimed to carry. He said in a low, savage snarl, "In
a minute I'll smack that smile off your—face."

Granier said mildly, "You're getting a little out of control,
boy, aren't you? That's not the kind of thing you would
say to me normally."

The moment was past. Max was calm again. "No," he
said, almost apologetically. "No. I'm tired. That's all.
Sorry, sir. You can smile as much as you want to. Why
not?"

"Two nights out," suggested Granier, "might be a bit
exhausting. Same girl?"

"There was no girl," said Max. His voice was even and
composed. He added, with a little smile, "This takes me
back, you know. They put a lighted cigarette under my
finger-nails. That was before they beat me. Ah well. As old
Wolff would say, *Ou sont les neiges d'antan?*"

This time it was Granier who was disconcerted. A dull

flush came to his cheeks. He began furiously, "Are you suggesting that I—" He met the dark, derisive eyes. He swallowed. He said, "All right, all right. Well. You say you were out for an hour. You were carrying a bunch of roses. I saw you, if you remember. They were very beautiful. She's a lucky girl. You must think a great deal of her to buy her a present like that. I shouldn't be surprised to learn you were thinking of getting married."

Max said in a smooth, soft voice, "There was no girl, Monsieur Granier. I believe I've already said that." And now he raised his head. He was no longer smiling. All the guards were up. The Nazi commandant would have recognised that face. Behind the cold lack of expression was a vast and monumental resolution.

Granier saw it. He knew the battle was on. "Yes," he said, "you've already said that. And I put it to you that you're lying. I put it to you quite simply that a young man does not buy a big bunch of extremely expensive flowers for his own amusement. An old woman might. Women like flowers. If they have no man to buy them, they go out and buy them themselves. But not young men, Max. Not broke young men of nineteen. It's against nature. I don't like to call you a liar, but really, you're carrying this prevarication to the point of absurdity."

The sweat was out on Max's face again. But his voice was steady. He said, "You're forcing me to discuss my most private affairs."

"It's my job, boy."

"I'm not reproaching you for being a scavenger. All right, damn you. I bought those flowers to lay by the memorial. For my parents. It was the anniversary of the day when I had the last news of them. The day when, as far as I know, they died. They have no grave. They have no headstone. I do not even know where they lie. But they were my mother and father. I don't respect much. There's little to respect. I certainly don't respect a filthmonger like you. But—" his breath was coming in gasps—"I respect them. They were good and honest and decent, and all the things that don't matter. I bought the flowers for them. Are you satisfied now, or would you like me to take a hacksaw and carve out a piece of my guts, to show you they're real guts and not just sawdust?"

It was all of course what Moishe had said. There was a terrible sincerity and pain in Max's drawn face. Granier averted his eyes from it, and spoke what seemed to him the most shocking thing he had ever had to say. "I don't believe you," he said.

There was a long silence. The town of Portelet-sur-Seine was asleep. The little girls slept their innocent sleep, and the boys opposite slept also. The moonlight spilled on to the Place du Triangle, making it white and cold. Max's face, in the glare of the lamp, was pitted with shadows. Then, to Granier's dismay, he laughed. He said, "That's too bad. What are you going to do about it?"

Granier said in an exhausted voice, "I'm going to tell you what I believe happened, Max. I've nothing to say to your story. If you feel you can use your dead parents to back up the lie to save your skin, well, that's your affair. I suppose I shouldn't even be surprised. I am, a little. There's a trace of naïveté in us all. Like the vestigial tail. Never mind. There's no call for me of all people to be starry-eyed." He met, almost unwillingly, the vast eyes that stared stonily at him. There were no stars there; the depths were black and bottomless. He went on, "I think this is what happened. You bought your flowers and you set off to meet this girl by the river. I know you went that way, because there was a little affair at a café. You knocked over a table. The man remembered you. One of the Jew-boys, he said. You'll forgive me. I'm merely repeating his words. Then—" He paused expectantly, but Max was silent.

"That of course is the way to the war memorial. Is that what you were going to say?"

"I was going to say precisely nothing."

"All right. But I don't think you were going to the memorial. I think you were making your way to the river, and I believe that there you met your girl. What happened then is of course your own affair. I suppose you met her to discuss the weather. And then Quiqueran comes along. He was always over-inquisitive. He sees you, discussing the weather. It interests him. As one to whom the weather was no longer of much practical importance, it would interest him very much. He was that kind of person. And so he watches, and then, Max, then you raise your head and you see him. I think you lost your temper. Perhaps your girl was frightened. Perhaps Quiqueran said something he shouldn't. I don't know. But I think you leapt out at him. And in the struggle, perhaps by accident, your knife went into him. Those flick-knives are confoundedly dangerous. I'm not saying you meant to kill him. I'm not saying he didn't ask for it. I am merely suggesting that that is what happened. And afterwards—You're used to that kind of thing, aren't you, Max? You shoved him in the river. Your girl must have been rather upset. But I suppose you took it in your stride. It's not the first time you've killed, is it?"

Max, not answering this, said calmly, "As a point of interest, Inspector—purely as a point of interest. You tell me it's not the first time I've killed—"

"Then you admit it!"

"Oh, come off it. You know I bloody well do nothing of the kind." Max gave a brief, hard laugh. His eyes were shining. "You're too clever by half, aren't you? I not only don't admit it, I deny it categorically. There's not a word of truth in it. But you say I've already killed. O.K. So I have. I once killed a couple of Bosches. They were camp guards. The war was over. They once flogged a friend of mine to death. Everybody knew I'd killed them, and why. No one minded. In fact, they patted me on the head and told me I was a clever boy. And now you accuse me of murder and, if you prove your point, you'll send me to the guillotine. What's the difference? Is one belly sacrosanct, and the other not? When does execution end and murder begin?"

Granier said wearily, "I don't know, and I don't care."

"That's a fine confession for a policeman."

"You're being smart again, Max."

"I should have thought you would have found the dialectics of murder a most interesting subject."

"Not at this hour. Besides, there are no such dialectics. Don't chop words with me. What I want to know is why you were so stupid as to leave the roses on the bank. Did you lose your head as badly as all that? Or was it that your girl, unused to dialectics, got hysterical and had to be hurried away?"

A muscle flickered in Max's cheek. But he only said in a cool, detached voice, "I was not on the river bank. There was no girl. I didn't kill Quiqueran. The roses are lying in front of the war memorial."

"Quiqueran was stabbed in the stomach."

"It's as good a place as any."

"Or was it the heart? But you wouldn't know. Or care."

"True."

"In fact, like Jean-Louis, you simply say, *Je m'en fous.*"

"Like Jean-Louis, I say, *Je m'en fous.*"

"I might be able to make things easy for you, you know. I imagine there were extenuating circumstances. We all know what Quiqueran was. He was a poor, cowardly creature, and a dirty old man at that. And we all know what a bad time you've had. A good lawyer could bring tears to the eyes. You might get away with it. If you tell me the whole truth, and give me the name of the girl to back it up."

Max gave him a broad smile. He said, "I've had a terrible time, haven't I?"

Granier eyed him warily. He said nothing.

"I'm a poor persecuted Jew."

Granier sighed, and grimaced.

"Oppressed and downtrodden—"

"Go on," said Granier grimly.

"Brutalised and tortured. I am bound to be maladjusted, even psychopathic."

"I suppose this amuses you, but frankly it doesn't amuse me. What's the point of all this?"

"I was just making my lawyer's speech for him."

"And I," said Granier, "am going to speak for the other side." He rose to his feet. He was a big man, and for all his heavy, exhausted air he looked formidable. He said, "I'm not going to soften this. I've known you for a long time. I like you. So does Anni. She refuses to believe you could do anything wrong. But I know you rather better than she does—No. Listen to me. This time I'm going to say my say."

"Okay, okay," said Max. He leant back, tilting his chair. He lit himself another cigarette. His half-closed eyes were fixed on Granier's face.

"I know more about you than you imagine. You keep strange company, boy. There's a small matter of black market that crops up from time to time when you're short of cash. You've been seeing these men recently. There was an awkward little episode, a couple of days ago. In a café. Something to do with a knife—I think you've always done a bit of fiddling on the side, one way and another. I'll admit there's never been a charge of murder, but you have a tough, dangerous reputation, and they say you're handy with your knife. There's a dossier on you. Nothing much, but it tots up. The police are not quite such fools as you imagine. I tell you this, Max, and I tell it you without embroidery. I believe you killed Quiqueran. I may never prove it. I'll do my best, but in any case, these things take a long time. I grant you that I have nothing to hold you on. Yet. But from now on you're getting away with absolutely nothing. Nothing, nothing, nothing. Is that clear? You've sunk yourself, you've really done for yourself, this time. It makes no difference to my personal feelings for you, but my personal feelings make no difference, either. I like you neither more nor less, and I've no doubt you will continue to come for supper with Anni and the kid, as I've no doubt we'll continue to play chess—"

"And I'll continue to beat you."

"Maybe. I shouldn't bank on it. But take care. My eye will be on you, all the time. You claim to be maladjusted. All right, if you must use jargon. I'm a plain man, and I can only see things as they are—"

"Then you are a most remarkable man, Inspector."

"But you are not, Max. You believe you are. You're thinking even now—I can see it in your face—that you can diddle the old fool, and go on just as before. That's where you're mistaken. This is the beginning of the end. You're finished. Why don't you admit it, and get it over?"

Max's lashes lowered, the thick, curling lashes that shrouded the disillusioned eyes in innocence. A faint smile caught at his mouth where the cigarette drooped, casting a black shadow across his jaw. His face was calm. Only the top of the cigarette was a mess of wet tobacco, as if his teeth had met through it. He did not answer. One hand, hanging down, brushed against the rung of the chair.

"Why don't you admit it?"

Max shrugged, not troubling to speak.

"Is it for the girl you're lying? No one imagines she did it. Girls don't carry knives. We shall probably find out who she is, in any case. You shouldn't depend on her too much, even if she does love you."

"I depend on no one," said Max. He raised his eyes. "May I go now?"

"All right. I shall certainly want to see you again."

"I'll be around. Don't worry. I won't run away. When are you asking me round to supper, sir? Patricia will soon be needing another bath."

"You can come whenever you like."

"Thank you," said Max. He rose to his feet. His eyes flickered contemptuously over Granier's exhausted, dyspeptic face. He said, "You're all the same, aren't you? The whole bloody world's the same."

"There's no point in dramatising yourself."

"Why not? It amuses me."

He sauntered out. Granier, at the window, watched him crossing the Place du Triangle. He moved with an easy, swaggering grace. He might have been any young man returning after a date with his girl. But his shadow followed on stilts after him, long and black in the moonlight, and the face he wore, the face that Granier could no longer see, was not a gallant's face—it was a face of horror and shame such as had not been on him for seven long years.

He looked at the writing on the wall, but did not see it. *Juif, go home.* It would not have touched him. He was home. He was back where he had started, in his own place, and the disconnected sentences jostled in his shocked mind.

I didn't mean it. It's an insult, but you must try to forgive me. I don't know when you died, I only know you're dead, the dead, one's own dead, should be sacred. Do you think I don't know that? It's not that I've forgotten, or could ever forget, you're all I ever had, I couldn't make mock of you. If I never bought you flowers, it's because it's not my way. I've used you for a lie, but don't be angry, don't think it's because I don't care. I didn't mean it, *mamalo*, you know

I didn't mean it. You shall have your flowers, you shall have all the flowers you want, only you must not be angry with me—

"Ah God," said Max aloud, and he spoke in Yiddish, "I wish I were dead."

And he walked upstairs to his room. He did not think of the wine that M. Wolff had left for him. He lay down on his bed, still dressed. His arms were folded across his chest. Only his fingers moved as if soft, golden hair were spilling on the pillow, and so he lay without moving, until the dawn light touched his eyelids and at last closed them.

*   *   *

Deirdre spent the greater part of the day at her drawing-book. She looked so white that Miss Pelham again refused to let her work. "I'm going to get the doctor to look at you, tomorrow," she said.

"I'm all right."

"I don't think you are, my dear. I had so hoped that our little talk—Is anything worrying you? Has anyone said anything to upset you?"

"Oh no, Miss Pelham."

"Well, we'll see what the doctor has to say."

"I don't need a doctor," said Deirdre. The sickness within her made her utter these words in a shrill, hard voice. She looked in despair at Miss Pelham's kindly, well-made-up face. She did not know it, but she was feeling what Max had felt—the consciousness of being lost in an alien, uncomprehending world. She no longer thought of going home. It was not possible. Such sweetness and sanity were now utterly beyond her reach. She thought of Max, with longing and revulsion. The thought of never seeing him again was unendurable, yet her flesh crawled at the memory of that dreadful little house, where the unspeakable had happened, where people had anguished and died. She could not begin to understand her own feelings. The pitiless force of the love that beat upon her was more than her frail spirit could stand, yet she dreamt constantly of his arms around her, his mouth on hers, and her dream led her into unchartered realms where she sickened and rejoiced at her own thoughts.

The sense of wrongdoing lay within her like a stone. This was sin, this was shame, this was damnation. What would Mummy say? What would they think at home? But her body was not concerned with her conscience, and through this the irresistible excitement ran like a flame. Before her eyes swam that ravaged, beautiful face, and then she was lost indeed, astray in a world where there was not one familiar landmark to guide her.

Her pencil began frantically to scrawl down the things that appalled her, so that Max beat upon her vision. "I am dreadfully, dreadfully wicked," whispered Deirdre in her room, and the wickedness flowed from her fingers, so that its glory blinded her. Face after face covered the page— smiling, tender, angry—"*Garce*" he had called her—the fallen angel face, so beautiful, so ruined, so unlike anything that home had ever had to offer.

She did not think of Quiqueran. The one drawing of that dead, stupid face was at the beginning of the book. She never turned back to it, either in the pages or in her mind. It had to be forgotten. It was too terrible to remember.

So it was forgotten, as was the fact that, entirely on her account, Max was in the gravest of dangers. But then she had never thought much of other people, and now she was entirely absorbed in her own violent emotions. When the appointed time came, she crept down the stairs, quite unaware that she was observed, utterly unsuspecting that a small, inquisitive shadow stole after her.

*   *   *

Nora was growing more and more bored as the days

went by. She was, as Miss Pelham not unjustifiably termed her, a difficult girl. In experience far older than the others, she resented both the restrictions and the constant, tedious company of her own sex.

It was just after six, and she was supposed to be changing for dinner. She made no attempt to do so. She gazed instead at the Place, bright still with sunlight, and her stubborn, sensual little face set in lines of sullen rage. For God's sake, must she spend her days surrounded by these giggling little girls, forced to recite damn silly poetry, compelled to do boring things like cooking and curtseying, and driven to bed at an hour when all civilised people should be enjoying themselves.

She could not even bring herself to write a letter. She was untidily dressed. The tight skirt that she loved was put away in the wardrobe. It was indecent. It was not nice. It was not becoming. Nora in no way objected to its being the first two, and found the last criticism ridiculous. What was the point in having a figure if you did not display it? She wore slacks at this moment, and a loose shirt blouse. Her dark fringe was rumpled on her forehead, and a forbidden cigarette hung defiantly from her lips.

The bad girl of the Fifth, that's what I am, she thought, made a rude face, and leant out of the window. The boys opposite were coming back from work. There was the big German boy—what a mountain! He looked as strong as an ox, too. She eyed him up and down. But he was not her type. Too solid and too stolid. She preferred the red-haired one with the cheeky clown's face. He had slanting green eyes with thick, white lashes; those eyes were suddenly raised to hers, and the owner whistled impudently as he turned into the doorway.

Nora grinned at him. It did not matter to her if he were a Jew or not a Jew. He was a young man, and, from the air of him, a young man who knew his way around; he looked, too, as if he had a witty tongue in his head.

Then she saw Max, and immediately all thoughts of the red-haired boy left her. Impelled by a feeling so violent that she did not so much as think of Miss Pelham, she ran out of the room, down the stairs and into the street.

Max stared at her as she came out, a little breathless, into the Place. It had been a merciless day for him. He felt as if his sanity hung by a thread; he could only think of what he was going to say to Deirdre in a few hours' time, how he could best put before her the decision that would change both their lives.

He did not at first recognise Nora, for other images stood against his eyes. He looked at her without liking or interest, seeing a small, dark girl, plump, high-breasted, with what seemed to him a sluttish face and black, greedy eyes. When she said, in an odd, husky voice, "I want to talk to you," he merely noted her surprisingly good French, shrugged, and would, if it had been possible, have pushed past her.

But she blocked his way. She said again urgently, "I want to talk to you." Then she cried out, almost in a rage, "Oh, why don't you listen to me? Why are you always so rude? Are you so bloody stuck-up that you can't even answer a girl?"

He noticed that she swore easily, as if it came naturally to her. It displeased him. But he said nothing, only stared at her.

She said, "You were abominably rude to me, the other day, and I still don't know why." Her voice changed. A cajoling note crept into it. "Look. I'm bored to death. I'm shut up in this ghastly hole like a prisoner. I'm not supposed so much as to look at a boy. It's not natural or right. Do you think so? It's all right for these kids. They're only babies and they don't know any better. But I can't take it any more.

Won't you come out with me, one night? Couldn't we go dancing or something? I'll pay. I've got plenty of money. You see, I like you. I think we'd get on together. What do you say? I promise I won't look like this. I'll doll myself up for you. After all, the risk is mine, not yours. The old bitch'd kill me if she found out, but she won't find out, I'll see to that, and if she did, it would only mean sending me home, and believe me, I shouldn't cry my eyes out over that." Then she smiled at him. It was a delightful, wicked smile. It had never failed in its purpose yet. "My name's Nora. You're Max, aren't you? Well, Max? What about it? I don't suppose you usually have young women on their knees to you. Or do you? You're not going to be rude enough to refuse me, are you?"

He was startled. He gave a brief, astonished laugh. His eyes moved over her. She recognised them as experienced eyes, and she did not like this appraisal; when he spoke with a deliberate and derisive courtesy, she stiffened. He said, "I'm sorry, mademoiselle—"

"My name's Nora."

"Mademoiselle Nora—but I don't find this a very good idea. There'll be hell to pay if we're found out."

"Why should we be found out? Are you afraid?"

He hesitated. Then he said coolly, "I'm not a gigolo. When I take girls out, I pay for them. And I choose my girls."

She flushed scarlet. She had not expected this. But she managed, with an effort, to keep her temper. She was thinking that he was even more attractive than she had thought. His dark looks excited her, and the contempt in his voice excited her even more. She said, "All right. Why don't you choose me then? I think you and I have a lot in common, Max. I think you and I are the same sort." She added, meeting his measuring gaze with one as calculating as his own, "Perhaps it's not a very nice sort. Perhaps we're not very nice people. But at least we won't frighten each other, and I fancy we'd get on rather well. You can pay if you want to. I don't care. I'd rather you did. I just want to go out with you."

His mouth set suddenly. The hardening accentuated the gaunt lines of his cheekbones, so that his face grew cruel, like some Eastern image. His eyes were black with anger. Nora was never to know how she had hit home, and in so doing, destroyed the last chance of receiving either pity or mercy from him. He recognised the truth of what she said. She and he were the same sort, and they were not nice people either. The recklessness in her was his, so was the wantonness and defiance. This girl would not weep if he kissed her. If this girl lay on a grassy bank and put her arms around him, it would be because she knew what she wanted, and she would see, too, that she got what she wanted. His golden-haired little Deirdre did not understand the half of what he said, but this bitch would understand well enough. This girl had fought in her time, as he had fought; if he wanted her—and perhaps if he did not—she would sleep with him, that very evening. She was a whore, and he no longer wanted a whore; she had virtually told him that this was what he wanted, and he did not want it, he would never want it again. It was as if she were dragging him back into the darkness with this monstrous acceptance of their kinship; at that moment he could have murdered her.

He said in a voice so ugly that it shocked even himself, "Why don't you go back where you belong? I don't want you. I wouldn't have you as a gift." He added brutally, "I don't know what your dragon would say if she knew that one of her nice little English girls was soliciting. You'd better hop it, hadn't you, before the Inspector puts you in jug."

She made no attempt to keep her temper now. Her cheeks were flaming. "You bloody little swine," she shouted at him. "You filthy little Jew—How dare you speak to me like that?"

He shrugged with the utmost contempt. He did not trouble to answer. He pushed past her, and instantly forgot her. Afterwards he was to remember. He went into the Hostel, and up to his room to change.

Nora walked slowly into the College. She was shaking with rage, and crying with something that was neither anger nor affront. Max had maligned her. Her offer had been prompted by a genuine liking, and she could not understand why he had spoken so abominably to her. The lacerating words he had uttered seemed to her utterly undeserved. And so it was that she had neither the heart nor the spirit to go out, and at ten o'clock heard Deirdre's door open, and saw Deirdre stealing down the stairs.

Nora's eyes widened. For the moment she forgot her own humiliation. She could hardly believe this incredible thing. She had regarded Deirdre as the dumbest of the dumb, yet here she was again stealing down the stairs, obviously on her way to an assignation; this appeared to be a regular intrigue.

Nora took off her shoes and followed her. In the street she put on her shoes again, and crept after her quarry, careful to keep at a discreet distance. This was something after her own heart. She meant no malice. She was delighted. Her respect for Deirdre grew. She saw her turn down a little street off the Place, and halted at the corner, flattening herself against the wall peering covertly around.

And then she saw the person who was waiting, and she gave a little gasp. Her eyes, enormous now, saw Max take Deirdre in his arms. She registered mechanically the fact that the gesture was one of extreme intimacy. This was by no means their first meeting. A passion of jealousy, rage and disappointment swelled up in her.

She watched them slipping off down one of the side

streets. She dared not follow. Max frightened her very much; God knew what he would do to her if he found her spying on them; he might even kill her.

The shock was such that for a little while she could not move. The tears of mortification were spilling down her cheeks. At last, sobbing angrily, her face puckered like a child's, she walked blindly back to the College. She was completely absorbed by what she had seen; her emotions so devoured her that she did not even see Miss Pelham until the cool, cultured voice spoke to her.

"Where have you been, Nora?" said Miss Pelham.

Nora was usually fertile in excuses, but this final blow was too much for her. She blushed and stammered, no longer a young woman of the world, but a naughty school-girl caught out in some misdoing; as she stuttered a lame and ludicrous explanation, she saw Miss Pelham's eyes surveying her with a cold, detached criticism that reduced her first to incoherence and then to silence.

Miss Pelham said, "It is too late to discuss this now. Go up to bed, please, Nora. I want to see you first thing to-morrow morning." She added, " Good-night."

Bitch, thought Nora, bloody bitch—She repeated these words several times as she tramped upstairs. The whole beastly world was against her, and the thought of going home was not so enchanting in fact as it had been in theory, for her father would be furious with her and would probably cut her allowance.

She climbed sullenly into bed. She tried to remember that she was eighteen, and felt as if she were eight. As she lay there on the pillow, wondering what Miss Pelham would say to her, she began to think again of Max and Deirdre.

So he preferred that dumb little creature, did he? The tears were falling down her cheeks. No doubt he would tell her all about it, and they would laugh together. She raised herself up and began to pummel the pillow with her fists. Damn him, damn him, damn him—Other boys liked her. Other boys were pleased when she was nice to them. Other boys did not accuse her of soliciting—Well, if she couldn't have him, she'd see that no one else did. He wasn't going to speak to her like that and get away with it. He'd be very sorry by the time she was finished with him.

But none of this stilled the ache in her heart; not even the thought of vengeance could soothe her bitterly hurt feelings. And so at last she cried herself to sleep.

*   *   *

Deirdre paused for one second by the passageway. Max came instantly to her side and put his arms round her. He kissed her, then stepped a little back so that he could look at her face. He thought, Oh, God, how little and pale she is. Is this what I have done to her? We must get away. This is no place for us. And Deirdre, seeing his haggard face, thought, He looks dreadfully ill, it must be bad news, have they found out about me?

She let him kiss her again. His arms swooped round her, holding her so tightly that they seemed to press into her bones; his cheek, newly shaven, yet still a little rough, was against hers. She whispered on a sob, "Oh, Max—" and they clung to each other, their feet slipping in the violence of their embrace.

They began to walk away. They were utterly oblivious of the black-eyed watcher who followed their progress with bitterly resentful eyes. They walked very slowly. Max said at last, "I thought you wouldn't come. I was sure you wouldn't come. If you hadn't, I swear I'd have called for you. I'd have dragged you down the stairs—Listen, darling, I've been thinking. This can't go on. It's impossible for both of us."

"Yes, I know."

"I want you so badly. I can't take it any longer. You want me too, don't you?"

"Yes." But it was a faint, distant whisper, like the voices of the ghosts in that hideous house near the Mairie. They had said, Yes. They had said it because they could endure no more. Yes, yes, yes. Only stop, because I'm at breaking point—Yes. Yes. Yes.

If he sensed the weakness in her, he would not admit it, even to himself. He said, "Old Granier's sure I did it. He'll pin it on me if he can possibly manage it."

"He doesn't know about me?"

"No, no, you're all right." The hysteria in his voice changed to gentleness; in that gentleness there was a hint of the old mockery; the face that looked down into hers held a certain bitter amusement. But he went on, calmly, "I've told you. He'll never even consider you. I'm the obvious suspect after all. But he's going to tail me. He'll certainly find out about us. Deirdre. Will you come away with me?"

"Come away!"

"Yes. Tomorrow."

"But I-I can't—I—"

The roughness returned to his voice. "We love each other, don't we?"

"Yes—"

It was all slipping away from her, the green hills, the deep dark lake, the innocent little churches where St. Kevin had preached. And Rusty asking for walkies, and scones for tea, and little talks with Celia on the phone. "Deirdre? Is that you? I say, the most exciting thing's happened—" Daddy, writing about the war, the silly old war. Mummy, rather tiresome, treating her as if she were a little girl—"Really, Dee, you are so untidy"—yet understanding in the matter of new clothes, so anxious for her to meet the right young men. The smell of wood fires and furniture polish and clean linen hanging on the line. The wind blowing down from the hills, the soft Irish rain—

All going. All so soon to be gone.

"It must be tomorrow. What's the point in waiting? We'll be so happy. I'll be good to you. I swear I will. I'll look after you as you've never been looked after before. I've got some money. We'll take a train to Marseilles, and then take a boat. I've got it all planned. I'll get the tickets in Paris, in the morning—"

"But tomorrow's so soon—I haven't packed—"

"You don't have to pack. We can't take much with us. I'll buy you clothes. I'll buy you all the clothes you want. Think, sweetheart. Tomorrow night we'll be together, and to hell with Granier and your Miss Pelham and the whole bloody lot of them." Then he said in a surprised voice, with the old tinge of mockery, "I'm marrying you, you know. It'll be all right. Leave it all to me—"

She said nothing, and he stopped, pulling her back against the wall. He stared at her. Even in his moon-madness he knew it was not like this. And suddenly he knew, too, that if they went to that house, with its dreadful memories and sad, tortured ghosts, it would be the end for both of them. He said, "I'll tell you what. We'll go to a cinema. Would you like that?"

"Oh yes, Max!" She did not know, would never know, how the eagerness of her voice, so different from that last faint, unwilling agreement, hurt him. But then she said, falteringly, "Suppose someone sees us—"

"Who cares? Tomorrow we'll be away. I want to see you laugh again. I want you to be gay. There's a Charlot film on. A revival. It's bound to be good."

"Charlot?"

"Your Charlot. You must know him. He's English. He's a Jew, too."

"Oh, you mean Charlie Chaplin—"

"I don't know what you call him. It doesn't matter. Come on, darling. It will do us both good."

The film was "Shoulder Arms". It was long before their time. Deirdre had never even heard of it. They sat in the back row, very close together, and presently their hands stole out to meet and entwine. They looked gravely at the screen, and watched as Charlie proceeded to capture the entire German army, with the Kaiser thrown in as make-weight. Deirdre heard Max catch his breath, as Charlie's uplifted foot kicked down German after German—then suddenly he began to laugh as she had never heard him laugh. The laughter swept his years away, and the ghosts with them; he laughed so helplessly that he rolled on his seat, convulsed with a glorious, wholehearted amusement so contagious that Deirdre at last began to laugh, too. The Germans went down like ninepins before the sad, impudent little fellow who with an indifferent, backward kick sent pomposity a-rolling; the shades of Auschwitz were briefly avenged in this magnificent onslaught which seemed to reduce the *Wehrmacht* to the thing of nothing that it really was. In that moment she truly loved him with all her heart; when his arm came round her, she leant back against his shoulder; he tried to kiss her but they were both giggling so much that the kiss was nothing but a noisy splutter, and this made them laugh the more so that his body shook and heaved beneath hers.

It seemed to her then that to go away with Max would be a magnificent adventure. The grim memory of the house with its tortured ghosts was gone; she forgot everything but the sheer physical delight of his presence; she was obsessed with him, could not bear to move away, pushed her body against his as they walked back, insisting that he should kiss her every few steps of the way.

When he whispered, between kisses, "Will you meet me, tomorrow? Outside the Mairie, at seven? So that we can catch the seven thirty to St. Lazare?" she said, "Yes, yes, oh yes," and in that instant his dream was hers; they would lie on some hot, southern shore, with no more need for concealment, no more need for shame.

Only when they stood once more at the corner of the Place du Triangle did a strangeness come upon her that she could not understand; the fear fluttered within her again. To her drawing eye it was as if the shadow of that sick, diseased building were across him, as if the memory of pain and torture and death were sucking him in, a whirlpool that relentlessly swirled between them.

He kissed her once more, briefly, without passion. His eyes were fixed on hers. The laughter had long left them. She felt unbearably remote from him, and this prompted her to speak as she had never spoken.

She said, "Max, I do love you. I love you so much."

"Do you?" he said. His voice was quiet. His face was a little twisted.

"Oh, I do. Really, really."

He did not answer as she expected. He did not touch her. "*Tiens, tiens!*" he said, and a slow, bitter, ironic smile curved his mouth. Then he said, "I'll see you tomorrow," and the defiance rang in those words, a defiance that dared the world to do him down.

She did not know how to answer him. Suddenly she was filled with such unhappiness that she felt ill with it. She wanted to say again, "I love you," but the words would not come to her lips. Then the fear gripped her, for it was as if this were something that might never happen again, something that she was losing, something intolerably magnificent that was sliding remorselessly from her grasp.

"Good-bye, Max," she said.

He did not even answer. Perhaps he did not wish to speak the word, good-bye. He only shook his head. He stood there, gaunt and motionless, the fallen angel who was letting heaven go, and at last she turned and began, stumbling a little, to retrace her steps to the College. He still did not move; she looked back at him once, and for her, despite his immobility, it was he who was retreating, swimming away from her into the shadows. She held out her hands to him in a weak, useless fashion, then suddenly began to run, not stopping until she reached her room.

He stood there, head a little bowed. He lit himself a cigarette. There was no rejoicing in him, only a violent, bitter excitement as if once again he would pit his wits against the whole, vast, hostile, hating world. *Tu vas crever*, they had said. But he had remained alive—skin and bone, with the lice crawling over him, yet undefeated and alive. His eyes turned like a torch over the white walls of the College at the other side of the Place, flaring out its corners, lighting up that prim and alien fastness. She was there now, his girl, his love. Tomorrow she would be away, and he with her. Tomorrow—A dreadful, cold consciousness of defeat seeped into him, gripping him so that he could not move.

He spoke aloud. All his will to live, all his strength, all his purpose, was in those words. "You must come," he said. "You must. You will."

Chapter Nine

DEIRDRE saw Nora go down to Miss Pelham's study after breakfast. It did not interest her. She had no idea that Nora had her notebook with her, that she had removed it from Deirdre's room while she was taking her bath. She was feeling almost numbed. She could not even begin to think of what she had to do. She supposed faintly that she should leave a note for Miss Pelham, that she should at least write a line to her mother. But she did neither of these things, neither did she attempt to pack.

She stood there, staring out of the window. When one of the girls knocked on her door she had no premonition of disaster, for indeed disaster lodged within her, so that she could not think beyond it. A voice was sounding in her ears that said, *You must come, you will*, and she raised a bleak, white face to the child who stood in her doorway.

"Miss Pelham wants to see you."

Even then she did not realise what had happened. She automatically smoothed her hair—"I like my girls to be well groomed"—and tucked her blouse more neatly into her skirt. There was not the faintest apprehension within her, for all that had occurred between her and Max was so utterly remote from the world and the College that she could not conceive of Miss Pelham's having any part in it. She did not even feel curiosity. She came quietly down the stairs. She was a little surprised to see Nora, who looked as if she had been crying, standing on the ground floor, staring at her.

"Is anything wrong?" said Deirdre.

Nora gave her a desperate look of mingled anger and shame, then without a word walked into the lounge.

Deirdre forgot about her. She knocked at Miss Pelham's door and went in.

Miss Pelham, for a minute, looked at her without speaking. She had just received the shock of her professional career. There had of course always been crises. You could not hope to deal with young girls without crises. There had been scenes, hysteria, violent quarrels; once, a rejected suitor had tried to force his way in. There had even been a girl who drank too much. Miss Pelham had coped with all this, and more; she had coped with Nora, too, whom she had recognised as a difficult girl from the beginning.

She stared at Deirdre. There was honest bewilderment in her eyes. Even now she could hardly believe it. The notebook lay on her desk. She had only had time to glance at it, but Max had leapt up at her out of every page—his violent face expressing every emotion, from despair to rage, from irony to love.

She could not but see that the child looked most dreadfully ill. It was all utterly scandalous, and of course she must go, there was no question of her staying, she would ring up Mrs. O'Brien immediately—but never had a culprit looked less rejoicing; she had the air of one staggering under an intolerable burden; she seemed desolate and entirely defeated.

But who would have believed it? If it had been Nora now. She could have believed anything of Nora. But Nora, though she deserved and had indeed received a severe scolding, had really done nothing, while this dumb little beauty who said nothing but, Yes, Miss Pelham, No, Miss Pelham, had achieved the doubtful glory of behaving as none of her girls had behaved before.

To indulge in secret meetings at night, with, of all people, that appalling Jewish boy who was now suspected of murder, who was notoriously of bad character, who was so plainly the type of young man no nice girl would want to be seen with—

She raised her eyes to Deirdre's. She saw there such hopelessness, such an infinite desolation, that the angry words dissolved, unspoken. She said, firmly but kindly, "I know all about it, Deirdre. I know that you have been meeting this boy, Max. You have behaved very badly, and I am afraid there is no alternative for me but to send you home. I shall be ringing your mother in a few minutes, but I don't want this to be a scene of recrimination. I feel that I myself am very much to blame. I have obviously not understood, and I want to understand, I want to help you. My dear, I should like you to sit down and tell me quite calmly exactly what has been happening, and why you have behaved in this dreadful and inexplicable fashion."

The colour rushed into Deirdre's wan face. She flung out her hands and swayed; if Miss Pelham had not caught her arm and pushed her on to the nearest chair, she would have fallen. Then she burst into uncontrollable crying, sobbing wildly and convulsively, the tears flooding down her face.

Miss Pelham had behaved with unusual restraint and common sense. She was an intelligent woman, but she was never to know that these tears were provoked by neither fear, shame nor remorse. They sprang from sheer, overwhelming relief. There was no longer the frightful burden of severance and enforced decision. There was no longer the appalling tug on her emotions. There was no longer the battering of Max's urgent and demanding love. Later, much later, there would be the awareness of an irreparable loss, the return of a longing that could never again be satisfied. But that was later. Now, simply, it was all over.

The grass was green again, and there would be scones for tea.

*　　　*　　　*

Inspector Granier saw with some astonishment that Miss Pelham was standing outside the Hostel's front door. Normally, this would have made him smile, only at the moment, what with overwork, the pain in his stomach, and general emotional disturbance, he was past smiling at anything. He had actually been looking at the chalked writing on the wall; he wondered why M. Wolff had left it there, and decided he must get it rubbed off. Perhaps, because he was concentrating on this, and wondering unhappily why human beings must always persecute someone, he allowed his powers of intuition, normally high, to let him down. He found the incident strange, but without particular significance. He assumed, correctly enough, that the *Anglaise* was lodging a complaint. Probably Jean-Louis "that infernal little boy," he had said to a colleague, "with more original sin in his little finger than you'd find in the whole nineteenth arrondissement"—had been making a nuisance of himself, or maybe one of the older boys had spoken rudely to the girls.

It never entered his head that Miss Pelham's upright figure in its superbly tailored black suit, contained not so much shocked propriety as a piece of information which could have shuffled into place the jagged jigsaw pieces that so obdurately refused to fit.

He forgot about Miss Pelham and walked on. He had added nothing to his knowledge so far except the certainty that everybody was lying, even Madame Dupont of the Café Niçoise, who admitted that Max often came there, but never brought a girl with him. So he plodded crossly on, trying to pretend that he felt no relief; in his mind was a surrealist confusion of roses and flick-knives and grave, young lying faces.

*   *   *

M. Wolff at once rose to his feet when Miss Pelham came

in. He thought ironically that this two-way passage between the institutions was becoming positively excessive. First he must cross the sacred virgin threshold, and now the lady was braving her way into the jungle. He nearly asked her if she were leaving her cards. But the irony was instantly submerged in apprehension; only something disastrous could provoke such a visit, and already disaster was far too near.

Miss Pelham began her story after the most perfunctory words of greeting. It was a measure of her extreme distress that etiquette for once went by the board.

He listened, head bowed. The kappel was as usual rakishly askew on his half-bald head. Occasionally he glanced from under his bushy brows at this English lady who sat there so upright on the hard-backed chair, her gloved hands—who but an Englishwoman would have remembered her gloves in such a crisis?—clasped in her lap, the tight-gripping fingers betraying her agitation.

"It is quite outrageous," she said. "It—Frankly I cannot understand how it could ever have happened. I have no doubt that you consider it is all the girl's fault, but if you are going to tell me she would encourage a young man of that—of that sort, I can only say you are wickedly mistaken. If it had been—But never mind. I've always thought her a rather simple girl—"

"No girls are simple," said M. Wolff. These were his first words, but they were instantly drowned in a furious deluge from Miss Pelham, who was by this time so upset that she was indulging in positively foreign vituperation. She was after all a kindhearted woman. She had meant to speak to Deirdre with the utmost sternness, but her scolding tongue had faltered before the white face and frantic sobbing, and now she felt that she had to take it out of someone. Mr. Wolff was at least an opponent worthy of her steel, all the more so because she could not bring herself to be harsh to this really extremely naughty little girl.

"What did you do?" she asked Deirdre, for like Max she did not believe that young men arranged to meet young women at nights solely to discuss the world's politics. She added, with a rather grim desperation, "I'll try not to reproach you, but you must tell me. How far has this disgraceful affair gone? I can only pray that you have not done anything really wrong." And Deirdre had cried out incoherently, "Oh, I have, I have," at which Miss Pelham, aghast, had shed all her gentility and demanded in basic English, "Have you slept with this boy?" "Of course not!" Deirdre wailed, and after this there had been such general confusion that Miss Pelham had for the first time in her life wished to seize hold of *sancta simplicitas* and shake some sense into its charming golden head. And now, with savage gusto, she turned all the indignation that should have been expended on this shocking and heartbreaking child on M. Wolff.

His face was impassive. He had learnt impassivity in a hard school, and could, if necessary, reduce his naturally mobile features to a mask. Behind that mask, anger, horror and sick apprehension were writhing like serpents. He could only pray—Oh, God, how he prayed—that this remarkably silly woman was not doing the same addition sum as himself. He, too, was kindhearted, but he recognised, as she did not, how regionalised his kindness was. For the reputation of her College she would gladly throw Max to the wolves; he, with a certain sick disgust at himself, knew that he would gladly break this pretty little idiot's neck if it would save his boy from the guillotine. But none of this showed in his face. He listened to the angry words, while his mind trundled feverishly along its own unhappy, tortuous path.

"Her trouble is that she's too innocent," cried Miss

Pelham. "This young man of yours, Max—I don't know his other name—"

"Wrzonski. Max Wrzonski."

"Well, it really doesn't matter. You must admit that he's a boy of bad character. He has already been in trouble with the police, and now I understand he may be facing a murder charge—"

I wish, thought M. Wolff quite simply, that God would strike her dead and her precious innocent with her. Then, for he was a deeply religious man, he was appalled by himself; for the first time the mask began to crack.

"Naturally she would have no defences against such a type. I saw him, if you remember. How you could even send anyone like that into my College, I shall never understand—I was most unfavourably impressed by my first sight of him. There was a kind of—kind of gutter impudence to him, coupled with those flashy good looks of his. She can't ever have met anyone like that in her life. She's an extremely well-bred child from an excellent family. Her mother's mother was Lady—" She met M. Wolff's eye, and the colour roared unbecomingly into her face. She rushed on in a brittle voice that was dangerously near a sob, "She has led a most secluded life. I've no doubt that your boy turned on all the charm, and of course she would find it romantic and exciting. Oh, I'm not entirely excusing her behaviour, and—and of course, I have no choice, I have had to ask her mother to take her home. Her mother is flying over to-night. By tomorrow she will be gone. It is quite obvious, for all our sakes, that she cannot stay here. But she did not realise what she was doing, and your boy realised only too well. Do you know, they were planning to run away together? Can you imagine what would have happened to my school?"

She broke off. It was as if that abominable old man were forcing her to say all the wrong things. She stumbled ungracefully to her feet, and walked across to the window.

For a while she did not speak, and neither did he. When at last she continued, it was with her back turned to him.

"I must ask you," said the brittle voice, with the emotion sparking and snapping behind it, "to keep a little more check on your young men, in future. As for this boy, Max, the treatment he deserves is a good thrashing. You will of course send him away, immediately—"

"No," said M. Wolff.

"What!" She swung round. The unbecoming colour was still high in her face. "Do you mean to tell me—"

"Madame," said M. Wolff. He, too, rose to his feet. He was shorter than she was, but the look on him made her fall silent. He said grimly, his eyes condemning her, "I do not send my boys away when they are in trouble. Max will stay here, as long as he pleases. Can't you understand anything? He'll hate it, poor devil, but he must stay. There is nowhere else for him to go. And may I add that I have never understood—I never will understand—why a good thrashing is considered a panacea. Apart from the purely personal factor that I have a dislike of physical violence, and know also that the person who tries to administer a thrashing to Max wouldn't have a very agreeable time of it—"

"You admit he's a gangster then!"

"If he's a gangster, madame, it is because the world has made him one. In the same way, I might add that if your girl is a confounded nitwit, it is because her world and your school have made her one—"

"Really, M. Wolff—"

"Do you deny she's a nitwit? Of course she is. There's more trouble caused by keeping the young in ignorance than by anything else. Though I think she was a fool to begin with—I by no means absolve this young lady from responsibility, though, unlike yourself, I do not wish to indulge in recrimination. To return to Max—I know him a great deal better than you do, but never mind that. The trouble with him, as you might see if you'd care to think about it, is that he's been thrashed far too much and far too often. But if you're so set on violence, why don't you thrash your young woman? I'm beginning to think it might do her a great deal of good. On the other hand, of course, it mightn't."

Miss Pelham said in a suffocated voice, "If this is meant to be humorous, M. Wolff, I can only say that I do not appreciate it."

He gave a half-laugh. "I didn't think you would. Well, I suppose there is no point in our blackguarding each other. How far has this business gone? Is your young woman likely to have a baby?"

"Certainly not. There's been nothing like that, nothing at all."

His eyebrows shot up. "You surprise me very much. I shouldn't have thought a gangster like Max would have been so overburdened with scruples. I cannot believe she would have put up much opposition." He added, with a twist of his lips, "I have no doubt you bring them up in the gooseberry bush tradition."

Miss Pelham said, with a desperate urge to fairness, and the utmost unwillingness, "She tells me that he asked her to marry him."

"Good God!" said M. Wolff. He was silent for a moment. Then he said, "And where did they meet, these poor, silly little idiots?"

"Oh, in a most shocking place. That house by the Mairie. The Nazi headquarters—"

He stared at her.

"Apparently—apparently, it was the only place where they could be sure to be undisturbed."

"Good God!" said M. Wolff again.

"I think they only met three times. One of my girls saw them. I don't approve of tale-bearing, and this particular girl, I'm afraid, is of a difficult temperament, but I am only thankful that I knew about it in time. They were going to run away tonight. To Marseilles—Can you imagine," cried Miss Pelham, "what I should have had to say to her mother?"

"I can indeed," said M. Wolff dryly. "You seem to have some very strange characters in your convent, my dear Miss Pelham. Well—This is all very distressing." His eyes for a second veiled themselves. "I suppose I had better report this at once to Inspector Granier, in case any more of your young aristocrats decide to take the night air with my gangsters. It would mean that we could stop any more nonsense at the very beginning."

"Inspector Granier!" Miss Pelham, in her excitement, came up to him. He could smell the perfume she wore. It was a very expensive one. It seemed to him strange that a woman so well dressed and so elegantly scented should be quite devoid of attraction. She said, her voice thin, "You're surely not going to tell this to the police?"

The fervent prayer of thankfulness that went up from M. Wolff's heart at that moment was such that it seemed like an angelic choir singing. But the look in his eyes was not angelic. She was not going to be let off so lightly. She called his boys gangsters, did she. All right. All right. His mouth twitched. He said, in the same dry voice, "But of course."

"But—"

"My dear lady, I have to think of my own reputation, and the reputation of my Hostel." Then he came grimly in to the attack. "This is all very fine, madame. I consider that I have listened to you with the most remarkable patience. You tell me, at some length, that one of my wicked boys has seduced—*en principe*—one of your innocent little girls.

233

But these things are not entirely one-sided, you know. Seduction is a two-way traffic. If you'll pardon the misquotation, there is one who seduces and one who lets herself be seduced. You are, not unnaturally, thinking of this entirely from your own point of view, but I think you should consider mine. I have always regarded your young English misses as a potential danger. Do you imagine I wish my Jewish boys to get entangled with your girls, for all the dear children are so impeccably well-bred and so irredeemably stupid—"

"M. Wolff, I—"

"They are Christian girls, madame. I am not, I hope," said M. Wolff, "a prejudiced man. Some of my best friends are Christians. It is, however, entirely unsuitable that there should be any intercourse—you will understand that I use the word in its most general sense—between them. My boys may or may not be gangsters, but they are still boys, and no amount of thrashing will make them any less susceptible to the charms of your well-washed, virtue-inoculated angels. Especially as some of the angels appear to be temperamentally a little unstable. Oh, there's no question of it. This must never happen again. I shall go and see Granier now."

"M. Wolff!" Her tone was positively imploring.

"Perhaps you'd like to come with me?" he said, thinking, That'll teach you, my girl, that'll teach you to call my boys gangsters and tell me I ought to thrash them.

"No, of course not. I must ask you," cried Miss Pelham desperately, "not to go to the police."

"Why not? I should have thought, for your own sake—"

"But can't you see—The publicity—It would mean endless questioning. It would be all over the town. The other girls would be bound to hear about it, and they would write at once to their parents. It would be the end of my College."

"Well, after all, it is a finishing school—" Then he relented. "Very well. If you say so. Though I must say, you surprise me. Only I think you'll agree that it's up to both of us to keep a sharp look-out, in future."

"Oh, I will, I assure you," said Miss Pelham.

He said, "So you're sending the young lady back to her mama?"

"What else can I do? It's not so much discipline as the fact that I daren't keep her here. Especially as you tell me you're not sending the boy away. This might happen again. You can't imagine I would ever have a moment's peace, with only the street between them. And you can't pretend he's a boy likely to be bothered with scruples."

"Oddly enough," said M. Wolff, "I might pretend just that. It surprises me a little, too."

"Well, perhaps—But I'm sure he'd pursue her."

"Very likely."

"And you must admit he's behaved disgracefully. I hope at least you're going to speak to him about it."

"No." He met her affronted face, and sighed. "Miss Pelham," he said, "you after all are a woman of the world. What good do you imagine it would do? He is, I'm afraid, going to be very unhappy."

"Unhappy!"

"Oh yes. Even gangsters have feelings. Max has never been devoid of them. He is not quite as wicked as you imagine. You'll be horrified, no doubt, if I say that he is really a good boy, with a good heart. But I don't expect you to believe that. It doesn't matter." Then he said with difficulty, as if the words hurt him, "And what, when you come to think of it, am I to accuse him of? What crime have they committed, our little boy and girl? Oh, I know it's very dreadful. It's disgraceful. They have presumed to act against their own upbringing. They have fallen in love with each other. It's shocking. Of course it is. But what the devil would you have me say to Max? 'How dare you fall in love'? My dear good lady, frankly I haven't the nerve. I run a Hostel, not a court of morals. And what's the point? Tell me that. Does it really matter any more? When is she going, your little blasphemer?"

"I told you. Tomorrow."

"So tomorrow it will be all over. There's nothing more that Max can do about it. I cannot see that any words of mine will improve the situation. Tomorrow, life will go on as usual. Your girls will promenade in their crocodile, and my boys will go to work. You and I will bow politely to each other from opposite corners of the Place du Triangle, while M. Granier goes about his business. This will never happen again. Mademoiselle Deirdre will marry some nice, English boy, from an impeccably correct background, and Max—"

"He'll probably end up in prison." Then the mean, spiteful sound of her own words shocked her, and she cried out impulsively, "Oh, I'm sorry. I'm very upset. I didn't mean to say that. I suppose, with his background, he really can't help it."

"Well, well," said M. Wolff, giving her a faint, wintry smile, "this is a day of concessions, is it not?" He opened the door for her. "You know," he said, "I think that all people who live in an institution tend to get things out of proportion. We are treating this as high tragedy—and perhaps it is for Max and Deirdre—but as far as we are concerned, we shall all go on precisely as before, and in a year's time we'll have forgotten all about it. Your girl may dampen a dozen pillows or so, and Max—There, of course, I do not know. But really, we're making a great fuss over nothing. Or don't you think so?"

"I certainly don't," said Miss Pelham. But she spoke with less that her usual assertiveness. She added, almost pleadingly, "You won't go to the police, will you?"

He said solemnly, "Inspector Granier shall know nothing about this." And, when she had set off down the path, he added to himself, Please God, please God, please God!

*　　　*　　　*

Max rang the bell at Rosedene College the next morning at nine o'clock. He stood there, waiting for the maid to answer. He was shivering as if with the ague. He was unwashed and unshaven. He had eaten nothing for nearly twelve hours.

He had not been home. He had spent the night wandering about the town, returning at regular intervals to the Mairie. He had waited till midnight in the little house next to it, standing up against the barred window so that he had a clear view of the street. He knew almost at once that she was not coming, yet he could not bear to believe it, he could not bear to go. And so he had stayed, with the ghosts for company, and a despair and rage within him so monumental that he believed he was going mad.

He talked aloud to himself. There was no one to listen, except the ghosts, and they no longer cared. They watched impassively this wild young man who had once, in this very room, received a whip across his back, and who was now receiving something infinitely worse.

He talked to Deirdre. He talked to Chaja. He talked to his parents. The bitter words were churned out of him. From time to time he struck his breast as if the pain were something he could not endure. He stamped across the floor, the thud of his footsteps like that of the *braunen Bataillonen*; he beat his hands until they bled against the sweating, stone walls. And all the while his voice soared up in an hysteria of passion and grief, for he knew this was the end, yet he would not, could not, accept it, he had never accepted anything, neither torture, nor desolation nor death.

Tu vas crever, they had said.

And now he felt as if he were dying indeed. The four walls were his cage, and around him nothing but sick evil memories; the weakness surging up in him corroded his spirit, so that it seemed to him as if he at last knew annihilation.

He looked now at the door of the College, and briefly closed his eyes. He had never in his life asked for mercy from anyone. The beatings, the kicks, the cold, the starvation, all that he had taken, and he had taken it without a word. But now he stood a supplicant; he asked in a voice that cracked if he could speak to Mademoiselle O'Brien.

He was left standing in the hall; a few minutes later he was ushered into Miss Pelham's study.

She had been prepared to speak her mind. This after all was the monstrous young man who had done his best to ruin her pupil, and ruin her school. This was the young gangster who had deliberately set out to seduce one of her girls. M. Wolff might have scruples about speaking to him, but she certainly would have none.

But she looked at him now as he came in, and it was no monster that she saw, nor was it a gangster. Here was a young boy, plainly half-dead with exhaustion and grief; he was shaking from head to foot, and his face was like that of a corpse, with eyes sunken back, and great, dark lines running from nose to mouth. It was not in her to be proof against such despair; her sentimental heart was touched, despite herself, and the look in the dark eyes raised to hers, startingly pricked the tears into her own.

She was sitting at her desk. She would not have admitted this to a soul, but the thought of Max at bay had frightened her, and the desk was a comforting symbol of authority. Even now, she automatically put out a hand to the great bowl of roses in front of her, as if their beauty would sustain her. But, for once, neither the authority nor the beauty helped her—both in the presence of this battered young outlaw, who looked as if he had not slept for a week, seemed to shrivel; for all his slightness, he dwarfed both her and the room.

She said, "Won't you sit down?"

He replied uncompromisingly, "No." He might be exhausted, but the defiance in his voice revealed that he was not yet beaten. He said, "I would like to see Miss Deirdre."

"I'm afraid that's not possible," said Miss Pelham.

"Why not?"

He was speaking to her as if she were a servant—She flushed a little, and rose to her feet. She said, "Deirdre has gone home." Then, "I know all about it, Max. She told me yesterday morning. I don't propose to waste time in useless reproaches, and I quite understand that you are very unhappy, but you must realise it was a dreadful and shocking thing to do. After all—"

He interrupted her in a harsh voice, "When is she going?"

"My dear boy, I've told you. She's already gone. Her mother—"

"That's a damned lie!"

This was too much. Nobody had spoken so to Miss Pelham in her life. Her sentimentality was swallowed up in anger. She said, "Don't be so impertinent, please. I tell you she has gone. It is your own doing. It was obvious that in the circumstances she could not stay here. And I think you should be bitterly ashamed of yourself. What you have done was most dreadfully wrong. To behave so with a young, innocent girl. She's never been away from home before. I should have thought that even you would have had the decency to control yourself. Why, think what you would have felt if your own sister—"

He was gone. He did not even trouble to answer her. The door slammed behind him with such violence that the curtains blew out from the windows. Only the look he gave her made her gasp, as if he had spat at her. She stood there, breathing quickly. Thank heavens the girl was off the premises. If he had come a few minutes earlier—He was obviously extremely dangerous. He might even carry a gun. She would put nothing past him. She glanced at her wrist-watch. The train left in twenty minutes. She wished now that she had kept Max, but he was already out of sight.

The thought of what might have happened made her feel a little sick. She sat down suddenly and, as she did so, her eyes lighted on the notebook which Nora had handed to her. It was the book she had given Deirdre for her diary. Half mechanically she began to turn over the pages.

*   *   *

Max walked round to the back garden, with the faint hope that Deirdre might be there, waiting for him. He would not have noticed Nora at all, if she had not so plainly wished to avoid him. The flurry of footsteps aroused his attention. He swung round on the well-kept lawn to see her terrified eyes, the hands flung out. Then suddenly, with the intuition of exhaustion and misery, he understood what had happened.

He sprang upon her and, as she tried to run from him, knocked her back against the wall. A shower of rose petals fell about them from a climbing bush, but neither noticed. She opened her mouth to scream, and he clapped his hand over it.

On the other side of the house, Miss Pelham was staring at Deirdre's drawings.

He said in a savage whisper, "You little bitch! So it's you who informed on us, is it? I remember you like wandering at night. Well? If you raise your voice, I'll kill you. I mean that. Well? You're the spy, aren't you?"

He removed his hand a little so that she could speak. But he remained standing against her, his fierce face a couple of inches from hers.

. She stared wildly around, showing the whites of her eyes. She stammered, "I d-didn't—"

He swung his hand out and smacked her hard across the cheek. "You bloody little liar!" he said.

She gasped, "I tell you I didn't—How dare you—"

He smacked her again, then shot out his hands to her throat, gripping it so that she could hardly breathe. He whispered, his breath hot on her face, "You said we were the same sort, mademoiselle. Do you remember? Well, if that's the case, you'll know I mean what I say. If you don't tell me where she is, I'll throttle you. And I am not being funny. I don't care what happens to me any longer, but I'll damn well see that you don't get away with it." And he began to shake her until she grew purple in the face. "You little bitch," he said, "you little whore. I've met your kind before. You'd sleep with anyone for a centime, and you'd betray half the world for less. You're the kind who went around with the Bosches. We used to shave their heads afterwards. If I'd a razor handy, I'd shave yours—Where is she? You'd better answer. You haven't got so long to make up your mind—You disgusting little slut—"

And still gripping her with the one hand, with the other he slapped her again and again, for he was raw with rage and grief, and no longer knew what he was doing. Nora, nearly out of her mind with terror, was only held upright by the strangling fingers at her throat. Her head twisted sideways to avoid the cruel rain of blows, she muttered in a hoarse, choked whisper, "She's at the station—You're too late—"

He released her so suddenly that she fell in a heap at his feet, her head cracking against the wall. He looked at her for one second. He said through his teeth, "If you tell Miss Pelham about this, I'll shave off all your pretty hair. And if you don't think I mean that, you're a bloodier fool than I take you for."

Then he whirled round and was off at such speed that the wind of his passing blew against her face.

She was sobbing with fear and anger and pain. She put her hands to her burning throat. She whispered savagely after him, "You're too late—I'm glad, I'm glad!—"

*   *   *

But he was not too late.

He ran down the street with bursting lungs and, as he pelted up the incline that led to the station, he heard the Paris train coming in.

He leapt on to the platform, shoving the ticket collector aside. He stood there, gasping so violently that it was as if his chest would snap asunder. His head was whirling; for a second he could see nothing but a grey mist, with the vast white letters of Portelet-sur-Seine jerking up and down before him. The sweat was pouring off him; his mouth was open as he gulped in the air.

Then he saw her.

She must have been waiting on the platform. She was walking towards the train which had now halted. An older woman was at her side. He knew it must be her mother. There was a strange, almost dismaying, resemblance between them. There was the same golden hair, only it was faded. There were the same features, only they were pinched and old. Deirdre's mother wore a blue-and-white floral silk, with a sensible edge-to-edge coat. The wide-brimmed hat was a white straw. She moved with a no-nonsense air to her, and Portelet's one porter followed, grumbling, behind, with a vast crate of luggage.

Max's desperate, burning eyes were now fixed on Deirdre. She walked behind her mother. She moved with her slow, indolent grace; her head was a little bowed. The golden hair that had entwined with his alien fingers blew back in the summer breeze. The soft line of cheek and throat—all he could see of her face—was so beautiful that it made him want to die. The shoulders that had borne the weight of his arms were a little huddled, as if she were cold.

He wanted to spring towards her. He wanted to seize hold of her, twist her round to face him. Never mind her mother. Never mind Miss Pelham. Never mind the whole damned world. *Darling. Come back with me. Don't be afraid. You want me as much as I want you. I know I frightened you. Forgive me, I didn't mean it. I love you so much, I can't exist without you. Come with me. You can't leave me like this. Come with me, oh come with me—*

But he did not move. He was silent. The colour slowly retreated from his face. There was a lump in his throat that was choking him. This was everything. This was Chaja saying good-bye. This was the last glimpse of his mother's face. This was the death of his friends, one by one. This was the final stroke of the lash, the last screw of the rack. The pain ripped the skin from him, turned in his guts like steel, flung him into the ultimate abyss.

And he could not say a word. He could not say one word. And the world was ending, and nobody knew or cared, and he was alone. He could only stare.

She knew he was there. She could not but be aware of those vast eyes fixed upon her. He saw her body shudder, come to a sudden standstill. He saw her head begin to turn with a hypnotised, reluctant slowness.

Then her mother spoke. Her voice, her clear English voice, rang in Max's ears like a bell. "Oh Dee, dear," she said, "do come on. What are you loitering there for? Do you want to miss your train?"

Deirdre's shoulders stiffened. Then without a word she stepped forward and climbed into the train.

He had a last glimpse of the long, slender legs as she mounted the high step, saw the last flutter of her skirt, saw her hand come out to shut the carriage door.

The whistle blew. The train began to grind out of the station. In a few hours' time she would be at Le Bourget.

I hate it when you go up, and somehow your inside is left behind.

That is what she had said, only a few days ago. For him there seemed to be nothing left, only a great, hollow emptiness. He raised a face so white and haggard that it was unrecognisable. The weak fury flooded through him. He whispered, *"Salope! Garce! Putain!"* And then the sobs began to bubble up in his throat, so that his breath whistled and sang with them—obscene, high-pitched, whimpering sounds that shamed his manhood, only his manhood was gone, it had gone up, and only a shell was left behind.

He flung his hands up to his face. He did not see that people on the platform were looking curiously at him. He did not hear a shrill voice calling out his name. He stood there, head bowed and hidden. Behind the hands was a monstrous upheaval, a convulsion and a tearing and a rending; the choking sounds emerged as if the framework of his body were cracking asunder. He had once said his tears were done. They were not done. It was as if they never would be, never, never again.

"Maxy! *Qu'est-ce-que tu as? T'es schické?"*

The hands came slowly down, the slender brown hands, elegant hands despite the cracked and black-rimmed nails. The face revealed was a mask, smooth, smiling, expressionless. The cheeks were wet, the thick lashes soaked, yet it was impossible to believe that tears could spring from those hard eyes.

"Who do you think you're talking to?" he said, his voice as hard as his eyes. "Drunk, indeed! You impudent little so-and-so." And he swung Jean-Louis, gaping up at him, round, and slapped his bottom, not very seriously. "You learn to respect your elders and betters," he said, then grinned as the little boy tried to hit him back with flailing fists. "That's enough," he said, warding off the blows,

"That'll do, now. What are you doing here, anyway? You ought to be in school."

Jean-Louis stared at him in silence. His eyes roved over Max's face. Then his lashes flickered down. He made no further protest. He did not point out, as he well might have done, that Max should be at work. Instead he stretched out a dirty little hand and caught hold of Max's unwilling fingers.

"What's all this?" demanded Max roughly, his eyebrows shooting up.

Jean-Louis did not release him; indeed, he tightened his grip. He said in a subdued voice, "There was a phone call for you, yesterday. You didn't come back last night."

"Well? Is that anything to do with you?" Max jerked his hand away, and shoved it into his pocket.

"No, Max. But it seemed very urgent. The man said you were to ring him today. He said you'd know what it was about. It was Jacques again."

"Oh. All right." Max turned his head, blinking a little in the sunlight. He began to saunter towards the exit, Jean-Louis tailing behind him. He looked round. "All right," he said, "you've delivered your message. I'll ring. You'd better go off to school."

"Yes, Maxy." But Jean-Louis still hesitated, his eyes always on Max's face.

"I said you'd better go off to school. What's the matter?"

"Nothing, Max."

"Then be off with you."

"Yes, Max."

Max began to imitate him. "Nothing, Max, yes, Max—Look. I told you to be off, didn't I? If you don't do what you're told—"

"*Je m'en fous*," said Jean-Louis, but without his usual spirit. He met Max's eyes, and suddenly smiled his most angelic, urchin grin. He began to back as if he were dealing with royalty then, when he was a little distance away, ran towards the school, hopping and skipping as he went.

"You ought to have a record made," called Max after him.

*   *   *

Miss Pelham was astounded by the obvious talent of Deirdre's drawings. She remembered that last good-bye. The child had hung her head, had scarcely been able to say a word. It was impossible to believe that so foolish a little girl could observe with such accuracy, and set down her observations with so deadly a skill. But then it was no more impossible than thinking that she had contemplated running away with that beautiful, wicked boy from the Hostel opposite.

Max's face stared up at her from every page. The diary had never got very far. Miss Pelham noted with a faint grimace the comments on herself, then continued to go through the portraits of Max. There was no denying his good looks. It was a long time since Miss Pelham had permitted herself to be stirred by young, masculine beauty, but she could not be entirely immune to the passion and vitality that flamed in these swift drawings; she remembered the ravaged face that had stared into hers a little while ago, and she frowned as if the memory hurt her.

She was wondering whether she should send the book on or whether, in the circumstances, it would be wiser not to do so, when her attention was caught by another drawing, and not of Max. She glanced at it idly, then her shoulders stiffened, and she bent closer to the page.

It was M. Quiqueran who stared up at her, only the up-turned eyes were unseeing. His mouth was open, his head flung back. From that loosely-opened mouth came a trail of rose-petals, with a knife-blade through the last. There was a terrible authenticity to the picture. Deirdre's appalled pencil had caught with accuracy the stiffness of a face from which the spirit had fled.

Miss Pelham stared at this drawing. The delicately applied rouge was startling on her cheeks. The disbelief in her eyes was slowly changing to incredulous horror. She sat there for a long time, with the drawing in front of her, and through her mind were passing such thoughts as had never before entered it.

Then she rose swiftly to her feet. Her mouth was set. She rolled the notebook up and stepped out into the hall. For a second she glanced through the window at the Hostel opposite, where M. Wolff was no doubt wrestling with the problem of Max. An odd, defiant look came to her face, which was still very pale. Then she walked into the kitchen, much to the cook's surprise, and went across to the boiler that heated the water. She seized the prong, lifted off the lid and thrust the notebook into the flames; she prodded it down until it was nothing but ashes.

She replaced the lid, and raised herself to smile at the cook. Then she returned to her study, and began to write a letter. "Owing to the illness of one of our girls," she wrote, "we now have a vacancy for another pupil. I shall be delighted to welcome your daughter here, and hope she will be very happy with us—"

*   *   *

Max picked up a sandwich at Madame Dupont's. She looked at him curiously, but decided to make no comment. She filled the bread, however, with breast of chicken, and charged him half-price. He ate it as if he did not know what he was eating, thanked her, and strolled off into the sunshine.

He saw Inspector Granier in the distance. He began to sing:

"Je me demande pourquoi, mon Dieu,
Cela vous derange si je vive un peu,"

then broke off, as Granier came up to him, to say cheerfully, "Hallo, Death!" Then, with a cracked smile, he held out his two hands as if for the handcuffs.

Granier gave him a sour, unhappy look. "Why aren't you at work?"

"Oh, I felt lousy when I got up. I've a foul headache. It's going off. I don't suppose it's anything much."

"You don't look very well."

"I'll survive. Aren't you arresting me, Inspector?"

"No. Not yet. Death! That's a fine way to address a man. Since you are here, you'd better come back and have lunch with us. You look as if you could do with a square meal. And it'll please Anni. Or have you something better to do?"

"I have nothing better to do."

"Well, come along, then. We can have a game of chess afterwards—Sir Max. Incidentally," said Granier, "I'd like to point out that you've got your story wrong. I was checking on it, yesterday. Your knight didn't beat Death at all. What he did do was to bargain with him for a life. He lost his own, and serve him right."

He was not looking at Max as he spoke, or he would have seen the faint contortion in those ravaged features. He went on, "Anyway, all that nonsense doesn't concern us. I suppose you haven't decided to make a clean breast of it, and tell me the truth?"

"The truth, Inspector?"

"You know very well what I mean. The truth about old Quiqueran. How you killed him."

"I've told you the truth. I didn't kill him."

"You certainly don't look well," said Granier. They were nearing the Place du Triangle. "I should like to think it was conscience." Then he burst out, as if in anger, "You won't get away with this, you know."

"I don't suppose I will," said Max indifferently, lighting himself a cigarette.

"How you can smoke those things—I know you're lying."

"What a clever man you are," said Max. "They'll promote you yet. Isn't the path to promotion lined with corpses? In your particular profession, I mean."

Granier said heavily, "I'm sorry about this, you know. I always hoped it would never happen."

Max's composure cracked. He whirled round on the Inspector, who surveyed him with oddly compassionate eyes. He shouted at him, "Ah, God damn your sanctimonious soul! You hoped! You always hope. You shut your eyes. You put the blinkers on. It's so easy. A few kind words, a pat on the head, get him to play with the baby, show him how nice and cosy home life can be. Perhaps he'll really settle down—But the cold wind still blows, you know. It blows down the cosy chimney. It blows under the painted door. It blows everything away, cradle, baby and all—I don't envy you, for all you think you've got everything and I've got nothing. You're smug and pompous and fat and old, your belly hurts you and serve you bloody well right. What have you got ahead of you? A nice retirement with nothing to do, and precious little to do it on. You'll have to occupy yourself by thinking how really decent people could be if only they'd let themselves, and never mind, never bloody well mind if they've been kicked to hell, bashed on the head, had the guts torn out of them in little pieces. They can forget all that, as easy as winking, there's no point in brooding, is there? It doesn't get one anywhere, and after all we all know that the world's divided up like a chessboard, and no one on one square gives a damn for how the other square gets by. The world's forgotten what happens, so why can't they forget it, too? Forget it, it's all over, remembering won't bring the dead back, they've rotted long ago. Be a good boy, and I'll give you a sweetie. If not—why then, it's: *Juif, go home!* Ah, to hell with you, you hypocritical old bastard, what do you know about it, what can you know?"

Granier looked away from him, screwing up his eyes. He said sadly, "You never used to indulge in self-pity, Max. It's the one thing I've always admired in you."

Max, for the one second, looked pure murder. He was shaking. He whispered, "How dare you?" Then, his face contorted, he rolled the saliva round his mouth and spat; the spittle landed on the toecap of Granier's shoe.

Granier said not a word. He stared at Max, and Max stared back at him, his breath whistling between his teeth, his half-naked chest beating up and down like a clapper.

Granier said at last in a gentle voice where the pity pulsated, "Well, Max? What about that lunch and the game of chess?"

"I'll beat you to hell," said Max. He was still white, but he was smiling now, a wide, gaunt, wolfish smile that bared his teeth, dented the muscles in his cheeks.

"I wonder if you will," said Granier.

And they crossed the Place du Triangle side by side.

Made and printed in Great Britain for
HODDER AND STOUGHTON LTD., by
T. and A. Constable Ltd., Printers
Edinburgh

For regular early information

about

FORTHCOMING NOVELS

send a postcard

giving your name and address

in block capitals

to

THE FICTION EDITOR
HODDER AND STOUGHTON LTD.
2 St Paul's House
Warwick Square
London, E.C. 4